A Mind's Eye Witness

Rosanne L. Higgins

Book layout by www.ebooklaunch.com

To The Turner Boys and all of the wonderful women who are still with them.

Your love and support through thick and thin are very much appreciated.

From the Trophy
Wife—
Peace & Joy
[illegible]

Prologue

Buffalo, New York, 1924

Captain Thomas McNamara began to think better of using his own car as he pulled up to the back of the massive sandstone asylum. It was a Model T sedan, an indulgence from when he served as the Chief of Police a few years back. Being one of three people living on Colvin Avenue who owned a car wasn't worth the stress of being Chief, and McNamara resigned the position in 1922, instead taking over as Captain of the Fourteenth Precinct. Would the Ford be recognized as his? He couldn't have used one of the Buicks from the police depot. At this late hour, it would have attracted attention. Patients were not typically transferred in police vehicles to the Buffalo State Hospital in the dead of night. It was well past curfew, so most of the inmates, attendants, and administrators were asleep. That made him feel a little better about his decision. Just Dr. Detweiller would be there to receive the new patient. They had been altar boys together, and McNamara trusted him to keep this secret.

As the car moved closer to the building, the passenger in the back seat began to get nervous. "I don't know, Captain. Are you sure this is a good idea?"

"They got to you already, Tocci. You're safer here than any place else at this point." McNamara seemed unable to suppress his mirth. There was some justice after all in the deal he had struck with this thug. Luciano Tocci and his cronies had broken the law more times than McNamara could count, but he was willing to offer evidence against Joey Saladino, the gang's leader, who had been identified in the robbery of Community National Bank on Hertel Avenue. During the course of the robbery, the bank's manager, Arthur Lemke, had been shot and killed.

Tocci was married to Saladino's daughter, Sylvia. Joey had warned him more than once to keep his hands off the booze and, more importantly, off his daughter. She had come to one too many Sunday dinners wearing dark glasses to hide the bruises on her face. Fearing for his life, Tocci was actually relieved when he was pinched by the police a week ago. He had been identified as the driver of a car seen speeding away from the scene of the crime three nights before that. To save his own hide, he admitted during questioning that Saladino had indeed pulled the trigger of the gun that killed Lemke. That wasn't all he had told McNamara; he knew many of Saladino's secrets. Captain McNamara saw this as a real opportunity to learn more about Saladino and his clandestine group of thugs, if he could keep Luciano Tocci alive long enough to put a case together.

Patrolman William Cooper, sitting in the passenger seat, had yet to speak. He wasn't about to side with Tocci in front of the captain. Hiding Tocci in the insane asylum seemed risky to him. Nobody really knew what went on there, but Cooper would never question

Captain McNamara. Willy would do what the captain asked of him, whether he thought it wise or not.

Dr. Detweiller was waiting for them when the car pulled up at the back of the administrative building. There was a quick nod between he and the captain as Tocci was handed off in shackles. Stepping aside to reveal Cooper, who wasn't exactly hiding, the chief said, "This is his cousin; he'll be around to check on him regularly." Both Cooper and Tocci were surprised that no more was said between the two other men, but neither felt the need to add anything, although they both had plenty of questions about daily patient life at the asylum.

What could go wrong? Cooper had asked himself that when the captain first told him of the plan. Tocci would hide out in the insane asylum until a case could be brought against Saladino. Cooper had reluctantly agreed to be the link between Tocci and the captain. He was fair skinned, with freckles and red hair, so nobody looking from the outside would guess the family member he visited weekly at the Buffalo State Hospital was really Tocci, who was, of course, no relation. Cooper had been publicly relieved of his position as a patrolman so that nobody would wonder what a policeman was doing regularly visiting the asylum. He was just a man visiting his cousin. Only the captain would know better. Plenty had already gone wrong and they hadn't even left the asylum.

Part One

Chapter One

May 1, 2020

Maude and Don Travers each took a seat in their usual booth at their favorite diner in North Buffalo. When they lived in the neighborhood, they ate breakfast there nearly every weekend. They enjoyed the 1950s theme and creative daily specials. This morning they returned to the neighborhood to celebrate. For Maude, it had been a full year without any vivid, historically accurate dreams of the past, revelations regarding past lives, or spirits from the other side with cryptic messages of unfinished business.

The past few years had been a whirlwind of adjusting on the fly to life-changing events for both of them as they came to realize Maude's unique abilities, and a return to normalcy was welcomed by both. To anyone who might ask, they would simply say they were in the neighborhood and had to stop by for a fix of the diner's famous homemade corned beef hash. It really was addictive. After all, few, if any, of their old friends would have even believed them if they had wanted to share their adventures since leaving the neighborhood.

Mysterious dreams of the past and visits from nineteenth century ghosts had been a regular occurrence in her life since Maude was involved with a study of the inmates of the Erie County Poorhouse during the nineteenth century a few years earlier. Over the last seven years, the messengers in these dreams and ghostly visitations brought to life a period of Buffalo's history Maude had studied most of her professional life as an anthropologist as well as the owner of an antique shop. The most startling revelation was that she had been an important figure in that time period. One of the spirits from the other side revealed that Maude had been a poorhouse inmate turned physician in a past life. It also became clear that she and Don were soul mates, destined to find each other throughout eternity, and, in this life, committed to accomplishing the tasks that Spirit placed before them.

While the couple had come to accept these otherworldly interruptions in their lives, it had become difficult to keep their adventures, which had taken them as far away as a remote island off the west coast of Ireland, a secret. Their two college-aged sons, as well as the rest of their family, friends and colleagues remained unaware of this aspect of their lives. Twelve months spirit-free was a welcome change. If Maude was being honest, it had been quite a year. A perfectly uneventful, dare she admit, boring year.

"I'm not sure we have ever been here without the boys," Don mentioned as he pushed the menu aside. There was no need to examine it; he ordered the same thing every time.

"We haven't," Maude confirmed. Their oldest son, Glen, was attending college in Ithaca, New York. Much to his parent's dismay, he still hadn't declared a major.

Billy was living at home and majoring in Education at Buffalo State College. "It seems kind of weird without them."

"This is just the beginning, Maudie. We're this close to being empty nesters." Don held up his hand with his thumb and first finger less than an inch apart. "Without those two hay burners to feed, we can eat out every night and still save money!"

"Who are you kidding? You'll be devastated when the boys finally leave the house and you know it."

"Maybe at first, but I expect I'll get over it when we start to realize the savings. Boys are expensive. There's food, sports equipment, and let's not forget private school and college tuition." Don's list of child-related expenses was interrupted when a tall woman with flaming red hair approached the table.

Their waitress recognized them immediately. "What brought you two back to the neighborhood?" she asked.

"Why, Lisa, you, of course, and the corned beef hash! How are things?" Maude asked, holding up her coffee mug to be filled.

"There have been some changes in the neighborhood. You should take a walk down Hertel Avenue if you have time. There's a lot of new shops and a few bars, too."

"That's a good idea," Don agreed.

"The big news is that the Italian Festival is being moved to Wilkinson Point," Lisa told them.

"Wow, I hadn't heard that," Maude said. The Italian American Heritage Festival was held the second weekend in July along Hertel Avenue in North Buffalo and had been for as long as Maude could remember. From Colvin Avenue to Delaware Avenue, the street was jammed with vendors offering cannoli, sausage, ravioli and other delectable Italian nibbles. "What's the buzz in the neighborhood?" Its relocation to the outer harbor, along the shores of Lake Erie, was bound to elicit strong opinions among North Buffalo residents.

"Some people are pleased, and some are not," Lisa reported. That remark prompted comments from a few of the other diner patrons. Conversations were seldom private there; it was part of what Maude and Don loved about the place.

"We lived west of Colvin Avenue, where the festival began. We were right on the corner, so it did get a bit noisy, but it was just for a few days each year, so it really didn't bother us," Maude explained.

"It was great to be able to walk out our front door and grab Italian sausage and a cannoli," Don added.

"On what street did you live?" The woman behind them asked. When Maude told her, the woman asked, "It wasn't by chance number 215, was it?" She had heard a few years back that 215 had sold and wondered whether its secrets had been passed from owner to owner.

"Yes, it was." Don's smile faded quickly as he watched the woman's expression change.

"Did you know someone was murdered in that house in the 1920s?" She had lowered her voice so as not to be heard by the other patrons.

"No." Maude and Don answered in unison.

"Oh, it was quite the scandal," the woman continued as she rose and moved to join them. "You see, we lived at number 221. My parents bought our house in 1950, just after they were married. Even all those years later, folks were still whispering about it. They had changed the name of the street, but that didn't seem to hush the gossip."

The woman went on to tell them that the owner of the house had been a doctor for a local crime gang. When he retired, he made it clear that he would no longer treat the gunshot wounds or stitch up the lacerations they had brought to his door in the dead of night so many times before. His decision angered the mob and they put a hit out on him. "Well, one day there was a knock on the door and the doctor's wife went to answer it. How was she to know the man on the other side had a loaded gun pointed at her? You see, he was expecting to see the doctor and he fired the instant the door opened. Of course, he fled immediately when he realized he had shot the wrong person. Can you just imagine that?" The woman sat back and sipped her coffee while her audience of two soaked in what she had told them.

"Did she die instantly?" Don asked.

"What about the hit man? Was he ever caught?" The words were out of Maude's mouth almost before her husband finished speaking.

"Oh, I really don't know," the woman answered. It turned out that the old woman could not recall any other details of the case. "Well, you see, I haven't spoken of it in ages, and of course, we're over in Elmwood Village now."

"Can you believe we lived in that house for all those years and never got any inkling that a person was murdered there?" Don said as they were walking up Hertel Avenue after breakfast.

"Yeah. Given the connection I have with the other side, I am actually surprised." Maude stopped to look in the window of one of the shops. It had been her favorite flower shop and was now a high-end dog boutique. Feeling stuffed from breakfast, she could imagine herself curling up on one of the luxurious dog beds for a nap.

"Maybe you weren't ready yet," Don told her as they continued down the avenue. "You may have had a dream or two and not remembered."

"Maybe." The intrigue of a murder in their former home faded as Maude took in all the changes in the neighborhood in the short time since they had moved downtown. They were pleased to see some fresh new restaurants and shops and relieved to see so many of their favorite places still thriving. "Remember, we considered opening our shop right here on Hertel Avenue."

"Yeah, but it appears that Spirit was leading us downtown," Don reminded her.

The building they currently worked and lived in downtown had been Nolan's Dry Goods Emporium in the nineteenth century. Another revelation from her dreams was that the building had been owned by Maude and Don in their past lives. Was Spirit now leading them back to North Buffalo, and if so, why?

Later that evening the story of the murder made its way into their after-dinner conversation. "A mob hit in Buffalo during the roaring twenties… It's a great idea for a book," Don suggested as he emptied the bottle of wine between their two glasses.

"I don't know if I want to get started with another book. I'm remembering how much I enjoyed being Maude Travers, antique shop owner. It's less work than Dr. Travers, anthropologist or Maude E. Travers, writer of historical fiction."

"Are you sure it's not because you are afraid to break the streak?"

"So, what if I am? Don, it has been a nice year, a quiet year."

"A boring year," he added. Don had always been more open to the beckoning of Spirit and considered himself a Modern Spiritualist, although it was his wife who had the ability to summon the past and communicate with the dead.

Maude had spent the previous two years frequenting Lily Dale, the Modern Spiritualist community just an hour south of Buffalo. Her mentor Charlotte Lambert and other gifted psychic mediums helped her to understand her abilities and learn their application and boundaries. Somehow while embracing Modern Spiritualism and her particular gifts - something she had previously been afraid to do - she had severed communications with the other side. There were no more dreams that pointed her in the direction of understanding some aspect of her past life in the nineteenth century and provided the inspiration for her novels. She had written a few books, which, it seemed, would never be enjoyed by anyone outside her small circle of friends and family. Perhaps that chapter of her life had come to a close, pun intended. In the year since she had limited her trips to Lily Dale to the summer season and occasional weekends, Maude had enjoyed embracing her former life as a wife, mother and business owner.

"Are you saying you would be happy if life continued on the way it has been this last year? No more insight into the past, no more research, no more writing?"

"Don, we don't even know if the story we learned today is true."

"There's one way to find out. Do a quick newspaper search. A murder would certainly have been reported in the papers."

With Billy on campus cramming for finals, they would have the evening to themselves and Maude didn't want to spend it arguing. "Alright. Tomorrow I'll do a quick search at least to verify the story." She picked up her glass and took a long sip for no other reason than to prevent her from crossing her fingers behind her back. She would not lie to Don. If things were quiet at the shop tomorrow, she would search the period newspapers. Of course, there was that closet in the back of the workroom that needed to be cleared out and the basement was long overdue for some reorganizing.

As she drifted off to sleep, it was not images of flappers and gangsters that occupied Maude's mind. Instead she was contemplating what she might find in the closet at the back of the shop. It was in the workshop where Don repaired and restored the antique lamps acquired during his travels or were brought in by their clients who trusted him alone to breathe life into a family heirloom. She had been after him for months to clean out that closet so she could use it to store holiday decorations. It was time to tackle the job herself. Tomorrow was the day, she decided.

The next day Maude was sitting on the floor of Don's workroom taking inventory of the boxes in the back of the closet. There were three, all still sealed. "I can't believe we never unpacked these," she said out loud to no one in particular. Whatever was in them hadn't seen the light of day in years, so she decided to open them and determine whether there was anything worth donating to charity.

The first box contained old linens, which Maude knew would be of use at the women's shelter downtown. The second box was full of Don's high school and college yearbooks, which went straight back in the closet. The third box had some old family photos wrapped carefully in well-worn towels.

Maude made herself more comfortable on the floor and prepared for an unanticipated trip down memory lane. There was Glen's kindergarten graduation; he looked adorable in his little cap and gown. Billy's third grade soccer team featured her son in the front row holding the championship trophy. Then there was Don's thirtieth birthday party. Maude smiled, remembering their own private celebration after the guests had left. She laughed out loud at the family camping trip to Algonquin in 2005. Each of them wore a broad brimmed hat draped with gauze to cover the head and neck. The bugs had been formidable that summer and they had to be completely covered head to toe to avoid being eaten alive.

Carefully placing the pictures to the side, Maude felt around in the box to determine whether she had found them all. There was one more at the bottom. The frame felt heavier than the others as she peeled away the layers of terry cloth. It was an old carved wooden frame. "Wow, I'd forgotten all about this," she said examining the photo. It was of a family: a husband, his wife, two older children of high school age, and two younger children. They were seated at a table in a restaurant, a fancy one by the look of it. Maude had never been any good at identifying the fashion trends of any particular era, so she carefully removed the photo to see whether it was dated. In tidy script was written *Twins graduation 1923.* She remembered now; they had looked at the date when they first found it in their old house nearly fifteen years ago.

The older boy and girl looked about the same age, so Maude assumed them to be the twins. The little boy looked to be older than his pint-sized sister, but not by much. Two boys and two girls… They looked to be the perfect family. It didn't make sense that Maude felt sad to look at them.

"Whatcha got there?" Don asked, peering into the workroom.

Maude hadn't heard him approach and looked up in surprise. She held out the picture. "I thought we agreed to leave this picture in the old house." They had found the picture in the basement when they first moved in, along with a few other treasures that had apparently been left by past owners of the house.

"Oh, wow! I'd forgotten all about that. Do you suppose that's her?"

"Who?" Maude asked.

"The woman who was murdered in the house."

Flipping over the photo to show Don the date, Maude replied, "I hadn't thought of that, but, yes,

I guess so. The photo was taken in 1923. They are celebrating the twins' graduation, so this would have been nearly a year before her death."

Maude looked at the photo again. "Well, now I understand why I feel emotional when I look at this picture. They seem so happy, but I felt sad just now, and I remember having the same feeling when we first found this picture. That's why I left it in the basement. I wonder how it ended up in this box. It was pretty carefully wrapped, so someone put it in here."

"Well, it wasn't me." Don took in the pile of old towels and the neatly stacked frames on the floor next to his wife. The picture of all of them draped in gauze caught his eye. "Now that's a blast from the past." He sat down next to her and began sorting through the photos. The next two hours passed quickly as they reminisced over each one. It was a very slow day in the shop and neither one felt the need to return to doing anything else.

When Billy came home that night, he saw the picture sitting on the dining room table. "I'm wondering how it got packed in with our stuff. We all agreed it should stay with the house, remember?" Maude asked him.

"I packed it," Billy admitted.

"Why did you do that?" Maude asked.

"I just wanted it." It was a typical Billy answer, to the point, with no explanation.

Later that night, as Maude thought about the woman in the picture, her curiosity got the better of her and she began to wonder about the events that had taken place in her old house all those years ago. She had spent months in guided meditation classes that had helped her shift her consciousness into the past, but could she direct it towards events she hadn't experienced in a past life? Perhaps it was time to find out.

Don was already fast asleep, and their bedroom was dark and quiet. After a few deep breaths, she began to think about what her old neighborhood might have looked like during the 1920s. There wouldn't be as many houses as there were now. The streets would be brick instead of asphalt, and trees would be much smaller. She imagined few, if any, cars parked in the driveways. Silently, she asked for Spirit to guide her to the events that transpired the night of the murder.

In her mind's eye she recognized her old house just off Hertel Avenue. Something was different; there were no trees on the front lawn, and the skinny saplings that lined the street couldn't be more than a few years old. A man was walking up the driveway. He had on an overcoat and a black derby, a large box balanced carefully in his arms. He was definitely not from the twenty-first century, but Maude didn't know enough about men's fashion to identify the time period. Certainly, it was twentieth century, but that's as close as she could get. She had asked Spirit to guide her to a specific time and she had faith that her attention was focused where it needed to be.

Thoughts of chronology left her mind as the sound of voices could be heard from the upper floor of the home. Somehow, she knew that the voice was that of the woman in the picture.

"Young lady, you will not leave the house in that dress!" Eva Barstow called out as her daughter, Nina,

tiptoed past the master bedroom just at the top of the stairs. "You'd better change before your father comes home and sees you."

The bedroom door was only open a few inches and her mother was seated at her vanity facing the fireplace on the opposite side of the large room. She had easily seen the dress reflected in her mirror, but Nina didn't need to know that. Eva rose from her chair, low, thick heels clicking across the oak floor. With shoes on, she could stand eye to eye with her most willful daughter. The rest of this conversation would be had standing up.

Nina had made the dress herself and hidden it in the back of her closet, removing it only just now to dress for the party she would be attending in an hour. "Oh mother, the only other party dress I have is from last year; please don't make me wear that old rag."

"You will catch your death in that sleeveless dress," Eva scolded, glad she had the cool April temperatures to bolster her argument. She had to admit the dress was stunning, red silk cut in the trendy princess line with the hint of a curvature of hip and breast, before falling loosely to mid-calf. Nina had seen the original in The Sample, a trendy new dress shop on Hertel Avenue. When her mother refused to pay the twelve dollars and seventy -five cents for the dress, Nina was determined to replicate it herself. While Eva was proud of her daughter's efforts, Nina's father would have a fit if he saw her in it.

"I'll wear a coat."

"For the entire evening? Don't be silly darling, now hurry up and change, Jonathan has been ready for over an hour."

Nina had hoped to be attending the party with Willy Cooper rather than her twin brother Jonathan, but that would just be another argument with her mother, which would involve bossy Jonathan for sure. Although their parents would never tell them which one was born first, Jonathan assumed it was he, and often felt the need to act the part of the older brother. No doubt he would try and make her wear that coat all evening when he saw her in that dress.

Nina also had no doubt that even if Willy attended the party, Jonathan would not have let her near him. Willy was the cousin of her best friend Nellie Finster, and a patrolman who walked the beat in their North Buffalo neighborhood…at least he was. Willy had been let go from his position with the police department for drinking on the job, which he was in no hurry to explain. Jonathan condemned his former friend and decided that Willy was no longer good enough for Nina.

Using an argument that was more volume than it was substance, he had managed to convince their mother of the same. As a result, Nina was no longer allowed to take her afternoon stroll down Hertel Avenue, where she would just so happen to see Willy walking his beat. At first there had been talk of forbidding her attendance at the party altogether, but both her mother and brother agreed that Willy would be too ashamed to show his face.

The sound of the backdoor opening sent Nina flying into her room. Eva smiled, listening to the deep murmuring of male voices as father greeted son. She took another quick look in the mirror. Confident she had blotted and powdered the burdens of the day away, Eva went to meet her husband downstairs.

"Darling, you're home." Eva smiled as she leaned in to receive a gentle kiss on her cheek. He smelled of cigar smoke and whiskey, familiar reminders of the trappings of his job. Conrad Barstow was a jeweler who owned a shop in the heart of the city. He was known to pull out his finest cigars and spirits to toast the young man who had purchased a lovely engagement ring, or the older gentleman who had chosen a stunning pearl necklace for a special wedding anniversary. Conrad was a kind and gentle man who delighted in sharing the joys of his clients.

"You look beautiful, as always," he whispered in Eva's ear as he kissed her cheek. She could feel his body go rigid as his head tilted toward the stairs. "Just where do you think you are going dressed like that, young lady?"

"Oh, daddy, don't be old fashioned." The words came from the little girl standing just behind Nina.

"Yeah, dad, she's a m-modern woman," said the little boy next to her.

Conrad's brows rose at the comments of his youngest daughter and son, who had followed their sister down the stairs. "What a loyal brother you are, Matthew. You must have practiced that line to have managed such a perfect delivery. I'm sure both of you have earned whatever your sister has promised you. Now off to bed. You, too, Amelia."

"But…" The two children took in the look on their father's face and through unspoken agreement decided not to protest further.

"Goodnight, father," Matthew said as he followed his sister up the stairs.

Conrad turned to see Nina putting on her coat. "Stop right there, young lady. You are not leaving the house in that dress, no matter who you recruit to come to your defense."

Nina looked her father in the eye as she fastened the last button on her coat. "Father, I am not a child anymore." She spoke with dignity, careful to avoid using her usual endearment, daddy. "I made this dress myself and I would like to show it off to my friends. You have raised me to act like a lady and I'd hoped you would have some confidence in my ability to govern my own behavior."

Jonathan looked as if he was about to add his own thoughts to the argument, but Eva spoke before he could. "She's right, Conrad. We have raised her well and now we must trust her. We have also raised our son to look out for his sister, which he has already shown he is more than capable of doing."

Nina was furious but had the good sense not to say anything. Jonathan would be watching her every move, no doubt to give her parents a full report in the morning. She should have known that an attempt to cross her mother would not end in her favor. Eva smiled, knowing she had regained the upper hand yet again. "Now you two hurry off or you'll be late. We'll leave the door open for you, so lock up when you come home."

• • •

William Cooper pulled out his pocket watch and held it toward the full moon. It was after eleven o'clock and Nina and her brother would be home soon. The plan had been to wait in her yard in the hopes that he might have a few quick words with Nina. He had been desperate to explain himself but was losing his nerve. What had he been thinking? There was no way to get her attention without also gaining that of Jonathan. What would he say even if he successfully stole a few moments alone with her? Captain McNamara had made him swear on the life of his dear, sweet mother that he would tell no one of their secret. Still, he wanted Nina to know he really hadn't been fired, though he couldn't think of a way to let her know without breaking his word to the captain and compromising their plan. He looked at his watch one more time and, before he could talk himself out of it, left, scaling the back fence into the night.

As Cooper reached Hertel Avenue, he turned the corner and walked quickly in the direction opposite Nina's house. Keeping his head down to avoid being recognized, Willy didn't see the four young men in a car on the other side of Hertel slowly turning toward Nina's street.

"That's it, right there." The young man pointing to number 215 was careful to keep his voice low.

"Are you sure that's the right house?" one of his companions challenged.

"He told me that's the place," another one said confidently.

"Shut up, you knuckleheads, before you wake up the whole street," A third man told them as he pulled

up in front of the house. "You two go around the back and see if there's a window open." He gestured to the fourth man, "We'll try the doors."

They quickly checked the lower story windows and back door to find all were locked. The ring leader motioned for the others to stay put while he crept up to the front porch. When the door opened, he waved the others forward. Upon entering the house, he motioned for them to follow him up the stairs.

Eva heard some noise downstairs. "They must be home." She rose from bed and put on her robe. "I'll just make sure they locked the door."

"Wait just a minute." Conrad sat up and canted his head as if he was straining to hear something. "Have you ever known those two to enter the house quietly? Let me go see what's going on."

"Nonsense, dear. They are past curfew. I suspect they are doing their best to sneak in. I'll be right back."

"Jonathan is that you?" Eva called, making her way to the landing at the top of the stairs. "Who's there?"

Conrad jumped out of bed, alarmed at the change in her tone. He was just out the bedroom door when a gun went off.

"Shit! Everyone out, now!"the ring leader shouted, as all four men scrambled out the door.

Conrad took in the scene from the landing. The front door had slammed shut, the younger children had come out of their rooms and little Amelia was screaming. Eva was crawling up the stairs, her robe and nightgown thoroughly saturated with her own blood.

• • •

"Shit!" Maude sat upright in her bed, the force of it sending the comforter flying.

"What? What's wrong?" Don was seated now, too, taking in the sight of his wife, who hadn't yet come fully back to the present. He could tell immediately. Her eyes were still focused inward and she was breathing heavily. He placed a hand gently on her back. "Come back to me, Maude, and tell me what happened."

There had always been some disorientation when she came back. Maude looked at Don and placed a hand on his shoulder as if to prove to herself that he was really there beside her. She sat back, brushed the hair away from her face and took a deep breath. "It wasn't a mob hit."

Chapter Two

"The murder at our old house, I don't think it was a mob hit - at least not in the way we were told."

"You had a dream about the murder at our old house?" As he asked the question, Don realized it was a stupid one.

"No, I was able to get there on my own. The house was unlocked because the older children were out at a party. There were intruders. I can't be sure, but it seemed like they were looking for something." Maude reached for the notebook she always kept on her nightstand, only to find a glass of water there instead. When had she removed her notebook? It was important to write things down immediately because important details would be lost come morning.

Don seemed to realize her dilemma and went out to the kitchen to grab the small spiral notebook they kept in the junk drawer for grocery and to do lists. "Here, use this." He handed her the notebook and then sat quietly for the next ten minutes while she transcribed her dream.

Maude had developed shorthand incomprehensible to others though it allowed her to record sufficient detail quickly, so she was not up half the night. Her dreams had occurred frequently enough that Don usually was content to go back to sleep and hear the details in the morning. She was surprised to see him still up when she had finished.

"So, you think the woman was killed by a thief?" Don asked.

"Maybe. It's hard to say. It was *thieves;* there were four of them. They had definitely targeted our house, but what for I don't know. I got the feeling that they might have been looking for something, but they could just have been looking for valuables to steal rather than something in particular."

"Maybe there will be more information in the newspaper."

"Yeah, maybe." Maude turned out the bedroom light knowing she had started down a new path. This time there was no trepidation. She had asked for the information that had been received and knew there would be something important to be learned in the end. Whatever it was, she would have Don there to help her make sense of it. She turned and looked at her husband, nearly asleep again, and then settled in to join him.

The next morning Maude was in her office with the laptop on and a steaming cup of coffee next to it before Don was even out of bed. They had quickly become accustomed to sleeping in when the boys no longer needed rides to school in the morning, but Maude's eyes popped open before the first glimmer of dawn, eager to place her dream in historical context. She was so absorbed in an article in the *Buffalo Courier Express* she didn't hear him coming down the stairs.

"Have you found anything interesting?" Don had to ask twice before she was able to pull herself from the article and answer.

"Yes, a lot." Maude reached for her notebook and quickly reviewed what she had learned thus far. "The family in the picture was the Barstows: Conrad, Eva, and their children. The twins were Jonathan and Nina; the younger two were Matthew and Amelia. There doesn't seem to be any connection between any member of the family and any crime gang. The police assumed the four intruders were thieves whose prowling was interrupted by Mrs. Barstow, but - at least as far as I can tell at this point - the murder went unsolved." She took a sip of her coffee before continuing. "I haven't uncovered any information that they ever apprehended the killer or the other three intruders. From what I read, four men were seen by a neighbor getting into a car parked in front of the house and speeding down the street. Willy Cooper, the man from my dream, was a suspect. He had been identified scaling the fence in the backyard around the time of the shooting. It never went anywhere, but some detectives in the BPD were convinced it was him. They knew he had a thing for the oldest daughter, Nina Barstow."

Maude's eyes seemed to linger on the page for a moment. Don had seen that look before. "So, what about Willy Cooper?" he asked.

"Well, I don't think he did it. He was there to try to see Nina. He was worried about what she might think after his firing from the police department. He was a patrolman; did I tell you that?" Maude spoke with confidence, knowing the details of her vision had actually played out on that evening back in 1924. There was a big difference in Maude today as opposed to when her dreams began years ago. She knew now they were quite real. The newspaper reports confirmed the details of the crime, although the new Maude didn't need that confirmation to be assured that what she had seen in her dream had really happened. "Anyway, there's something about Willy Cooper. He's caught up in this somehow."

Don held her gaze for a while before he spoke, trying to determine if she understood the significance of this latest journey into the past. Finally, he asked, "So, what's your plan here?"

Maude knew what he was asking, because the importance was not lost on her. This was the first time she faced one of these mysteries of the past in full possession of her abilities. "Well, there's more. I think we're somehow embroiled in this. The car seen speeding down the road was stolen. Guess where it was stolen from?"

She had his full attention and he did not take his eyes off her while considering the question. Finally, he asked. "Where?"

"Just around the block…"

Don's eyes grew wide and he laughed out loud. "It wasn't, was it?"

"Yup, our old apartment! Can you believe it?" Maude was all smiles. In the past it had been frustrating and a bit scary as both the details of her past life and her extrasensory skills unfolded more with each adventure. This time she was enjoying the hunt.

"Of course, I can believe it. So, again, what's the plan?"

"I want to see if I can track down any more details about this case. Also, I need to know more about Willy Cooper. I think for now it will be mostly phone calls and online searches."

"Okay. Let me know if I can help."

"I imagine I'll be spending a fair amount of time in the old neighborhood snooping around. You can drive the getaway car!"

Don smiled. "It's good to see you excited about this, Maudie. It's time to take all your new skills out for a spin and see what you can do!"

Maude's own grin became brighter as she relayed how easy it had been for her to connect with their old house. "I have to admit, I'm actually looking forward to pursuing this."

"It will certainly make a fascinating story. Who knows? It might be time to start writing nonfiction." Don regretted that last suggestion when he saw the smile leave his wife's face.

Maude shook her head. "Not gonna happen, Don."

"Maybe not now, but you should consider it in the future. What you are experiencing will be of interest to others. You should share what you're going through."

"It's not that simple, Don, and you know it. I would become a joke to my university colleagues." She could see that he wanted to argue the point, and so finished her statement with more conviction. "If I stick to fiction, people will just think I have a creative imagination. If I suggest my experiences are real, they will think I'm delusional."

"Okay, I'm sorry I brought it up. Seeing as though you won't be needing a getaway driver this morning, I can handle the shop until Christine comes in if you want to keep working."

"That would be great, thanks." Maude looked at her watch. Christine, their part time employee, fellow local history enthusiast and busybody, would be in around noon. Maude would finish up before then or face the inevitable interrogation for working in her office behind closed doors.

All Christine would have to hear is that Maude was researching a murder in her old house. She would not be able to resist telling whoever came in the shop that day. It would be all over the city by the end of the week. That might be handy when the time came to market a new book, but right now Maude wanted to keep it between herself and Don. Christine was naturally suspicious, and Maude was a terrible liar. If she let something slip from her connection with the past, Christine would pursue it relentlessly until Maude admitted she had spent the last few years working with Modern Spiritualists refining her inner senses. Maude certainly wasn't ashamed or embarrassed about her abilities, or her pursuits to better understand them, but she was not quite ready to announce them to the world, or even the neighborhood.

"Okay, I've got a few hours to get some things done. Let's see if there are any surviving case files surrounding this murder." Maude did a quick search to find the phone number for the Buffalo Police Department's D District.

Much to her dismay, the case file had long since disappeared. It was more than likely the restructuring of the Buffalo Police Department and the relocation and renaming of the Fourteenth Precinct was responsible for the file's disappearance rather than any nefarious attempt to keep secret the details of the crime. Still, the detective with whom she spoke promised to do some digging and get back to her soon.

Maude had come to a moment where her previous self would have been frustrated by the lack of historic documents available to provide her with answers. Now, with an understanding of the range of her gifts and how to use them, she knew she might be able access the information in a different way. During her training, Maude had learned how to connect with the energy of past people and places. She had come to understand when she was writing previous novels that she could slip into a meditative state while writing and, in doing so, actually channel the past, and while her books were marketed as historical fiction, much of what she wrote had actually happened.

There had been a picture of Captain McNamara of the Fourteenth Precinct in a few of the articles she had read in the newspaper. She pulled up the one with the highest quality image in an effort to connect with him. Placing her fingers on the keyboard, she reached out to Captain McNamara, picturing him seated behind the desk in his office. An image of the man formed in her mind and her fingers began tapping the keys.

Captain McNamara sat straight up in his chair with his head raised, eyes toward the door and ears sharply focused. He recognized the sound of footsteps coming down the hall, heavy, yet quick, agitated. Something was wrong. As they drew nearer, he braced himself for the knock on his door. "Come!" Something must be very wrong because the desk sergeant had already started turning the doorknob before the command to enter had left the captain's lips.

"What is it, Wellesley?" The captain would wait to hear the news and then decide if the man deserved to be chastised for his breach of etiquette.

"There's been an incident over at the poor farm, sir."

The Erie County Home, formerly the Erie County Poorhouse, stood on the edge of the city in an area known as Buffalo Plains. In the previous century it served as an almshouse, hospital and insane asylum. The institution's name was changed, the inmates now referred to as residents. Still, most people called it the poor farm, although it had become more of a home for the aged and infirm than a refuge for the downtrodden. In recent years, much of the property had been sold off to the University at Buffalo and the campus was growing rapidly, enveloping the aging complex. A newer facility, one more suitable to the current elderly population in need, was being built in Alden, but the Buffalo Plains institution was still in use.

McNamara had been afraid there might be an incident and left instructions with the Deputy Commissioner of Charities and Corrections to bring word to him immediately should anything out of the ordinary happen. "What kind of incident?"

"I don't know, sir, but something must have happened there. The Deputy Commissioner is waiting to see you."

That last sentence triggered a flurry of thoughts, all of which were kept hidden behind a mask of professional interest as Captain McNamara tried to make sense of them. If Deputy Commissioner Fisher had come to the precinct, whatever had happened was more than just out of the ordinary. It also meant that he was looking to avoid having the captain of the Fourteenth Precinct come to the poor farm, but he was willing to risk being seen calling on the captain himself. None of this bode well. It took only seconds to process, and a mischievous smile spread across his face as he spoke. "If the deputy commissioner has come all the way to the Fourteenth, you can be sure that he is here at the behest of his lovely wife, my good sister, to collect on the donation Mrs. McNamara has promised for the orphan asylum. Please, Wellesley, show the man in."

Sergeant Wellesley returned with a tall older man dressed in a wool coat and holding a black derby. "Mr. Fisher, come in, sir. Our wives do keep us busy. I sometimes believe they forget that we have important jobs! I had intended to leave Mrs. McNamara the funds you seek for their meeting on Friday, but it appears the ladies cannot wait that long." He smiled, vigorously shaking the man's hand.

Miles Fisher just laughed. The remark did not surprise him, although he knew not what the captain was going on about. He had taken a gamble that McNamara would find a way to explain his unorthodox visit to the precinct. Fisher made himself busy removing his coat and placing his hat on the chief's desk while Sergeant Wellesley took his time exiting the room.

"That will be all, Wellesley," the captain said.

"Of course, sir."

The two men continued to exchange pleasantries, all the while listening for Wellesley's footsteps to recede before getting down to business. They both remained standing, and when McNamara spoke again, all levity was gone from his voice.

"What brings you to my office, Miles?"

"Tocci has killed a man." The deputy commissioner held his hand up to forestall the question he knew the captain would ask. "It was self-defense, of that I'm sure."

"They found him."

"It appears so. We had him in one of the solitary rooms on the third floor of the hospital, but they found him. There was a struggle, but your man was able to get the better of his assailant. He managed to suffocate him with a pillow."

"When?"

"About an hour ago. We have some time to think this through, but not much I'm afraid. Tocci was alone in his room when the man entered."

"Did anyone else see or hear anything?"

"The intruder chose his time well. The staff was having their lunch, so there were no attendants on the ward. Lucky for you that I check on him personally around that time. I daresay, if I hadn't been delayed by a telephone call, I'd have witnessed the act in progress."

The captain thought it more likely that one of Saladino's men placed the call to keep Fisher away. Tocci had only been there a few days. It hadn't taken long for word to travel to Saladino. "We must act quickly."

Fisher nodded in agreement. "The body is in our morgue. As far as the ward attendant knows, he had occupied the room next door." When McNamara seemed surprised at how easy it had been to remove the body, Fisher simply replied, "The residents are old and in frail health. Death is not uncommon at all hours of the day and night. The attendants go about their business amiably enough, but they seldom really see the people before them. When asked to remove a body to the morgue, the task would be accomplished efficiently, without regard for the identity of the person or cause of the death. My only regret is that the county will have to incur the cost of the man's burial so that we can keep the whole matter quiet."

"I know I've caused you considerable trouble, Miles, and I have no right to ask any more of you."

"But you will, Thomas, and, as I'm happily married to your sister, that makes us family. For that reason, I'll help you."

McNamara thought for a moment. He needed to keep Tocci alive long enough to make use of the information he had provided that would put Joey Saladino and a few of his friends behind bars. He had thought it a stroke of genius to hide Tocci in the Erie County Home. The institution on Main Street had outlived its purpose, most of its residents were old, feeble of mind, and without friends or family. It should have been the last place anyone would look for him. The odds of someone from the hospital recognizing Tocci and being able to get word to Saladino about his whereabouts were slim. That meant someone from the precinct had squealed. "We've got to get him out of there."

"I have an idea."

McNamara leaned back in his chair. "Don't keep me waiting."

Fisher had also deduced that there must be an informant at the Fourteenth Precinct, and so went over to the door, opened it and checked down either direction in the hall before returning to his chair. "Well, we could make public the murder and have Tocci transferred to Matteawan. Surely nobody would pursue him at the hospital for the criminally insane, and, even if they did, it would be next to impossible to get to him in solitary confinement."

"No, it's too risky. I don't want to involve anyone else in this; besides, they could get to him during the transport to Matteawan. I need him here, where I can keep an eye on him."

"I see." Fisher thought for a few more moments. "It would be helpful, then, if his enemies thought him dead."

"Indeed, it would. How could we do that without adding to the mess you have already been kind enough to sort out for me?"

"As I've said, death is something we deal with every day. The question is how do we get Tocci's enemies to believe him dead with his attacker dead as well." Without waiting for an answer to that all-important question, Fisher continued. "I think you'd have no trouble hiding Tocci in the asylum on Forest Avenue." He saw the skepticism in McNamara's eyes. "Just hear me out. The institution is massive, but patient life is much more strictly scheduled and regulated than it is at the Home. It's also more difficult for visitors to come

and go." As an afterthought, he added, "Still, it seems that there is someone on your staff not to be trusted. If this plan were to work, it could only be known to one or two highly trusted individuals."

McNamara thought about it for a moment. The Buffalo State Hospital was altogether a different place than the Erie County Home. The Home was for the aged and infirm, the State Hospital for the insane. Most people were reluctant to walk by the massive complex that ran along Forest and Elmwood Avenues, let alone walk through the large wrought iron gates. Inmates could often be seen all about the meticulously manicured grounds, as daily chores and exercise were considered an important part of most treatment plans.

It could work if they kept it quiet. Dr. Albert Detweiller was the physician there. Bert Detweiller had served as an altar boy at St. Marks Roman Catholic Church with Tommy McNamara. They had once been thick as thieves. Would Bert keep his secrets now?

Chapter Three

Maude stared at her screen, dumbfounded at what she had just written. "Of course - it had to be the poorhouse." There had been a connection to the Erie County Poorhouse each time she had explored her supernatural attachment to the past. Still, she had not expected the institution to be involved in this current mystery. Her link to the poorhouse had always been through the Sloane sisters, who were long dead, having arrived in Buffalo during the early nineteenth century. "Now what?" It was a question she was almost afraid to ask. Each time she had forged a connection with the past, she learned something important, even life changing. What was yet to be revealed through the massive institution?

"Now what, what?" A blonde head popped around the door frame.

"Christine. It can't be noon already, can it?"

"No, it's only ten o'clock. The shop is not even open yet."

"Oh." Maude was a bit disoriented, and at the same time very concerned. Often, when she slipped into her writer's trance time would fly, so that it could be hours after when she came back. Also, she was known to talk out loud to herself while pondering the clues presented to her by Spirit. Had Christine overheard anything important? "Well, then, what brings you here so early?" Maude was hoping she sounded casual.

Christine seemingly pranced into the office and bounced into the chair opposite Maude's desk. She was in a good mood. Maude was hoping it was good enough to keep her focused on the purpose of her visit. "I was wondering if you really needed me this afternoon, or can I come in a few hours later?"

Maude was immediately relieved. Christine had chosen to come in person to make a request that could have easily been handled with a phone call, or even a text. She was all smiles, so there wasn't any unfortunate reason she needed a bit of extra time this afternoon. That left only one reason for the request. "What's his name?"

"Ha! How did you know?" Without waiting for a reply, she continued speaking in that fast and breathy way one spoke when they had wonderful, life changing news to report. "Sam, Sam Stockwell. We met last night at the zoo fundraiser. He is my soulmate, I'm certain of it!"

Maude had heard this before. Christine was in her early thirties and had had a few soulmates in the decade she and Maude had been friends. Still, she would listen, offer encouragement and, ultimately, understanding when the relationship didn't work out. "How exciting! Tell me all about him."

"Well, he's my age for a change, and not at all tall, dark and handsome. He's more like my height, strawberry blond hair, and cute as a button." Christine was blushing as she described her latest love interest.

"He is an animal lover - I mean, we met at the zoo, after all. Oh, and he likes history."

Thus far, he seemed a departure from her usual type: tall, dark, and handsome, for sure, but also mysterious or downright shady. Maude was intrigued. "Dare I ask what he does for a living?"

"OMG! He's a Marine! Can you believe it?"

"Wow! I wasn't expecting that. You think a Marine is your soulmate? Who are you and what have you done with Christine?" Sam Stockwell was a departure indeed, and although Maude hoped for the best, she was fairly certain the relationship would fizzle out sooner rather than later. Christine was beautiful, smart, kind and funny, but she was also a disorganized slob. Sergeant Sam, or whatever his rank was, wouldn't last an hour in her apartment. Beyond that, she didn't exactly see black and white when it came to the law. She had even dated an international jewel thief.

"I know, he is completely different from the other men I have dated, but there is just something about him. I felt it the moment we met, and he did, too. We went out for coffee and talked until after midnight. He wants me to meet him for lunch, so can I come in late?"

Maude laughed. "Who am I to stand in the way of you and your soulmate? Try to get here by two."

Christine popped out of the chair. "Awesome, thanks. Now, what am I going to wear?"

"Where are you going?"

"I suggested the pub up the street, so I could get back to work quickly."

"What you have on is fine." Maude was absolutely fascinated now. Christine liked to be wined and dined, regardless of the meal time. It was unusual for her not to suggest a more upscale restaurant.

"You're right. I guess I don't have to change my clothes." She was wearing designer jeans and a long sleeve red cotton V-neck. She didn't typically wear jeans to work, let alone on a date, and Maude's brows shot up in surprise.

"Wow, you *are* in love! So, when do I get to meet the man who you are meeting in a pub wearing jeans and a t-shirt?"

"Soon, I promise!" Christine said as she pranced out the door.

Perhaps the most peculiar thing about the whole encounter was that Christine never followed up on her original question. She had overheard Maude talking to herself, asking, of all things, 'now what?' No matter how preoccupied Christine might be with a man, her curiosity always got the better of her, especially when it came to Maude. Christine always seemed to know Maude was hiding something juicy from her, quick to connect seemingly unrelated comments to help her deduce the mystery. That she walked into the office just as Maude was trying to determine what to do next and let it go in favor of discussing her new romance, that was odd indeed.

Pondering the earlier conversation with herself allowed Maude to answer her own question of how to move forward in this investigation. It would be easy to become preoccupied with the role of the Erie County Home in this murder mystery, however experience had taught her to stay on track. If the institution was important to the story, more details would be revealed as she moved forward. The immediate question was: what did the scene she had just written, the scene she was confident had actually played out in the past, have to do with the murder in her old house? Who was Tocci and why was he at the Erie County Home, and why was Captain McNamara so willing to cover up that crime? Maude sat back and pushed all thoughts and questions from her mind. William Cooper stubbornly refused to leave her consciousness. Somehow, he could provide some answers.

It didn't take long after typing his name into a genealogical database to find out that William Cooper was named for his grandfather on his mother's side. He was the son of Weldon Cooper, who had come from Ireland just before the turn of the century, and Susan Abbott of Albany. Someone had done quite a bit of work on the Abbott family, but there were a few details about the Coopers as well. Weldon Cooper came to Buffalo from Ireland with his parents and younger sister in 1895. He was nineteen at the time. He joined the Buffalo Police Department a few years after his arrival in the Queen City and married Susan in 1901. William was born in 1904. Weldon had risen to the rank of sergeant just before his death in 1914.

There were two period newspaper articles among the digital files associated with William Cooper. One was the report of his father's death. Sergeant Weldon Cooper had been shot in the line of duty. The second story made Maude laugh out loud. Evidently Patrolman William Cooper had foiled a robbery at the Buffalo Zoo. Two thugs had actually tried to steal a reindeer in December of 1923. Patrolman Cooper caught them in the act while walking through the zoo, as part of his normal beat. There wasn't much after that, just a listing in the City of Buffalo Directory on Commonwealth Avenue in 1924. Maude found no record of him after that.

She clicked back to the article about the attempted reindeer theft to look at the picture of Cooper printed along with the story. He looked so young, his expression a mixture of pride and pain. He had caught the thieves, but the reindeer had been injured in the struggle and had to be put down. Looking into the grainy image, Maude knew he felt responsible for the animal's death. "What happened to you, Willy?"

Maude looked at her watch. The shop opened at eleven o'clock and Don had promised to cover her until noon. It was ten-thirty now. She exited the office and spoke to Don as she trotted up the stairs in search of her car keys. "I've got some field work to do. I'll be back at noon and tell you all about it."

Pleased to see Maude so enthusiastic, he merely gave her the thumbs up. "Bring back lunch!" He called as she ran back down the stairs and out the back door.

Putting on her blinker, Maude got off the Parkside Avenue exit of the expressway. The intent was to head to the old neighborhood and let Spirit guide her. Maude glanced at the zoo on her left-hand side, regretting they hadn't renewed their membership. They had kept it current when the boys were younger. It was walking distance from their old home, the house in which Eva Barstow had been shot. Maude wondered if people from the neighborhood frequented the zoo back then. There was no cost of admission in those days and people were free to enter from several gates, including the adjoining Delaware Park. Without thinking, she turned into the zoo's parking lot.

Maude entered through the main admission gates at Parkside, uncertain what this exploration would reveal. Heading toward the herd animals made sense, as it was likely the reindeer story drew her to the zoo...but that didn't feel right. Instead, she was drawn to the polar bear dens. She noticed a bench nearby, took a seat and pulled out her laptop. Taking a deep breath, Maude began to think about the fair faced young man who made it his business to keep the zoo animals safe. A variety of bears were part of the menagerie early on, so the area upon which she focused wouldn't have looked that much different in the 1920s as it did today. With thoughts of Willy Cooper fixed in her mind, her fingers began moving madly across the keyboard.

Patrolman William Cooper walked through the East Meadow entrance to the Buffalo Zoo. He had convinced himself and others that a trip through the zoo grounds was just part of walking his beat. Truth be known, Willy was more concerned for the animals there than for any potential dangers to the people strolling the grounds. Someone had tried to steal one of the reindeer last year at Christmas time. The poor thing stumbled and broke its leg as Cooper tackled the robber to the ground. It had been shot by one of the keepers, butchered and served up as Christmas dinner at one of the local orphanages. Willy could only hope the children remained ignorant to the identity of their meal.

Since the reindeer incident, he'd noticed that some of the other patrolmen from the Fourteenth had made it a habit to pass through the grounds at the end of a shift. He'd even seen the desk sergeant regularly making a careful inspection of the grounds. By unspoken agreement, they'd all made sure the zoo was protected from further mischief.

The antiquated menagerie stood on seventeen acres in Delaware Park and hadn't seen any significant improvement since the building of an elephant house in 1912. The two wooden sheds which had been built years earlier as temporary shelters still stood bravely, providing shelter to birds, reptiles and other four-legged creatures that made up the zoo's collection. Willy was heading toward the bear dens when he recognized Captain McNamara looking down at the brown bears. He was about to call out to the captain, but the man looked up and his expression made the young patrolman slow his pace. The last time he had seen that look was when the captain had come to the house to tell Willy and his mother that his father had been shot and killed in the line of duty. Willy had been just a boy then, but he remembered it well. His legs felt as though cast in concrete, and it seemed to take much longer than it should have to cover those last few steps to the bears.

"My mom…" Willy couldn't bring himself to ask the question.

"She's fine, Willy." The captain only now realized what showing up on Willy's beat in the middle of the afternoon must have looked like to him, but there really wasn't another way. Not with a snitch somewhere in

the precinct. "Walk with me a minute. I have something I need to ask you."

As they walked, Captain McNamara told Willy about Tocci and what had happened at the county home. Willy's eyes grew wide as he listened to the plan to hide Tocci at the asylum on Forest Avenue. They grew even wider as he learned of the part he would play in this plan.

"What do you mean, I'll have to be let go? What will ma say?"

"I'm sorry, son, but you can't tell anyone, not even your ma. It's just for a few weeks, until we can put together a case against Saladino. When it's all over, you'll have your job back and we'll clear your record of any wrongdoing."

Willy Cooper hadn't done anything seriously wrong in his life, and now it appeared he would be fired from his job. The reality was that he would be working undercover in the insane asylum of all places. He would check on Tocci and serve as a go-between for the criminal and the captain. It was a good plan. Few knew about McNamara's relationship with the Cooper family since the death of Sergeant Weldon Cooper a decade ago. The captain had quietly put in a good word to get Willy assigned to the Fourteenth Precinct but had left the young man to sink or swim after that. It was how his father, the captain's friend, would have wanted it. Willy was an exemplary patrolman, which had made his mother proud, and now he was about to be fired.

"What exactly will I have done wrong?" he asked the captain.

Captain McNamara looked at the young man he had known all his life, seeing the boy who only wanted to make his ma proud. This was the part he dreaded telling Cooper. "Just before you report for duty tomorrow, pour yourself a wee dram from the bottle your da kept on the top shelf of the pantry. If I know your ma, it's still there; she'd not part with the bottle brought by your father's father straight from County Clare." The captain smiled as he recalled a time when he and Weldon Cooper had taken a nip from that very same bottle, the last that his Da had brought with him to America nearly forty years ago.

"Pour just a splash on the collar of your coat, just a splash mind you; it's a shame to waste fine whiskey. Find a reason to stop by and have a word with the desk sergeant. He has a nose like a hound and loyalty only to himself. You'll be called into my office before the morning briefing begins." For all it was a crime to manufacture, sell or transport alcohol, it was not illegal to possess or consume it. Willy would be fired for drinking on the job, but he would not go to jail for it.

Willy dropped his head as if the shame of it were already upon him. He knew he could not refuse Captain McNamara, but the thought of facing his mother after having been fired for drinking on the job made him physically ill. Drinking on the job was both immoral and irresponsible. Would he ever recover from the humiliation? "How long until people will know the truth?"

"Just as soon as Saladino is behind bars. I'll see to it personally that your name is cleared."

Willy drew in a deep breath and nodded. "Okay, then, I'll see you tomorrow."

"Tocci will be transferred tomorrow night. I'll need you to come along to meet him face to face, and to meet Dr. Detweiller. Can you get out of the house after midnight without any trouble?"

"Ma's in bed long before then. It shouldn't be any trouble."

"Meet me at the corner of Hertel and Delaware." Not many people in their neighborhood owned cars so pulling up to Willy's house on Commonwealth Avenue in the middle of the night would surely draw attention. He waited for Willy's nod and then turned to take his leave.

Willy decided to take an extra lap around the zoo, thinking he would use the time to figure out how he would face his mother.

• • •

Willy Cooper stood quietly outside his mother's bedroom door listening to the gentle snore coming from within. He wasn't so sure she would ease into her usual bedtime routine after the discussion they had earlier over dinner. It would have been better to wait until the next day to tell her he'd been relieved of his position at the BPD if for no other reason than to insure she slept soundly this evening, but fate would not allow him that luxury.

Captain McNamara had been correct in his prediction that if Willy had found a reason to be near Sergeant Wellesley with just a hint of whiskey on his breath, the lad would be dismissed before the briefing began. What Willy didn't count on was how fast the news would travel. Wellesley wasted no time telling Jonathan Barstow, whom he knew would pass the information on to the one person Willy was hoping to keep in the dark for as long as possible: his sister Nina.

Willy had been a year ahead of Jonathan at St. Marks, but the boys had become friends. Willy had watched Nina evolve from a pesky sister to a beautiful young woman. Often, he lingered in the few blocks closest to her street as he walked his beat, hoping to run into her as she ran errands on Hertel Avenue for her mother. He had finally worked up the courage to ask her to his cousin Nellie's birthday party tonight and was hoping to keep the news of his departure from the BPD from her until after that.

Jonathan Barstow showed up at Willy's house just before dinner. Willy's day went from bad to worse as not only was he told in no uncertain terms to stay away from Nina, but his mother had overheard the argument and was devastated to learn of his termination. She had cried herself to sleep, Willy was certain of it. If there had been any way to get word to the captain, he'd have begged to put Tocci's transfer off just one more night. What if his ma woke up in the middle of the night and found Willy gone? She would assume the worst after what she had learned of her son today. He wasn't sure the woman could take any more disappointment.

Her breathing was slow and steady. He waited just a few more minutes just in case a way out of this mess would become apparent, but today just wasn't his day. "Sleep well, ma," he whispered as he headed back downstairs to leave. A glance at his pocket watch as he closed the back door told him there was plenty of time before he had to meet the captain, and so he walked in the direction of Nina's house. With any luck, she'd be home soon.

• • •

Captain Thomas McNamara began to think better of using his own car as he pulled up to the back of the massive sandstone asylum. It was Model T sedan, an indulgence from when he served as the Chief of Police a few years back. Being one of three people living on Colvin Avenue who owned a car wasn't worth the stress of being Chief, and McNamara resigned the position in 1922, taking over as Captain of the Fourteenth Precinct instead. Would the Ford be recognized as his? He couldn't have used one of the Buicks from the police depot. At this late hour, it would have attracted attention. Patients were not typically transferred in police vehicles to the Buffalo State Hospital in the dead of night. It was well past curfew, so most of the inmates, attendants, and administrators, were asleep. That made him feel a little better about his decision. Just Dr. Detweiller would be there to receive the new patient. They had been altar boys together, and McNamara trusted him to keep this secret.

As the car moved closer to the building, the passenger in the back seat began to get nervous. "I don't know, Captain. Are you sure this is a good idea?"

"They got to you already, Tocci. You're safer here than any place else at this point." McNamara seemed

unable to suppress his mirth. There was some justice after all in the deal he had struck with this thug. Luciano Tocci and his cronies had broken the law more times than McNamara could count, but he was willing to offer evidence against Joey Saladino, the gang's leader, who had been identified in the robbery of Community National Bank on Hertel Avenue. During the course of the robbery, the bank's manager, Arthur Lemke, had been shot and killed.

Tocci was married to Saladino's daughter, Sylvia. Joey had warned him more than once to keep his hands off the booze and, more importantly, off his daughter. She had come to one too many Sunday dinners wearing dark glasses to hide the bruises on her face. Fearing for his life, Tocci was actually relieved when he was pinched by the police a week ago. He had been identified as the driver of a car seen speeding away from the scene of the crime three nights ago. To save his own hide, he testified that Saladino had indeed pulled the trigger of the gun that killed Lemke. That wasn't all, he had told McNamara. He knew many of Saladino's secrets. Captain McNamara saw this as a real opportunity to learn more about Saladino and his clandestine group of thugs, if he could keep Luciano Tocci alive long enough to put a case together.

Patrolman William Cooper, who was sitting in the passenger seat, had yet to speak. He wasn't about to side with Tocci in front of the captain. Hiding Tocci in the insane asylum seemed risky to him. The place was scary, and nobody really knew what went on there, but Cooper would never question Captain McNamara.

Willy would do what the captain asked of him, whether he thought it wise or not.

Dr. Detweiller was waiting for them when the car pulled up at the back of the administrative building. There was a quick nod between he and the captain as Tocci was handed off in shackles. Stepping aside to reveal Cooper, who wasn't exactly hiding, the chief said: "This is his cousin; he'll be around to check on him regularly." Both Cooper and Tocci were surprised that no more was said between the two other men, but neither felt the need to add anything, although they both had plenty of questions about daily patient life at the asylum.

What could go wrong? Cooper had asked himself that when the captain first told him of the plan. Tocci would hide out in the insane asylum until a case could be brought against Saladino. Cooper had reluctantly agreed to be the link between Tocci and the captain. He was fair skinned, with freckles and red hair, so nobody looking from the outside would guess the family member he visited weekly at the Buffalo State Hospital was really Tocci, who was, of course, no relation. Cooper had been publicly relieved of his position as a patrolman so that nobody would wonder what a policeman was doing regularly visiting the asylum. He was just a man visiting his cousin. Only the captain would know better. Plenty had already gone wrong and they hadn't even left the asylum.

Chapter Four

Don refilled both of their wine glasses before giving the contents of the wok a good stir. He wasn't surprised to get a call from Maude earlier in the day asking if he could handle the shop for a few more hours. This sort of research had a timetable all its own and he knew once she jumped down the rabbit hole, there would be less room for her responsibilities at the shop. She had returned to work just in time to allow him to leave for the appointment he'd made with a client on Windsor Avenue needing a brass floor lamp repaired. When he came back, there were customers in the shop, so he had waited until dinner for an update on her field research. "So you have more questions than answers. That's usually how it goes in the beginning."

Their kitchen was small but efficient. They had updated it when they moved in, removing layers of paint from the wainscoting, replacing the linoleum floor with ceramic, and the plywood cabinets with beautiful refinished oak salvaged from a pantry on Richmond Avenue. It gave the kitchen a clean, antique look, with all the modern conveniences. Maude sat at the table, allowing Don to move freely between the stove, cabinets, and the refrigerator as needed. "That may be, but it doesn't make the situation any less frustrating,"

Maude replied, swirling the red liquid around in her glass. "How weird is it that the poorhouse is somehow caught up in this?"

"Given your particular history with the institution, not weird at all, but if you look at it just within the context of the facts you have learned so far, it's actually a great place to hide a witness. I mean, by then it had lost significance as a major safety net institution and had become a home for the aged. It would have been the last place anyone would look."

"You'd think, but somehow Saladino's men found out. There had to be someone at the BPD passing on information to them."

"Transferring him to the insane asylum was a pretty slick move, too," Don said, taking the wok off the stove. "I don't even like driving by that place now. I can imagine back then it was pretty scary and I'm betting it would not have even occurred to your crime boss that his son-in-law would be taken there."

"A part of it has been renovated into an upscale hotel now. Christine says the restaurant is to die for. I've actually been meaning to suggest we try it out."

"Only because I love you will I have dinner in a former insane asylum, but I refuse to spend the night."

"Chicken! I'll bet you twenty dollars you would love it." Maude continued as she helped herself to the stir fry. "Creepy though it may have been back in the day, you're right. It is unlikely that anybody would have gone looking there for Tocci after the trouble at the Erie County Home."

"How do you know that? Oh, before you sit down, can you grab the tamari sauce from the fridge?"

"The reason I asked you to cover the shop until this afternoon was because I stopped by to see my friend at City Hall. I wanted to take a look at the death certificates filed in the days before Eva Barstow's shooting. Tocci's was among the six deaths reported from the Erie County Home on April 12, 1924. Four men and two women. Two of the other men and both women were sixty years old or older, and the other man was a John Doe, estimated to be about 45 years old. I'm thinking the John Doe was the man who went to the Home to kill Tocci."

"So, the idea was for Saladino to assume that both men had died in the struggle."

"That's a safe assumption. They talked about it, the police captain and the assistant superintendent at the Home."

"So, if there was a leak at the BPD, then news of the incident at the Home and the death of the two men could have easily found its way back to Saladino."

"I don't have any confirmation on that, but it makes sense." Maude speared a piece of beef with her fork and smeared it around her plate for longer than was necessary to soak up the tamari sauce.

"What are you thinking?" Don asked her.

"Well, all of this is certainly interesting, but it doesn't tell me anything about Eva Barstow's murder."

Don drained his glass and rose to grab the wine bottle off the counter. "You spent some time with the young patrolman today, so let's start with him."

"I know he was interested in Eva's daughter Nina. His willingness to help Captain McNamara hide this witness seems to have cost him any chance with her."

"Do you think he could have actually done it? I mean maybe he wasn't after the mother. Maybe he was after the brother and shot the mother by mistake."

"I don't think so. The dream I had the other night was very clear. He hopped over the Barstow's back fence before the men who killed Eva arrived."

"Well, the good news is that you seem to be able to connect to the energy of these events pretty easily. I think it is just a matter of mapping out where you think you are likely to get answers and then going to those places to see what you can find out."

Maude laughed out loud at both the simplicity and the absurdity of the plan. "Do you think the people who bought our house will notice if I set up in their back yard? Better yet, the original Main Street location of the Fourteenth Precinct no longer exists. Don't you think I'll attract attention sitting in the parking lot of the landscaping business, or the lofts, or any of the other businesses located nearby, typing feverishly on my laptop?"

"Okay, it will take some planning, but I still think it's your best shot. You were able to connect with Captain McNamara just by looking at his picture. You were also able to guide your connection to our old house just from your memories of living in it. Why don't you try looking at a picture of the old Fourteenth and see what you get? Better yet, let's take a ride over there now. The landscaping place is closed so nobody will see us if we park there."

"I'll take a ride over there tomorrow. We're too far into this bottle of wine to even consider another journey into the past and I'm exhausted."

"Fair enough. I'll come with you if you want." Don looked at the empty bottle and then at his wife. "In the meantime, let's start on another bottle."

"Don Travers, are you trying to get me drunk?"

He flashed that devilish smile, the one that had convinced her to go on their first date over twenty years ago. "No, I'm trying to get me drunk in the hopes that you will take advantage of me."

Maude returned a cheeky grin of her own as she lifted her glass to drain its contents. "Getting drunk and having sex…isn't that how we started this relationship?"

Don laughed out loud. "We've come full circle, haven't we?" Instead of getting another bottle, Don took Maude by the hands and pulled her into his arms. His kiss was cautious at first. They still were not used to having the apartment to themselves in the evenings. More than a few passionate kisses were interrupted over the years by one or both boys needing a glass of water or help with their homework. Such was the life of raising children. It was a gift to be able to act spontaneously, and they both enjoyed it. They seemed to be reminded at the same time that Billy was out for the evening, and the kiss deepened.

Maude had enjoyed her college years. There had been many boyfriends, and even a few hookups where only first names had been exchanged and phone numbers had been lost or discarded, but once she met Don, it was his kisses alone she craved. Even after more than two decades together she wanted him as badly as she did when they first met. They stood there in the kitchen, shedding clothes between long, deep kisses. Were they moving? They must have been, because they were no longer in the kitchen. In the hall, he pressed her up against the wall. They had made love in less comfortable places back in the days when they had to steal moments alone. But now they had time. He picked her up and she wrapped her legs around his waist. They were both grinning, the tips of their foreheads resting against each other.

Other than a bit of silver hair at the temples, Don still looked like the man she married, lean and muscular. He carried her easily down the length of the hall, with one hand on her bottom and the other outstretched to open the bedroom door. There was no need to close it behind them. He sat on the edge of the bed, Maude seated in his lap, her legs still wrapped tight around him. He lowered his head, trailing kisses along her jaw, neck and breast. It went on like that until they were both gasping. She burned with every touch of his lips, every caress of his fingers, giving back the same until the need to be one overtook them both.

It was still light out when they both had regained the ability to speak again.

"What?" she asked in response to his cheeky grin.

"The night is young, Maudie, and we have it all to ourselves."

Maude laughed out loud. "The night may be young, but we are not. I think we have to at least catch our breath before we attempt that again."

"Speak for yourself!" Don pulled her close, feeling the need to prove his point, and so the next few hours were filled with passion, punctuated by pillow talk, laughter, and a bit of roughhousing, as it had been so many nights before the kids came along.

• • •

Maude pulled up in front of the lot on Main Street that once housed the Fourteenth Precinct. The shade of a nearby tree would keep the car cool for a while if she worked with the windows opened. She pulled on the lever to adjust her seat, moving it far back enough to accommodate the laptop comfortably in front of the car's steering wheel. With fingers poised over the keyboard, she began to consider the immediate aftermath of the shooting. She imagined that the officers called to the scene would have been up most of the night examining the crime scene, questioning the family, and canvassing the neighborhood for witnesses. She pictured two bleary-eyed men at the morning briefing making their report to Captain McNamara.

"There's no denying him, sir, what with that flamin' red hair," Detective Malloy told the captain.

"He walked that beat every day, sir," Detective Schneider added. "Folks know him well."

"He's had his eye on Nina Barstow," Sergeant Wellesley chimed in from the back of the room. The smug satisfaction of Wellesley's face could only be seen by the captain, since the others had their backs to him. The sergeant had made no secret about the reason Willy had been fired, as McNamara had predicted and the gossip had already begun to fly around the neighborhood.

Having Willy questioned about a shooting so soon after he had been fired would surely push Susan Cooper over the edge. The captain owed it to her late husband to do what he could for the boy. After all, this was a former patrolman of the Buffalo Police Department who was identified leaving the scene of a crime. It would not be unusual for the captain to want to question the suspect himself. "Leave Cooper to me. There were four people seen getting into a car just after the shooting. The rest of you find out who they are!"

Later that afternoon, Captain McNamara set out to question Willy Cooper. He considered his approach as he turned off Main Street onto Hertel Avenue. Going to the house would only upset Susan, and, if McNamara was being honest, he would have trouble looking her in the eye after having just seemingly fired her son the previous day. Willy was due to check on Tocci, and it was nearly visiting hours at the State Hospital so the captain drove slowly up the street, hoping to catch him along the way. He knew Willy would walk the few miles to the asylum rather than catch the street cars. He was a beat cop, after all. Approaching the intersection of Delaware Avenue, McNamara saw Willy about to cross the street.

Willy was as surprised to see the captain as he had been that day at the zoo. It had been made clear to him that McNamara would meet him at the end of the week in the cemetery at his father's headstone, so that they could exchange any important information about Tocci or the case against Saladino. If the captain was seeking him out, something was wrong.

"Get in the car." McNamara made no attempt to ease Willy's mind as he had the day he found him at the zoo. He drove in silence toward Forest Lawn Cemetery. They had planned to meet weekly at his father's headstone because it was less likely anyone would find it

unusual if they happened to be seen there together, so Willy wasn't surprised when the captain pulled the car up along Mirror Lake in the center of the plot.

If the captain's intent was to put a good scare into Willy, he had succeeded. When McNamara turned the car off and looked toward Willy, he was pale and all but shaking. The captain was determined to show the boy no sympathy. "What the devil were you doing at the Barstow house last night?"

"What? How did you know I was there?" Of all the reasons the captain might seek out Willy ahead of schedule, this was not one of them.

"You were identified by a neighbor approaching the house and by another one living behind them climbing over the fence around eleven o'clock. What the devil were you doing?"

Willy was completely baffled. "Did the neighbors call the police? I just cut through the yard, I swear, Captain."

"Oh Jesus, you don't know, do you?'

"Know what?"

"Mrs. Barstow was shot by an intruder last night. She's at Sister's Hospital. It's bad, son; they don't expect her to make it."

Willy was panic stricken. "Mrs. Barstow shot? Who? Why? Do you have any leads?"

The captain could see how much this news had rattled the young man and worked to keep the edge off his anger. "You are not getting it, Willy. You are the lead! You were identified fleeing the scene; now tell me what the devil you were doing there!"

Willy ran his hands through his hair, taking a deep breath in an effort to calm himself. The steely eyes of Captain McNamara may as well have been those of his father, and the look of both disappointment and anger in them burned through him. "I went there to try and see Nina. She was out at a party; we were supposed to have gone together, but..." He ran a hand through his hair again. "Anyway, I knew she had to be home by eleven and I was hoping to talk to her for a minute before I had to meet you." Observing no change of the captain's expression, Willy quickly continued, "After a while, I realized there was nothing I could say to her that wouldn't betray my promise to you, so I left. I knew she would be home at any minute by then, so I hopped the back fence."

"Did you see anyone else near the house? Mrs. Barstow was shot just before midnight. Four people were seen piling into a car just outside the house and taking off down the end of the street."

Willy sat back, stunned by the realization of those words. "I must have just missed them! If I had stayed just a few more minutes, I might have done something to stop them. If I hadn't been a coward and hopped the fence, they might have seen me and thought otherwise of breaking in."

The captain's anger gave way to compassion as Willy continued to berate himself for leaving. "Listen lad, if you hadn't left, they may have shot you instead. I told the boys I'd question you and this will be the end of it, I hope."

Confusion set in again and Willy asked, "They don't think I shot her, do they?"

The captain knew he meant his colleagues at the Fourteenth. "They are trained police officers, sworn to uphold the law, as you are yourself. You were identified fleeing the scene. They'll want answers, as you would if it were one of them who'd been identified. So, I'll ask again: did you see anything, anything at all?

Willy sat back again and considered the question. "It was very late. I didn't notice anything unusual when I approached the house. I looked up at the house and saw a light on in one of the upstairs rooms. I assumed it was Nina's parents' room, so I was very quiet when I walked up the drive and into the backyard."

"What about when you came out from the neighbor's yard and on to the street? Did you see or hear anyone then?"

"No, and I looked carefully before I walked out to the street. I walked up to Hertel and then toward Delaware. There was nobody on the street except me."

The captain said nothing while he pondered Willy's report. "Mrs. Barstow was shot close to midnight, and the neighbor has you sneaking through his backyard just after eleven. It's tight, but it works."

"What will you say? Will Nina know I was there?"

"Don't worry about this, Willy, you still have a job to do." Willy looked like he wanted to interject, but McNamara didn't give him the chance. "Get going now and check on Tocci. Find out what you can and I'll meet you back here in a few days."

Willy did his best to walk off his anger on the way to the asylum. In just a few short days his entire life had been turned upside down and now he was suspected of shooting Mrs. Barstow. Nina would surely hear about it and he was helpless to defend himself. He couldn't even bring himself to think about what his mother would say, and all to protect some two-bit, wife-beating thug.

Approaching the entrance gate on Elmwood Avenue, Willy took a deep breath before entering. From here it didn't look like a bad place. The grounds were well kept and resembled a park with tree-lined walkways and manicured lawns. The massive complex of buildings that included men's and women's dormitories, separate kitchens, outbuildings, stables and livestock barns was set far off the street, and Willy used those final minutes as he strolled up the curved road towards the administrative building to shake off the rest of his mood.

He met first with Dr. Detweiller, who assured him that Tocci's admission had raised no eyebrows, although he arrived in the dead of night. He was settling in on a ward with other non-excitable inmates. He would be offered a job in the greenhouse, as all inmates were encouraged but not compelled to add structure to their day with honest work. The doctor excused himself when the attendant brought Tocci into the room.

"You stick me in the nut house and you want me to work on top of that?" Tocci later complained to Willy. "You gotta be kidding me!"

"Both the captain and Dr. Detweiller said it would be best if you blended in. The best way to do that is to do what everyone else is doing. Dr. Detweiller says that you can choose between a few daily chores or a good strong dose of chloral hydrate." Willy had no sympathy for this man who was here rather than in jail because he was willing to rat out his boss.

"Knockout drops, that's what the nut jobs call them. No thanks."

Willy had no intention of telling Tocci that knockout drops were only used for the most excitable inmates. He thought it would do the man some good to engage in an honest day's work for a change and simply thought to bully him into it. "Just do the chores. You're safer out and about where others can see you, rather than squirreled away, alone in a room. Besides, an honest day's work won't kill you."

Although Saladino's men had attacked him in his room at the County Home, Tocci wasn't sure he agreed with the notion that he was safer out and about. Saladino thought he was dead, so it seemed foolish to do anything that might jeopardize that assumption. Sticking to the ward seemed the safest option now. Each one was a self-contained unit. In addition to the patient rooms, there was a dining room, sitting room, and lavatories. There was no need to ever leave it if one was so inclined. It also had the additional bonus of limiting his interactions with the other patients. What did he have in common with a bunch of nut jobs, after all?

There hadn't been any time to question Tocci after the attack at the Home, and Willy had been tasked with finding out what he could. "They knew where you were. Somehow Saladino knew where we stashed you."

"He's got a man inside, but only he knows who it is. Saladino don't trust nobody." In answer to the skeptical look, Tocci continued, "What? I got no reason not to be straight with you."

"Yeah, and I got no reason to trust you," Willy fired back. "Did you know the guy they sent after you?"

Tocci snorted out a laugh. "Yeah, no great loss to humanity there, I can tell ya that." The smirk faded from his face. "Saladino's got more where he came from, you can be sure of that. So, I gotta ask, who else besides you and the captain know I'm here?"

Willy could have answered the question and put his mind at ease but being the trusted confidante of Captain McNamara had cost him everything that was important, and Tocci wasn't remotely worth the sacrifice. "You'd better think long and hard about who in the precinct is tipping him off. The sooner we find the leak, the sooner we can plug it." He hoped knowing his life could still be in danger would make Tocci remember something that might help identify the snitch.

The visit with Tocci was brief and left Willy feeling no less angry or frustrated than when he had arrived at the asylum. He did not want to head straight home, so he walked down Forest Avenue toward the zoo. Just because he was temporarily prevented from walking his beat didn't mean he couldn't still check in on his favorite North Park residents. He entered through the main gate and made his way to the primates, hoping that by staying indoors, he might avoid the patrolman who had taken his place. No such luck. He hadn't been at the exhibit of Japanese macaques longer than five minutes before he heard a familiar voice.

"You got some nerve showin' your face around here, Cooper."

It was Nick Brown. He had been a year ahead of Willy at St. Mark's, and a bully. Of all the men who could have replaced him, why did it have to be Nick Brown? Willy steeled himself and turned toward the patrolman. "Last I knew the zoo was open to the public."

Brown laughed out loud. "I guess you have a lot of free time on your hands these days. Still, you ought to head home; the captain is looking for you. Fired less than a day, and now the lead suspect in an attempted murder. You've broken your mother's heart, Cooper."

There was no time to react to the taunting comments of his childhood nemesis. Willy realized that if Nick knew he had been questioned by the captain about the Barstow shooting, he would have blabbed it all up and down Hertel Avenue as he walked his beat. It was only a matter of time before his mother would find out. Willy had to get home. Without so much as a glance back at Nick, he was gone.

"You can run, Cooper, but you can't hide," Nick called out as Willy broke into a trot.

Caught up in her usual writer's trance, Maude hadn't noticed as the light faded. It was nearly dark when she returned home. As she climbed the stairs to her apartment the delightful aroma of simmering marinara sauce floated down to greet her along with familiar sounds she hadn't heard in a long time.

"Glen, if you keep tasting that sauce, there will be none left for dinner when your mother gets home."

"I can't help it; it's so good, better than mom's."

"Don't tell her that," Billy chimed in, pushing his brother aside and swabbing a large piece of Italian bread across the bubbling surface of the pan.

"We were saving that loaf for garlic bread," their father reminded them as he took what remained of the second loaf of bread over to the cutting board to slice it and slather the surfaces with melted butter and garlic.

"We're hungry," the boys said in unison.

Maude smiled on the other side of the door. They rarely had dinner as a family these days, and she hadn't expected Glen home for the weekend. The boys had loved to help cook when they were younger, and although it usually produced a bigger mess in the kitchen, their help was always encouraged and enjoyed. She was tempted to sit and listen for a few minutes longer, but the chances of there being garlic bread for dinner diminished with every minute she waited.

Maude opened the door to the three of them surrounding the stockpot on the stove. "Hey, what are you doing home?"

"All my finals were during the last week of classes. I'm done," Glen replied, giving his mom a hug the likes of which she hadn't felt since he was in grade school. Being away at school seemed to help him appreciate the comforts of home these days.

"Oh, that's right, I forgot."

"You know how mom gets when she gets going on one of those secret quests," Billy reminded his brother.

"Secret quests? What are you talking about?" Maude was taken aback by her younger son's remark.

"Oh, c'mon, mom, we're older now. Won't you finally tell us what has you running back and forth to Lily Dale?" Glen wasted no time piling on with a very frank question.

Maude exchanged a look with Don in the way that husbands and wives do when both simultaneously realize they had been fooling themselves all this time thinking that their sons had been completely oblivious to their adventures. Don raised his brows, daring her to come clean with the boys.

"Alright, let's get dinner on the table first," she told them.

Conversation shifted to the normal reporting of their respective days while the pasta and salad were prepared. Sadly, the garlic bread never made it to the table, as each of them ripped off a hunk as pots were stirred and vegetables were chopped. When everyone was seated, Maude cleared her throat. "Have you heard of Modern Spiritualism?" When each of the boys nodded, she went on to explain the changes that had occurred in her life, starting from the whispering skeleton of Frederika Kaiser, whose bones had given Maude vivid flashes of her nineteenth century life when Maude touched them. She learned that the woman had been brutally beaten by her husband, and eventually sought refuge in the poorhouse after his death.

The boys listened intently as their mother confessed to having detailed and historically accurate dreams of the past after they had found the antique ring hidden under the floorboards of her bedroom when they first moved into the apartment above the shop. Those dreams, she told them, had helped her understand how the ring had come to rest there. The mystery surrounding that ring had led to the revelation that she had been Martha Sloane Quinn, a physician in the nineteenth century, in a past life.

Maude did her best to hold back tears while describing the events at the marina on the Outer Harbor a few years back and how their father had nearly drowned when events of their past life together had caught up with them in the present. She explained that she and their father had been together in many lifetimes and would likely find each other again in future lives.

Focused on the methodical telling of her tale, Maude hadn't really paid attention to the expressions on their faces while she spoke. When she was done Glen looked disappointed. "That's it?"

Don laughed. "Did you think maybe she was working for Homeland or the FBI, or something?"

"Sorry, pal, nothing quite that glamorous," Maude confessed.

"Can you at least talk to dead people?" Glen looked hopeful that his mother might have an awe-inspiring super power after all.

"Not in the way that you mean." Maude answered. "I get information from people on the other side, like the visions from Mrs. Kaiser..."

"I can." Maude was unable to finish her reply when Billy interrupted. "I can talk to dead people," he repeated when they all turned and looked at him. "Yeah, ever since I was little. Aunt Mabel came to me the night she died."

"No way, I call BS on that," Glen argued.

"No, seriously," Billy persisted.

"You're a little old for imaginary friends, bro," Glen taunted. "I guess I shouldn't be surprised you made up a few, since you don't have any of the regular kind."

"Aunt Mabel? Why didn't you ever tell us?" Don asked, ignoring Glen's teasing. His great aunt had passed the year Billy started kindergarten.

Billy rolled his eyes, and pointed at his brother, who was shaking his head in disbelief. "This is why I never mentioned it before." A stern look from their mother stilled Glen and then Billy continued. "At the time I thought she came to everyone. She seemed really happy and told me not to be sad. It wasn't until later that I realized I was the only one seeing these people."

"When was that, and why haven't you said anything?" Maude tried to keep the accusation out of her voice. This is what she had been afraid of, the reason she had held off telling the boys. It was just easier to believe highly developed inner senses didn't run in the family.

Don placed a hand on her arm, knowing that small touch would offer her the reassurance that he could not give with words right now. Turning to Billy, he said, "It's no big deal, buddy, but since we're sharing, we'd like to hear your experiences."

"Yeah, what do you see? Are they glowing and see through, or oozing with rotted flesh, like zombies?" Glen pulled down on his lower eyelids to show the whites of his eyes while groaning and growling, not sure which noise was appropriate for a ghost.

Billy ignored his brother's antics. "Well, occasionally I'd see spirits; I guess that's what you call them, you know, at places like Old Fort Niagara, or Mikey Griffin's house when his grandma died. They are sort of… foggy. It wasn't until we moved here that I realized that these people were communicating with me because nobody else was able to see them."

Seeing dead soldiers at Old Fort Niagara changed Glen's tone from mocking to envy. "Dude! You never told me. You can talk to dead people. That is totally cool!"

"Well, it's really no big deal," Billy insisted. Seeing the look on his mother's face, which he interpreted as disappointment, he continued, "I mean, what was I going to say? *'I see dead people'*? 'cause that worked out so well for the kid in that movie."

Billy's posture, his expression and the tone of his voice said no big deal, but Maude knew otherwise. He was just like her, and Glen was a carbon copy of Don. He would have thought it was a very big deal in the beginning. Maude had the support of her husband when she realized that she possessed abilities that most other people did not, but Billy had been apparently dealing with it on his own. It was selfish of her to have kept this secret from the boys. She could only hope it hadn't been too much of a burden for Billy to shoulder alone.

Maude tried to sound casual as she questioned him further. "So, you're saying that there are spirits here in this building that are trying to communicate with you? Can you tell me about that?"

"I guess. What do you want to know?"

"For starters, how many people attempt to contact you and how often?" It was getting harder for Maude to keep the interest from her voice.

Billy didn't seem bothered by his mother's enthusiasm. "Well, it was a long time ago, before we moved in here. There was an older woman and an older man." He thought for a moment before continuing, considering how best to describe the couple. "Their clothes were old, I mean like from a long time ago. They used to live here, and they died here, too, both of them."

He said that last part with confidence. "Do they communicate with you?" Maude asked.

"I guess the short answer to that question is yes. I'm not sure I can explain how, though."

Don shot her a look to prevent what he knew would be a series of questions asking her son to elaborate. "How often do you see them?" he asked.

"I saw them a few times when I was a kid, but they freaked me out, so I told them to leave me alone. I also told them to tell any other ghosts that might be around to do the same. I'm not sure if they did or not, but I haven't seen anyone here since then."

"They just left you alone because you asked?" Glen asked. "Where did they go?"

"I don't know, and I really don't care as long as they stay out of my bedroom."

Glen was clearly envious of his brother's ability and would have grilled him in much the same way his mother would have if Don had not intervened. Later, when he and Maude were getting ready for bed, he cautioned her not to persist in questioning Billy. "He needs time to come to terms with his ability, like you did."

"Although it was not how I was expecting that conversation to go, I have to admit I'm not surprised to hear he is gifted this way. He is so much like me," Maude admitted. "I want to help him, but I don't know how."

"The boys have always come to us when they had any worries or problems. Billy handled this by telling the old couple to leave him alone, so he didn't need our help."

Maude laughed. "Yeah, I'm wondering why I didn't think of that. It probably would have saved me a considerable amount of stress."

"I think if you really didn't want your gifts, you'd have found a way to make them go away. That connection into the past was too much for you to resist. Billy doesn't have the same interest in history that you do. He may choose to do nothing about developing his ability. He might just tell every spirit who tries to make contact to stop bothering him. We have to respect that."

"So, are you suggesting that I just leave it alone?"

"I'm suggesting that you trust him to come to us if he needs help. Maude, he's a pretty well-adjusted guy already, and he's been having these experiences since he was a small child. It seems to me that he's done pretty well on his own."

Standing by and doing nothing was that part of being a boy's mom with which Maude was never comfortable. She had learned from the other sports moms to stay on the sidelines and let the coach sort it out if they took a hit during a game. When it came time, it was Don who took the lead on the birds and the bees talk and dating advice. Once again, she found it was required that she stand aside and act only if needed. Thus far that strategy had resulted in two confident and independent young men, so, hard as it would be, she nodded in agreement. "You're right…I know you're right."

"Just go be you. Let him see that this really hasn't changed who you are. If he wants to embrace it, he will, and if he doesn't, that's okay, too."

"Okay, well, I'm going to go be me in the old neighborhood tomorrow and see if I can gain any insight into this murder mystery. Stand by in case I'm picked up for loitering near our old house!"

"Will do!"

CHAPTER FIVE

The bell above the front door announced Christine, who had agreed to come in early. There was an unmistakable spring in her step that told Maude that things were still hot and heavy with Sam. It would be too easy to get caught up in a conversation about the juicy details of their love affair, which Maude didn't have time for, so she began gathering her things to leave.

"You look like you're about to head out," Christine observed as Maude picked up her purse and keys.

"Yeah, I've got a few errands to run," Maude answered vaguely.

"Do these errands have anything to do with 'Now what?'?" Christine was immediately suspicious that Maude was not inclined to stay and chat.

Recalling their brief conversation in her office the other day, Maude couldn't help but be impressed with Christine's ability to retain a clear memory of any question Maude had previously managed to avoid answering. The woman could sniff out intrigue from a mile away. "Yes, as a matter of fact," she replied with a smirk and headed out the door without further explanation.

"I'm sure I'm going to pay for that when I get back," Maude mumbled to herself as she climbed into her SUV, knowing now that Christine would make it her mission to find out what Maude had been up to while she was out of the shop.

She turned on to her old street, but kept driving past the house, feeling drawn to the end of the block. There was very little activity on the street late in the morning, as those who worked had already left, and those who didn't were still enjoying their morning coffee. Maude found a place to park two houses from the end of the block. As she pulled out her laptop, she recalled what she had read in the newspaper reports of the Barstow shooting. In her mind's eye, she tried to picture the neighborhood in 1924. The residential area ended just before what is now Tacoma Avenue, with a large open field beyond. The getaway car had been abandoned hastily when it became stuck in the mud and she pictured four men quickly exiting the vehicle and trudging as fast as they could across the muddy field. There would not have been much in the dark of night for the investigating officers to see, so she assumed they returned to examine the field more thoroughly the next day. After a few deep breaths, the scene became clear in her mind.

Two police officers and a portly gentleman, the owner of the stolen car from the next block over, watched as a tow truck hauled the Chevrolet sedan out of the mud. "And just who is going to pay to have it cleaned?" the portly man asked.

"Don't worry, Mr. Greco. The car will be returned to you as good as new."

"It had better be, sir. It had better be or your captain will surely hear from me!"

"I'll see to it personally, Arturo, you have my word." The three men turned as Captain McNamara approached, hand outstretched to shake on the deal. "Now why don't you go home? I'm sure Doris has your breakfast ready for you."

The two patrolmen looked grateful as the captain walked with Arturo Greco, continuing to offer assurances that his car was in safe hands and would be returned to him soon. "The old man would have surely followed us to the precinct garage," Patrolman Brown said as the captain returned.

"That he would have," McNamara agreed. "What have you got here, Brown?"

The young man pointed north. "Multiple footprints heading that way, sir. We followed them for about a quarter of a mile, to the railroad tracks."

"I've got a street car conductor who can put four men in mud-spattered clothes on his car just after the time of the shooting. They got off at Main and Hertel. Why don't you two head over there and see if you can identify them. I'll see that Mr. Greco's car gets to the garage in one piece."

"Yes, sir," the patrolmen said in unison and headed north across the field.

Captain McNamara was just about to return to his car to accompany the tow truck when he caught a man waving out of the corner of his eye. Bracing himself for another discussion with Mr. Greco, he was relieved to find it was someone else.

"Excuse me, captain," the man said, approaching at a brisk walk, still waving his arm, not trusting that the captain would wait for him. Out of breath when he finally reached the edge of the muddy field, it took a minute for him to speak again. "Captain, my name is Gabriel Lucchesi. I live just over there." He pointed up the block, on the opposite side from the Barstow's home. "Your patrolmen told me to contact the precinct if I remembered anything further about the incident… terrible, just terrible. That poor woman. Mr. Barstow, he stays by her side. He's a good man. My Juliana has looked in on the children, she helps where she can. Terrible, just terrible."

"Yes, yes, it is, Mr. Lucchesi. You say you have remembered something about that evening?"

"Yes, well, I was out walking just before it happened. I don't sleep well." He rattled on about his insomnia, refocusing only after some gentle prodding from the captain. "Oh, yes, I'm sorry. I was out walking, and I saw a young man approach the house. I believe it was young Mr. Cooper, but you already know that part. There was another man just up at the corner," he pointed up toward Hertel Avenue. "I only saw him briefly, that's why I didn't recall it at the time. Hearing about Mrs. Barstow was such a shock. The poor woman…they don't expect her to make it. Four children… It's such a shame, and two so young."

"Mr. Lucchesi, was there anything else about the other man that you needed to tell me?" McNamara had years of experience dealing with witnesses whose minds wandered, so he waited patiently for the man to focus again.

"Oh, that's right, yes, the other man. As I passed him, he quickly turned around, and hurried off in the direction he had come." Lucchesi pointed again in the direction of Hertel Avenue. "Is that important, do you think?"

"Where exactly were you, and where were you headed, Mr. Lucchesi?"

"I was about there," he pointed towards the street, about two houses past his own, "heading towards Hertel Avenue."

"You say the man was walking toward you?"

"Yes, I saw him turn from Hertel Avenue onto my street. I can't be sure, but I think something in the direction of the Barstow house caught his attention, but then he turned so fast and hurried off in the direction he had come from. I can't be sure, it all happened so quickly."

"Did the man speak to you?"

"No. I watched him coming toward me, and then he just turned and ran past me."

"Just like that, with no words or warning? Can you describe him?"

"Yes, without a word. Maybe he forgot something? In any event, he was tall, with dark hair…" Lucchesi thought for a moment. "Well, it was dark out, and he turned so quickly."

"How about just the basics? Was he older or younger, thin or fat?"

Lucchesi thought for a moment. "He was younger, I'd say. I don't move that quickly anymore," he admitted. "He was lean, tall and lean."

"Do you remember what time it was?"

"Well, I left the house at ten, and it was just after that," Lucchesi answered with confidence.

Captain patted his coat, searching for his pocket watch. "That's good, Mr. Lucchesi. Will you be home later this afternoon? I'd like to send a patrolman by to take down your statement in more detail." The other man nodded that he would. "That's good, sir; think on it some more and I'll send a man by after lunch."

"Good enough, Captain. Good day to you."

McNamara thought about Mr. Lucchesi's observation as he drove back to the station house. All the eyewitness accounts agreed that four people fled the crime scene, and although some claimed one was a woman, and others had seen four men, the number of individuals was the same. He doubted that the person Lucchesi had seen was implicated in the Barstow shooting in any way. Still, he'd send Brown over to take a statement and see if they could put a face to the tall, lean, dark haired young man who rushed off toward Hertel Avenue.

• • •

"Whatcha lookin' at, mom?" Billy had come in through the back of the shop and stuck his head into the office before going upstairs.

Maude looked up from her laptop. "It's an old map of the street car routes in the city. I wish I had a hard copy. It's brutal trying to read it on my screen."

"Email it to me. The screen on my desktop is twice the size. We can look at it in my room."

"Okay, thanks." Maude sent the image and shouted to Christine that she would be upstairs if needed.

"So, why are you looking at an old street car map?" Billy asked as he opened the file.

"Wow, that's much better." Maude smiled, realizing that she could answer her son's question truthfully now that he knew about her special skills. "I was in our old neighborhood this morning. It helps me connect to a specific time and place if I am near it. Anyway, I learned that the murder suspects fled the scene in the direction of the Erie Railroad tracks." She pointed to the map. "Everything beyond Tacoma Avenue would have been an open field. Evidently the getaway car got stuck in the mud beyond where the pavement ended. The suspects headed north, toward the tracks. A conductor reported that four men in muddy clothes got on his streetcar just after the time of the shooting. I don't know where they got on, but they ended up at Main and Hertel, so I'm trying to figure out what streetcar they may have caught. I was looking at the map hoping for some clarification."

"Would looking at the map give you the same kind of connection with the past that going to the old neighborhood did?"

"I had hoped so, but so far it hasn't," Maude admitted.

Billy looked at the map, tracing his finger on the lines representing the Erie Railroad tracks. "It looks like there was a route on Virgil Avenue. It seems like it would have been the closest." He removed his finger from the screen and turned toward his mother. "What difference does it make? Are you actually trying to solve this murder?"

"I'm trying to understand why it has been brought to my attention. I'm assuming it's because I'm supposed to figure out who killed Eva Barstow."

"Why, what good would that do anyone now?"

Maude hesitated before answering, mostly because she wasn't exactly sure what good might come of her efforts to understand and possibly solve a murder that occurred ninety-three years ago. "I'll admit I'm not sure, but some good always comes of these things. Some good has already come of this. I know now that I'm not the only one in the family with these special gifts."

Billy didn't have a response to that. Instead, he asked, "So, what did you plan on doing if you discover which direction the murderers took?"

"I'm not sure. I thought I might take a ride over in that direction and see if I pick up on anything. I'm having some success channeling the past through my writing. I drove over to our old street this morning and sat with my laptop for a few hours. That's how I learned that the four suspects may have hopped on a streetcar. I'm hoping if I can locate the area where they might have jumped on, I might learn something else. It feels a bit like a scavenger hunt, each clue leads me to the next."

"So, what are your plans for this long term? Will you hire yourself out as a supernatural detective?"

Maude could tell that underneath the cheeky grin, Billy's question was sincere. She laughed, not wanting to blow his cover. "Maude Travers, Supernatural Sleuth. I don't know about that. I can't see myself profiting from my gifts, although other people do."

"Why not? What's the point of having abilities other people don't if you can't make a few bucks? After all, mechanics charge to fix cars, lawyers charge for their services. I don't see this as any different."

"It's not that I think it's unethical. There is nothing wrong with legitimate psychic mediums making a living using their gifts, as long as they do so under reasonable moral, ethical and legal guidelines. I was happy with my life before all of this happened. I don't mind making a bit of room for the changes that have occurred recently, but I have no interest in leaving the shop to pursue other professional interests."

Maude paused for a moment, trying to decide if the moment was right to ask a few probing questions. They were enjoying a rare moment of mother-son bonding, so she took a risk. "Let me ask you something." He seemed receptive, so she continued. "Are you at all curious to explore your gifts?"

Billy didn't pause for thought before answering the question, which surprised Maude. "I hadn't really given it any thought recently. It has been a few years since I've seen anyone, so I assumed it wore off, or something." It was hard to tell if his shy smile indicated comfort or discomfort with the conversation.

"I don't think it works that way, pal," she returned the smile, giving his shoulder an affectionate squeeze. "My guess is that you are very focused on not seeing anything outside the physical world, and that's why you are not seeing spirits. There's nothing wrong with that, if you are happy."

"You can really go to a place and see what it was like there over a century ago?"

"Well, I don't actually see it, like a movie, but I am able to channel it through my writing. I suppose you could say that I see it in my mind. Does that make sense?"

"Sorta. So, everything you have written about actually happened?"

"That's a good question. I'm not able to verify every detail, but I've been able to find many of the people and events I have written about in the historic record."

Billy was clearly impressed as he considered her answer. "Would I be able to do stuff like that?"

"I don't know. If you were really interested in learning more, I could introduce you to a few people in Lily Dale and you can talk to them." The idea of visiting Lily Dale to speak to strangers changed the look on Billy's face from admiration to reluctance and so Maude quickly added, "You don't have to decide now. Think about it and let me know. I'll respect whatever choice you make."

The discussion ended when Billy's phone rang. "Sheri! Hi, hey, thanks for calling me back." As Billy turned away from his mom, the ear to ear grin indicated that he had been eagerly anticipating this call. Maude gave him his privacy, grateful to have had a few moments with her son. She'd planted the idea in his mind and could only wait to see if it would take root.

Chapter Six

Nina Barstow stood in front of the cabinet range, match stick in hand, but not yet ready to light the stove. Staring back at the reflection in the black enamel surface, her mind had wandered to the conversation she had overheard between Mr. Lucchesi and her father. Willy Cooper had been in the yard that night her mother was shot. Mr. Lucchesi had seen him walk up the drive, past the front door. What was he doing here? Could he have come to see her? How could she find out without asking her father, who wanted her to have nothing to do with Willy? The last thing she wanted to do was upset her father, but Willy wouldn't have intruded so late in the evening for nothing.

"Darling, do you need help?" Conrad Barstow asked, taking the match from his daughter's hand and turning to light the stove.

"Oh, thanks, daddy. I guess my mind wandered. I'll get your breakfast started right away."

His smile was bittersweet as he took a seat at the table. "Your mother would be proud of the way you have stepped into her shoes."

Nina kept her attention on the stove. "How is she?" She was afraid to look at her father as she asked the question, fearing his face would let on more than his words.

"There's no change, I'm afraid."

"Oh Daddy, won't you please let me go and see her." As Nina turned to face her father, the mature young woman was replaced by a scared little girl who needed her mother. "I know you don't want to frighten Matthew and Amelia, but I must see her." She did not want to argue with her father, but she would question the decision to allow Jonathan to see their mother, and not her if she must.

Conrad looked at his daughter, making no attempt to hide his grief. He knew when he left the hospital he'd have to tell the rest of his children the truth. Nina had fallen asleep on the sofa when he arrived home after midnight. He walked quietly passed her, relieved he'd have a few more hours before he had to tell Nina her mother would likely not survive the upcoming day. "Yes, darling. You must get your brother and sister ready after breakfast. It's time you all have a chance to see your mother."

Nina's spirits quickly rose, thinking there must have been some improvement if he was allowing the children to go and see their mother. Her joy was short lived as Nina read the despair in her father's eyes. "Oh, Daddy, oh, no!"

"They don't think she'll live." Jonathan stood in the doorway of the kitchen, trying desperately to keep his voice neutral.

"She's lost a lot of blood," their father reported, unable to look his daughter in the eye.

"Oh, daddy, what will we do?" Tears were streaming down Nina's face as she turned to meet her father's embrace.

Conrad reached out for his son as well, folding his eldest children against his chest. "I don't think I know, my darlings." Conrad clung to them, seeking the comfort he was unable to offer in return.

It was Nina who pulled away when she heard the younger children beginning to stir upstairs. "We mustn't let them see us this way," she said, pulling out a handkerchief to dry her eyes.

"What will you tell them, father?"

"The truth, Jonathan; they deserve no less."

Conrad would have waited until the children had finished their breakfast before telling them of their mother's grave condition, but he knew they would want news straightaway.

"You've been so brave, my little wonders." He had referred to his youngest children as little wonders just after he found out that Eva was expecting Amelia and Matthew was just learning to walk. Although they had wanted a larger family, they were content with Jonathan and Nina, and so to be blessed with two more children more than a decade later was nothing short of a wonder. "I have news that will require you to be braver still." He beckoned each of them to sit on his knee and told them, struggling to keep his composure as each child broke down and began to sob.

• • •

Willy slowed his pace as he approached Nina's street. He could see the Barstow house from where he was. Captain McNamara had informed him that it was unwise to seek out any member of the family to express his sympathy or to explain his presence in their backyard the night of the shooting. Although he was desperate to see Nina, he had no desire to see Jonathan or their father. There was no decision he made that night that could be forgiven. It was wrong of him to seek out Nina's company so late at night, especially after she had been forbidden to see him. On the other hand, if Willy had stayed, he might have driven off the intruders.

As he continued to stare at the Barstow's house, Willy hadn't noticed that he stopped walking. He was standing in this very spot not two weeks ago watching Nina and her little brother walk toward him from her driveway. She had waved, and hurried toward him, but then slowed her pace when she felt young Matthew dragging along behind her. Evidently, he was in no hurry to get where they were going.

Willy waited until they were closer to call out. He stooped down and addressed her brother first. "Hi, Matt. Where are you off to in such a hurry?"

"We're off to Mr. Wilkie's to pick up my trousers." The boy spoke as if they were going to a wake.

"It can't be as bad as all that," Willy told him.

"Don't let him fool you, Willy," Nina informed him. "I've already told him that if he walks with me to Mr. Wilkie's and doesn't fuss, we'll continue on to Parkside Candy for a treat after."

"Well, that's a fine deal, isn't it?" Willy said.

Matthew's expression brightened at the reminder. "Can we stop at Mr. Fawke's for some root beer barrels along the way? It's an awfully long walk all the way to Main Street." While it was a special treat to go to Parkside Candy for ice cream, Matthew also loved a trip to the North Park Pharmacy because he could usually talk his mother into buying him some root beer barrels. In fact, he knew just about all the stops on Hertel Avenue where his mother or father did business and where some sort of treat could also be had. Mrs. Cobb, the hat maker, always had caramels in her pocket, and Mr. Doersam, the tailor, was known to give him licorice. Mrs. Skoczelos, the dry cleaner's wife, oftentimes had cookies. When doing errands with their mother or father, Matthew and Amelia were only allowed one treat. It would be a grand day indeed if he could manage ice cream and root beer barrels.

"I don't think Mother or Amelia would be pleased if you had root beer barrels and a chocolate soda," his sister told him.

"They don't have to know," he countered.

When Willy seemed to support the plan, Nina gave her brother a conspiratorial smile. "Maybe, if you don't make a fuss at Mr. Wilkie's and you walk the rest of the way without complaint."

Matthew's face lit up. His prospects for the afternoon had improved considerably. He turned to Willy and asked, "Will you join us?"

Willy was pleased to have an excuse to spend a bit more time with them and even more pleased at the smile on Nina's face after her brother's request. "Well,

I'm on duty now, but I can walk you as far as Mr. Wilkie's."

It was just a few short blocks between Nina's house and F.B. Wilkie's shop near the corner of Hertel and Norwalk Avenues, and Willy used the time to work up the courage to ask her to his cousin's birthday party. Matthew raced ahead as they approached the shop, wanting to get the boring part of the afternoon over with quickly, which gave Willy a few moments to pop the question.

"Nellie turns nineteen next week," he commented, casually.

"Oh, I know. It's all she can talk about. I've helped her pick out her dress for the party."

"So, you're going?"

"Of course, silly. She's my best friend."

"Oh, right. Well, I'm going too."

"Well, I should hope so. You are her cousin, after all." Nina giggled, pleased to be with Willy and even more pleased that she might get a chance to spend more than just a few minutes with him at Nellie's party. Yet, she seemed completely unaware that he was working up to something.

"So, do you want to go together?" He was too nervous to look her in the eye while he asked, and so missed the radiant smile that spread across her face as he did.

"I think that would be lovely."

"Really?" He couldn't keep the surprise from his response, and Nina giggled again as his voice pitched higher than she had ever heard it. "I mean, that's great. Really great." Her mirth was intensifying; was he making

a total fool of himself? Making an effort to regain composure, he said, "Well, then, I guess I'll see you then. I mean I'll pick you up of course... the night of the party I mean." He was truly hopeless and decided to stop talking before she changed her mind.

After seeing her into the shop and saying a quick hello to Mr. and Mrs. Wilkie, Willy practically skipped along his beat for the rest of his shift. That day felt like it had happened years ago, he was so far removed from that feeling of elation. Willy focused his attention back on Nina's house, wanting so badly for her to skip down the drive again on her way to somewhere, anywhere. It was selfish, he knew, but he was eager to see her and explain himself.

It was nearly lunch time and his mother would be expecting him. He tried to spend as little time at home as possible. Susan Cooper had a sixth sense when it came to her son. She hadn't believed a word of it when he'd told her why he'd been fired and any attempt to explain himself just strengthened her conviction.

"That bottle of whiskey has sat on the shelf untouched since the day your father passed, and you expect me to believe you had yourself a wee dram before you started your shift? You're a police officer; you don't have it in you to be so irresponsible."

"It was stupid, I know. I was just thinking of Da, and I remembered the last bottle of Grand Da's whiskey he had hidden in the pantry. I just wanted a taste." He had expected her to be ashamed of him, or at least angry. He hadn't expected this.

"I'll never believe you are that foolish." She went on to insist that Captain McNamara would tell her the

truth of it, were she to confront him, and it took the better part of an hour to convince her not to. She tried everything to get him to admit the truth, alternating between anger, tears, and guilt. Eventually they just stopped talking, the uneasy silence continuing for the rest of the evening.

Their conversations since then either consisted of her continued attempts to get him to tell the truth, or an interrogation of his whereabouts. "And just where are you rushing off to this morning?" Susan Cooper asked that very morning, not turning from the cast iron skillet she was tending on the stove. "You're not dressed to be looking for work."

Nothing got passed her, and Willy had often thought his mother would make a great detective. Why hadn't he worn his best suit? "I'm going out for a walk, ma."

"The look on your face is that of a man who has a place to be, but no wish to be there. What is it you're hiding from me, Willy? It's not like you to keep secrets."

He looked his mother square in the eyes - to not have would only confirm her suspicions - and lied. "Nothing, ma. I don't have time for breakfast." Willy was anxious to get away lest she manage to drag a full confession out of him. He turned to leave, stopping dead in his tracks at her parting words.

"You're killing me, son." She wasn't trying to be dramatic and the anguish in her voice nearly brought tears to Willy's eyes. "I overheard Mrs. Lucchesi at the druggist yesterday telling anyone who would listen that you were sneaking around the Barstow's yard the night

that poor woman was shot. You've got yourself into some mess and it's caused you to lose your job, and the girl you're sweet on. If that woman dies, you'll be suspected of murder! I'm telling you right here and now, you'll lose me in the end, too, because I'll worry myself straight into the grave!"

Willy's own distress soon turned to anger as he realized the full impact of what his choices were doing to his mother. She would undoubtedly overhear more such discussions as she went about her business in the neighborhood. Being fired for drinking on the job would have been enough to keep the gossip flowing like the Niagara River, but the shooting of Mrs. Barstow and his potential role in the crime would keep the rumors circulating for the rest of the year. Every time she stepped beyond her own door there would be whispering in her wake. There would also be plenty of folks brazen enough to confront her directly.

"Ma, please don't worry about me." It was all he could think to say. He had been awake most of the previous night considering whether he should defy the captain and confide in his mother. In the end, he couldn't trust that she could keep his secret. Susan Cooper was not the type of woman to betray a confidence, but if she were provoked and felt the need to defend her son, details could easily slip out.

"Don't tell me not to worry about you. You are my son. You are all I have in this world and you are in trouble. I can feel it in my bones."

Neither of them broke eye contact, Susan trying to get her son to confess, and Willy determined to stay silent. Finally, he took a deep breath and slowly blew it out. "I'm not a little boy any more, ma. I'm a grown man and I can take care of myself. Trust me." He held her gaze for just a moment longer, hoping those two words would make a difference. She had nothing to say in return and so he left.

The conversation had rattled him, and he was agitated all the way to the asylum, taking his bad mood out on Tocci. The visit was short, and Willy took his time on the way back. To continue to avoid his mother would only raise her suspicion, so reluctantly he headed home.

• • •

Back in her office, Maude read over what she had written. When she came to the discussion between Gabriel Lucchesi and Captain McNamara, she paused. "What about Conrad Barstow and his family?"

"What about Conrad Barstow and his family?" Don stood in the doorway, his hands cradling something large and encased in copious amounts of bubble wrap.

"Is that what I think it is?"

"You first."

"Okay…but put that down carefully. If it's what I think it is, it's worth a fortune."

A sly grin slid across his features. "It is and there's a great story attached to it, but it can wait." He ducked out for a second and returned empty-handed. "So, the Barstows?"

"Yeah, well, it occurred to me while I was reading over my latest chapter that I hadn't learned much about them since the night of the shooting."

"What do you make of that?"

"I'm wondering if maybe they are not as important in all of this as Willy Cooper is. I keep seeing this story from his point of view. The shooting added significantly to his troubles."

"In the short term, it certainly did, but we don't yet know how this ended. The murderer was never caught, but what happened to Willy?"

"True, but I'm fairly sure he never returned to the Buffalo Police Department. In fact, there is no mention of him in the BPD municipal reports after Eva Barstow's death, although the reports detail all promotions, dismissals, deaths and resignations. There is no mention of Willy at all, even though he was apparently fired."

"I know you don't want to hear this, but you'll know what this is all about when you are supposed to."

Maude blew out something between an exasperated sigh and a laugh. "You have always been so much more patient with the process than I am." She glanced back at her screen as she spoke. "I guess now that I know I don't have to wait for dreams to give me direction, I'm not sure where to focus my inquiry."

"Well, what drew you to this?" When she looked confused, Don tried again. "There is a reason you are spending time and energy trying to learn what happened in our old house back in 1924. What is it? Do you want to solve the murder? Do you want to know what became of the people involved? Are you just interested because it happened in our house?"

Maude glanced at the Barstow family photo, which she now kept on her desk. "All of the above, I suppose.

The Barstow murder was presented to me at this time for a reason, I think, but I have no idea what it is."

"If you asked Charlotte, she'd tell you that you are ready to learn what you are supposed to learn from this experience and to use that information accordingly." He held up his hands as if to ward off any objects she might throw at him. Maude was often frustrated by her mentor's wisdom and Don's easy acceptance of it. "Just keep going. You'll find out what you need to know."

"Yeah, yeah, yeah, easier said than done." She would give the focus of her inquiries some more thought later. "Now tell me about your bubble wrapped treasure."

Don's eyes lit up as he popped up from his chair. "I nearly forgot about that. Let me go get it."

"How can you forget about a Louis Comfort Tiffany lamp? That's what it is, right?"

"Indeed, it is, Maudie. Wait until you see it! I think it's more beautiful now than it was when we found it!" Don was talking as he left the room, returning with the lamp still wrapped. "Mrs. Houston called me on my cell phone and asked me to stop by this morning. It was already wrapped up when I got there."

Louis Comfort Tiffany was the son of Charles Lewis Tiffany. At the turn of the nineteenth century, he was considered a world leader in the Art Nouveau movement, whose exquisite lamps, jewelry and stained glass continue to be highly sought after in the present day. This particular hanging shade featured delicate red and gold maple leaves set against rust, brown, and yellow-green background, suspended by a single bronze chain.

Maude had picked up on the fact that Mrs. Houston had called Don personally, resisting the urge to ask why. "Oh, Don, it really is exquisite. I can't believe she wants to sell it." Maude recognized the lamp right away once the protective packaging had been removed. It belonged to Alexandra Houston, a longtime client and one of Maude's favorite people.

"It's a good thing you're sitting down because she doesn't want to sell it." He looked like he might just burst, like a boy who knew a great secret and was torn between the big reveal and stringing along his audience for a while longer.

"It doesn't look like it's in need of repair. Why did she want you to take it?"

"Maudie, she gave it to us!" Don laughed out loud at the look on her face.

"She did what? Why on earth would she do that? She loves that lamp. I can still remember the day she came into the shop and recognized it." The lamp had belonged to Alexandra's great-grandfather, who commissioned it from Tiffany Studios in New York City at the turn of the nineteenth century. It was designed specifically to hang above the card table in the billiard room in the home he had built on Chapin Parkway in Buffalo. It was removed years later when the house was redecorated in favor of the more modern fashions of the 1920s and found its way, of all places, to Maude and Don's old basement. They discovered it, along with the Barstow family photograph, in the root cellar when they moved in. The previous owners knew nothing about it, having never actually used the root cellar at the back of the basement. It needed a bit of

TLC at the time, but Don still thought he had won the lottery.

Authentic Tiffany lamps sold for tens, or even hundreds of thousands of dollars. Given the condition of the lamp, Don had estimated it to be worth at least twenty thousand dollars. It hadn't hung in their shop very long when Alexandra Houston walked in and recognized it. She came in a second time with pictures of her home in its early days. They were black and white, of course, but the hanging lamps design was unmistakable. She offered to purchase it, but Don didn't feel right about taking her money knowing it had been commissioned specifically for her family home. In the end, they settled on a price below market value and all parties were pleased to see the lamp returned to its rightful home. Mrs. Houston became his best client and referred everyone she knew to the Antique Lamp Company, which had been able to grow into The Antique Lamp Company and Gift Emporium as a result.

"That lamp really put this business on the map," he remarked, admiring how the stained glass sparkled in the sunlight.

"It sure did. I can't believe she gave it to you."

"To us - she gave it to us."

"Okay, but why?"

Don handed her a small envelope that looked as expensive as it felt when Maude received it. "She's been trying to find a way to thank us."

The slightest hint of White Linen by Estee Lauder drifted up as Maude removed the page from the envelope. She would have known the note was from

Alexandra from the scent alone, as it preceded the woman wherever she went and lingered after she departed.

Dear Maude and Don,

It's been twice now that you have found my lost treasures against all odds. I can think of no other people who would have done what you have for me under either circumstance. 'Thank you' hardly seems adequate. It occurred to me recently that I've had my time with this beautiful lamp and now it's your turn to enjoy it...

Maude looked up, "Don, we can't accept this..."

"Keep reading," he told her.

I won't hear of you returning it, as I know you love it as much as I do. You saw it returned to its rightful home and now please allow me to do the same. We were both meant to have it, I think, and it's your turn. You'll know, I'm sure, should the time come to pass it on again.

Fondly,
Alexandra

Maude stared at the note and read it over again. "There is certainly no need to thank us for selling her the lamp. All we did was find it in the root cellar."

"This is why she sent for me and not you. She knew you would refuse her gift."

"C'mon, Don. We haven't done anything to deserve gratitude of this magnitude."

"Well, I agree, but it's really for her to decide. She was very happy to have her jewelry back."

"That was really Christine's doing."

If intrigue didn't find Christine, she was known to go looking for it. A few years ago, she had no idea she'd be placing Maude and Don in danger by attempting to entrap the thief who had stolen Alexandra Houston's family heirlooms. Maude had been held at gunpoint while Don had nearly drowned in Lake Erie. The memory sent a cold chill down Maude's spine.

There was a lot of baggage attached to that unwelcome memory, and it showed on both of their faces as each silently recalled the revelations of that evening. They had learned that something similar had happened in one of their past lives, lives they had shared as husband and wife. In the nineteenth century, Martha had lost her husband Johnny, who drowned trying to save a woman who had been kidnapped by the Keeper of the insane asylum. How often Maude and Don had been separated throughout time by that event, or something like it, was anybody's guess. Such events seemed to repeat themselves in each lifetime until someone did something to break the cycle. This time Maude had jumped in and pulled both Don and the jewel thief out of the murky depths of the Great Lake. This time, Don had survived, and the other man received punishment for his crimes, which was centuries overdue.

"I almost lost you that night, Don. I'm not sure I want anything around to remind me of that."

Don smiled and took her hand. "That's not what you'll think of when you look at this lamp. You'll think of Mrs. Houston, who is one of your favorite people, and you'll think of that day we found it in the root cellar."

That was a much more pleasant memory, and Maude laughed out loud as it played in her mind. "Neither one of us could believe our eyes! I still wonder how something that valuable lay forgotten in a root cellar."

"What amazed me was that the previous owners had lived in the house for so long, they had forgotten they even had a root cellar."

"Don, this was meant to hang in the billiard room on Chapin Parkway, not in a small apartment on Main and Chippewa. We have to insist she take it back."

"I tried to politely refuse the gift, but she won't hear of it." He held the handwritten note out and the perfume once again wafted up as if to remind them of the woman who wore it. "I think she honestly believes the lamp belongs with us for a while, and she as much as said so. Try not to look at it in terms of its monetary value. You know at this point we'd never sell it. Accept it in the spirit in which it was given, with the understanding that one day we will pass it on, like she says."

Maude blew out a sigh; she knew Mrs. Houston could be very stubborn when she insisted on something. "Where do you suppose we should hang it? In the shop or upstairs?"

"It's not for sale, so I don't think we should hang it in the shop. The dining room is the only place it's suited for."

Maude nodded in agreement. "It's too bad we don't still live in the old house. It would have looked great on the landing in the front hall."

"What would look great?" Billy popped his head in the office.

"Hey, pal, what are you doing home early?" Don asked.

"I'm not home early. It's after five. What's for dinner?"

Maude couldn't have said where the day had gone. "Yikes, I had no idea it was that late. Why don't you go up and rummage through the takeout menus while your dad and I close up here?"

"Wait a minute," Don called as Billy turned to leave. "How'd it go today?" Billy shot his father a look that clearly indicated he did not want to talk about how "it" went.

"How did what go today?" Maude asked.

"Nothing," Billy answered, and turned to exit before any more could be said.

"What was that all about?" Maude turned to Don, her expression making clear she wouldn't allow him the same exit strategy.

Don considered for a moment if he should betray his son's confidence. Ultimately, he decided that in the long run it would be better for Billy if he told Maude now, knowing if he didn't, she would drag it out of her youngest son one way or the other. "There's a girl who sits in front of him in Statistics. From the look on his face, I'd say he still hasn't worked up the nerve to ask her out."

"Would this girl's name be Sheri, by chance? He seemed very pleased that she returned his call the other day."

"Yes, but I can't remember her last name. She's a sophomore, too; I think she's a business major."

"How come I didn't know about this?"

"There are certain things you just need to ask your dad. Don't worry Maudie; he'll need your advice, too, at some point."

Maude smiled, but was always a bit disappointed that the boys confided in their dad more often than they did her. "The things I can help him with don't seem to interest him."

Don knew what she meant but thought it wise not to get into a discussion about Billy's inner sensory abilities while he was within earshot. "Just wait. Eventually he will work up the nerve to ask her out, and then he will definitely need you for a wardrobe consult. You know I'm useless when it comes to fashion, and so is Glen."

Maude chuckled, nodding in agreement. "Yes, you are all hopeless without me." She rose to lock the front doors. "Why don't you bring the lamp upstairs and we can decide where to hang it?"

"Sounds good," Don agreed. "How about Thai food tonight?"

"Works for me." Maude looked around the shop before she twisted the bolt lock. The proceeds from the sale of that Tiffany lamp had gone a long way toward adding the "Gift Emporium" to the Antique Lamp

Company and Gift Emporium. Other lamps came and went, some valuable enough that they added a security system, but none as unique as the Tiffany Maple Leaves. That lamp started it all, and now they had it back. What did that mean moving forward?

Chapter Seven

Willy got the sense that someone was watching him as he entered the gates of the cemetery. He was there for his regular meeting with Captain McNamara, and he couldn't shake the feeling that someone was close by. He stopped to right a bouquet of flowers that had fallen away from a headstone about one hundred feet from his father's grave. He spent a minute propping the flowers against the smooth marble monument, and then casually looked around again. There was no one else in this part of the cemetery, so he walked on.

McNamara always arrived after Willy and he was confident the captain would not approach if he thought they were being watched. He arrived within minutes, and greeted Willy as he did each time, as if he were surprised to see him. Neither man saw a third figure observing them from behind a large mausoleum on the hill as they shook hands. The third man was dressed rough, like he might have been a groundskeeper rather than a bereaved soul there to pay respects to a departed loved one. Had the two men he surveilled actually seen him, they'd have known him immediately.

Willy gave his report, stating that nothing had changed. "He still insists he doesn't know Saladino's source in the BPD. He says nobody knows."

"And do you believe him, lad?"

"No. Why would I believe anything he says? He's a thug."

"Keep trying, Willy. I don't like the idea of a rat in my precinct."

"I will, sir, but I think we'd have a better chance of making him talk if life became more unpleasant for him at the asylum. He gets three squares a day, and other than spending a few hours in the greenhouse watering plants, he spends the rest of his day reading in the dayroom of his ward. Put him in with some of the real crackpots and he'll tell us what we want to know. He'll be begging us to send him back to the greenhouse."

McNamara considered the suggestion. "I suppose something could be arranged. I'll speak to Detweiller."

Willy felt a perverse sense of pleasure in the hopes that Tocci's experience was about to become much less pleasant. Why should he get to hide from all his troubles, troubles he had caused, when Willy had to lie to his mother and face her heartbroken stares from across the dinner table each night? He was too angry over all this plan had cost him to feel ashamed of his feelings of ill will.

"I've got to head back now."

"Is there any news on the Barstow case?" Willy asked.

"She died yesterday, so it's a murder investigation now."

Willy's face was a mixture of grief and fear. He had been in and out of the Barstow house as he had the homes of other boys in the neighborhood growing up. He had always known Mrs. Barstow to be kind, and he would grieve for her loss. "Any new leads?"

"Nothing new. They pulled two .32 Longs out of her gut. Every thug in the city carries a Colt 32, so no help there. No fingerprints on the front door, vague eyewitness accounts… The only positive identification is you jumping the fence in the backyard."

"Am I still a suspect?"

"Not as far as I'm concerned, but there are others in the precinct who don't like the look of the situation."

"What exactly does that mean, sir?"

"It means you're not to worry about it. Just do your job, Willy, and I'll handle things at the precinct."

Willy gauged the captain's expression and dared one more question. "The Barstows, Nina, does she know…"

"Now, Willy, you must stay away from that girl! The last thing you want to do is ruffle Conrad Barstow's feathers. The man's lost his wife, and you were seen in his backyard near enough to the time of the shooting to draw suspicion. He'll not welcome you anywhere near his daughter."

That was answer enough for Willy. If Mr. Barstow knew he had been in the yard the night of the shooting, Nina did too. He kept his face neutral as he assured the captain he would not go anywhere near the Barstow house. If he couldn't call on Nina, there were other ways to find out what he needed to know.

When he parted ways with Captain McNamara, Willy headed in the direction of his cousin Nellie's house on Forest Avenue, considering how best to enlist her help to get word to Nina. He had promised not to go to Nina's house, but did not swear that he wouldn't attempt to see her. Willy was so focused inward that he neither sensed nor saw the man skulking around the cemetery following at a discreet distance behind him.

The man pulled his hat down and pulled the collar of his jacket up as he crossed the street and headed down a side street to Elmwood Avenue. He'd seen enough to know he was right in the first place.

A car pulled up alongside the man. "Get in!"

He couldn't see the driver's face, but the deep baritone told him it was Joey Saladino. The man opened the passenger door, gingerly moved the revolver resting on the seat to the floor and sat down.

"Whata ya got for me?" Joey asked.

"I was right: the captain is up to something and it includes Willy Cooper. I saw them together in the cemetery, and they weren't cryin' on each other's shoulder." He knew he was already in hot water with Saladino, who was furious over Tocci's disappearance, and he would accept nothing short of a confirmation one way or the other regarding his son-in-law's supposed death. The man did his best to offer an explanation that didn't sound like an excuse. "Captain McNamara suspects a rat in the precinct. He's been pretty tight-lipped about the killing at the old poor farm. Besides, he's got just about every available man on the Barstow case."

Nothing of what Saladino had heard improved his mood. "You follow that kid until you find out if Tocci is alive or dead."

The Barstow case...it was a murder now. The informant had been keeping him up to date on the case, as he did with any information that might be useful to the gangster. The Barstow murder could be a lucky break for Saladino. With all attention focused on finding the killer, nobody in the Fourteenth would think it odd if an officer spent long periods away from his desk, thus allowing the informant plenty of time to tail Cooper.

Saladino was driven from his thoughts by the agitated voice of the man in the passenger seat. He hadn't heard what the man said, and he didn't care. "Just follow him, or you will be the next person who goes missing!"

• • •

Willy Cooper stood under the Ivy Arch at the edge of Rumsey Woods. It was just after the dinner hour and that part of Delaware Park was all but empty. He had declined the meal his mother had prepared, knowing that rushing out of the house without an explanation would only add to the tension between them. Nina had agreed to meet him and he would let nothing, not even his mother's broken heart, get in the way. He heard the sound of footsteps coming up the path and peeked out to see who was coming toward him. When he saw it was Nina approaching alone, he stood out in full view.

As soon as Willy made eye contact he regretted his decision to ask her for a meeting. Would she believe him when he told her he hadn't been fired, but could tell her nothing more? Would she blame him for her mother's death? All the many ways this conversation could go wrong rushed into his mind. He was surprised to see she looked relieved to see him and even more taken aback as she rushed into his arms.

"Oh, Willy, thank God you're alright. I've been so worried." Nina could not hold back the tears and buried her face in his chest as she wept.

She was worried about him? It was the last thing that Willy had expected. "I'm so sorry about your mother." It was all he could think of to say, and that reminder had made her cry all the harder. She was shaking with grief, and all he could do was just hold her, but it felt so good to have her in his arms, to offer the comfort she so desperately needed.

It went on like that for some time, all the shyness that had prevented them from admitting how they felt about each other had vanished. Their forced separation and the need to connect right here and now had driven it away. Their emotions were in full control, not their rational minds, which would have forced each of them to act differently out of shyness and inexperience. Nina was hurting and the person she wanted most to comfort her was Willy. Later he might realize what that meant, but right now it just felt right to hold her and let her take what she needed.

Finally, Nina calmed enough to dry her eyes and speak. "I've been so worried since Nellie told me you lost your position. I didn't believe for one minute you'd been drinking, but Daddy forbade me to see you."

It was still a shock that during what must have been the most horrific days of her young life there was still a place in Nina's thoughts for him. It would have warmed his heart if concern for her hadn't taken the upper hand. She was thin and pale, her eyes red and swollen from too many tears. "No, Nina, don't worry about me." Willy had been so determined to explain himself and now that he saw there was no need, he was at a loss for words, so he just drew her in again and held her. "I'm fine. Shhh, don't worry about me."

She squeezed him just a little bit tighter and then pulled away. Looking up to meet his eyes, she said, "I know you had nothing to do with mother's death. Daddy and Jonathan know, too; they just can't see past their grief right now."

He brought both hands up, gently cupping her face. "I was just coming to try to explain things to you, but then I lost my nerve. Had I stayed a few minutes more, I might have seen the men who entered your house. I might have been able to stop them. Can you forgive me?"

Nina took his hands and held them together between her own. "If you had stayed, you might have been shot, too. I couldn't bear to lose you as well."

Her expression was heartbreaking: love, and grief and need all at the same time. Was it right to want to kiss her just now? He angled his head closer, giving her a chance to pull away. When she didn't, he gently touched his lips to hers, still offering a chance for retreat. Instead, she stood on her tip toes, twined her fingers together at the base of his skull and kissed him back.

It was a sweet kiss and, after, he held her, his forehead resting against hers, both of their eyes closed. They could have stayed like that forever, but Willy heard footsteps and abruptly pulled away.

Nina felt as if a small piece of her heart broke when he stepped away. "What is it? What's wrong?"

"I thought I heard someone." Willy ushered her underneath the arch and stepped out to look around. It was getting dark, but he could make out the shadow of a figure disappearing into the trees beyond the arch. It was hard to see, but it looked as though the person was moving at a leisurely pace. Perhaps someone just out for an after-dinner constitutional.

"What's wrong, Willy?" Even in the fading light under the arch, she could see his brow creased with concern.

"Nothing. Whoever it was is well on his way and no threat to us."

It was an odd choice of words, and Willy's comments brought back the worries Nina had been wrestling with since she had found out he was fired. "Willy, are you in some sort of trouble? Tell me what happened with the police department. Why were you fired?"

Willy took both of her hands in his and looked to the ground, trying to determine how much he could say. When he stayed that way for longer than she was comfortable with, she gently prodded him to confide in her. "You can trust me, Willy. You can trust me to believe what you tell me is true and to keep whatever it is just between the two of us."

He looked up and met her reassuring smile with one of his own. "I do trust you; it's just that I've sworn an oath of secrecy, which I'm obligated to uphold." He thought for another moment before he continued. "I'll tell you this: I've not really been fired, but no one must know that, not even my ma. I'm involved in something that nobody can know about. That's all I can tell you for now." Willy hoped that would be enough, his eyes pleading as he looked down into hers.

"Are you in any danger?"

"I don't think so. As long as people believe I'm no longer with the Buffalo Police Department, I should be fine."

Nina took a deep breath and nodded her head. "Alright, I can't say I won't worry, but I'm relieved to know there is more to the story than the rumors would suggest."

"I don't want you to worry. You have enough to deal with. I'm so sorry I can't be there to help you through your mother's funeral."

Tears pooled in Nina's eyes at the mention of her mother. She brushed them away, determined to be strong. "I miss her so much. It's up to me now, the running of the house, the raising of Matthew and Amelia. They are so young. Will they even remember her when they are grown?"

Willy gathered her in and tucked her head under his chin. He felt he had to absorb her uncertainty and grief, or she would overflow with it. "It's not all up to you. You still have your father and Jonathan. Matt and Amelia are young, but you will keep the memory of your mother alive in their hearts."

Nina sniffled as she brushed still more tears away. "Thank you for getting Nellie to arrange this. I've got to get back. It's nearly time to tuck the little ones in."

"Can I see you again?" Willy was still a little uncertain where things stood, even after such an outpouring of emotion between them, but there was no going back. He needed to see her again, to hold her again.

"The funeral is Wednesday. I won't be able to get away before then. I could meet you early Thursday morning, before everyone else gets up."

Willy couldn't hide his relief. "Will you meet me behind the casino near the lake?" The casino and boathouse overlooking Delaware Park Lake had been constructed for the Pan American Exposition in 1901, and offered a more private and comfortable place to meet. It was also less likely that there would be anyone else around early in the morning, unlike the woods, which was a popular place to stroll throughout most of the day.

"Yes, Thursday morning, at dawn. I'll be there."

He smiled and realized that this meeting was the beginning of something special. "Things will get better," Willy told her, and in that moment, he genuinely believed they would.

Maude was sitting under a tree by the very same Ivy Arch where Willy met Nina. She had awoken that morning with the strong feeling that something happened there. It was getting easier to follow her instincts, and so she headed to Delaware Park after lunch. The laptop was growing warm on the top of her thighs. On its screen was the transcription of a secret meeting, which had been observed by a third party. Willy was being followed. Maude lifted her head to catch the breeze on her face and began to wonder about the implications of that when her cell phone rang.

"Have I been promoted to a management position?" Christine asked. "Because I seem to be running the place alone more and more these days."

"Hi, Christine. What's up?"

"A crystal chandelier, and it has two burned out bulbs. I can't find any replacements."

"You can check Don's workshop. There are probably more in there."

"You know he doesn't like me to go in there. The urge to clean up after him is too strong. He'll lose something in that mess and blame me for sure."

Maude laughed, knowing Christine was right. Although her home could never be described as tidy, she was meticulous on the job. Don's work space drove Christine crazy and she was always trying to put tools and loose wires in what she thought were more appropriate places. "I'll be back soon. I'm just finishing up."

"Where are you? Do I hear birds? Are you outside?"

"I'm in the park. I was meeting an old friend." It was best to stick as close to the truth as possible when trying to deceive Christine.

"Hmm, did you need your laptop for this meeting? I couldn't help but notice that it's not in your office."

Christine really was relentless, and for a minute Maude considered just telling her the truth. She was silent for long enough that Christine thought the line had gone dead. "No, I'm here, and yes, my laptop is with me. I'll fill you in on my adventures this afternoon when I get back." That Maude had made a decision was evident in her voice. She was tired of sneaking around. It was such a relief not to have to pretend with the boys, although over the last few years, they had kept their suspicions to themselves. Christine could sniff out a half-truth a mile away. It was exhausting, and Christine would be of more help if she knew the truth.

"It's almost closing time, but if you're serious, I'll wait."

Maude came in through the back door and found Christine in Don's workroom sorting through wires and electrical tape. "I couldn't help myself," she said as Maude poked her head in.

"You know he's going to be furious with you." Maude looked out into the shop. The door was locked, and the main lights had been turned out. Only the lamps in the window display remained on, and Maude noticed that the bulbs in the crystal chandelier had been replaced.

When she returned her attention to the workroom, Christine was giving her a pointed look. "So, how was your day? I'm excited to hear about it."

Maude laughed. "What I have to tell you requires wine. Do you have time to come up for a drink?"

"Sam's got other plans tonight, so I have nothing but time."

It turned out to be a good night to confide in Christine. Don was playing cards with his old college pals, Glen was out with friends from high school and Billy was still on campus studying for his last final. Maude took her time selecting a bottle and two wine glasses from the dining room. Christine waited patiently, realizing that she was finally about to have all her questions answered. "Maude, I hope you know that my friendship with you and Don is very important to me. Whatever it is you have to tell me will stay between us. You have my word."

Maude filled each glass generously, handed one to Christine and sat across from her at the kitchen table before replying. "Thank you; that means a lot. It really has never been an issue of trust. I had to come to terms with a lot before I could share it. I only just told my boys recently."

Over the next hour, she told Christine everything in the same methodical way she had the last time this topic had come up at her kitchen table. Afterwards, she sat back and waited for the flurry of questions, but for once, Christine had no words.

Maude took a long sip from her glass. "Of all the reactions I might have predicted, silence was not among them."

Christine laughed, agreeing there wasn't much that could render her speechless. "My God, Maude, what a gift you have. It's just a lot to process, and if I'm being honest, I'm a little hurt you didn't want to include me on this journey with you. I wouldn't have kept something this big from you."

This time it was Maude who had nothing to say. She hadn't expected hurt feelings and took a minute to evaluate Christine's words, trying to gauge how much of a dent this put in their friendship. She took the time to refill her glass and noticed Christine had barely touched hers. "Christine, please try and understand that you and I are very different people. You are comfortable sharing personal details, where I am not. I only really began to understand what's been happening to me recently. It was important for me to have a handle on things before I shared my experiences."

There was silence again while each of them took a drink. "I get it," Christine finally said. "A lot of things make sense now."

Maude knew she was referring to that night at the marina where Don had almost drowned. He'd gone there to rescue Christine, neither of them aware that their actions had triggered an event that had been following Maude and Don through many lives.

"I've often wondered if we have been a part of each other's lives before," Maude told her.

Christine picked up her glass and drained it in one long gulp. "We'll need more wine if that's the direction this conversation is going!"

Later, when Don came home, Maude was alone. There were two empty wine bottles, and she was working on a third. "You're up late on a school night." He nodded his head toward the half empty third bottle. "Are you willing to share some of that?"

Maude smiled, aware of what it must look like, being up so late surrounded by wine bottles. "Actually, I've been sharing for most of the evening, and not just the wine." She got another glass and poured some for Don. "Christine came up after work and I told her everything."

"Wow! How did that go?" Don tucked the bottle under one arm, pulled Maude up from her chair, and steered her into the living room with the other.

"C'mon. I've been sitting on a folding chair all night and need something I can recline on while I listen to the details of this story."

They sat curled up together on the couch while Maude recounted her conversation with Christine. "That's not the response I would have predicted," Don replied when she had finished.

"I know. I told her as much myself. I wasn't expecting her to be more hurt than surprised. I expected shock, and disbelief. I expected thousands of questions, but instead the conversation got really deep. We talked more about the possibility that we knew each other in former lives than anything else."

"I hadn't thought about that, but it makes sense," Don agreed. "So, things are okay between the two of you?"

"Yeah, I think so."

"Then why the third bottle?"

Maude's smile had a guilty edge to it as she moved to refill her glass. "I guess I just feel so exposed now that other people know. I thought it would be a relief not to have to hide what I'm doing, but now that I don't have to be so careful, I'm afraid I'll slip up in front of someone else."

"Who? Do you mean our clients, or our friends and family? Would that be so awful?"

"Maybe, I don't know. Christine is pretty open-minded and readily accepted what I told her, but I can't pretend everyone I meet will be as receptive. A lot of people think Modern Spiritualism is blasphemy, while others might just think I'm nuts, or, at the very least, a liar."

Don knew being called a liar would be the worst in Maude's mind. "You're borrowing trouble."

"I don't think I am."

Don shifted so that they were face to face. "Can you at least put this aside until something actually happens? Try and focus on the Barstow murder. Did you learn anything new today?"

Maude recognized that Don was trying to distract her and couldn't decide whether to be put out or grateful. They had been down this road before and he knew that once Maude's worries got the upper hand, no amount of wisdom would ease her mind. It was best to give her something else to think about, and she had to admit it usually helped. "Yes, it seems that Willy and Nina are falling in love - or were at the time. They met secretly the day before her mother's funeral. She knew he had nothing to do with her mother's death."

"So, how does knowing that move you forward?"

"I'm not sure. I would have continued working if I hadn't decided to talk to Christine. I'll review my notes tomorrow and see what I can find out about Nina Barstow."

Their discussion was interrupted by the sound of footsteps coming up the front hall steps. The family usually entered and left the apartment through the shop during the day, but after hours, when the alarms were on, they used the front entrance from the street. Billy came in, clearly not expecting to see anyone else.

"Hey, what are you guys doing up?"

"Just talking," Don told him. "How are you feeling about Statistics tomorrow? That's your last final, right?" Billy broke into a smile that told his father that something important had changed. "I take it you weren't studying alone."

"No, Sheri met me at the coffee shop just off campus."

"Did you get any studying done?" Maude asked, Billy's sheepish grin giving her the answer.

"I'm beat. Don't you kids stay up too late." Billy made a hasty exit before they could extract any further details.

When Don was sure Billy was beyond earshot, he turned to Maude. "I don't think he ever had any intention of studying. Billy could pass that exam in his sleep."

"Ah, to be young and in love."

Don smiled, the twinkle in his eye making him looked about twenty years younger. "Being old and in love isn't so bad either!"

Chapter Eight

The small apartment above the Antique Lamp Company and Gift Emporium seemed very crowded in the middle of May. The semester had ended for Billy and Glen, and for the first time in a long time, the boys were home every day for long periods. As children, they lived in a large house in North Buffalo. When the family moved above the shop, the boys were teenagers, heavily involved in sports, even during the summer, and seldom around.

During the first few days of summer break, they had wandered downstairs to the shop wondering what was for lunch, or if Maude knew the whereabouts of a particular item of clothing or the remote for the television. Don had given his sons until the end of the month to get part time jobs. Maude, thinking more practically, had shown each of them how to use the washer and dryer and enlisted their help in dinner preparation during the week.

With some household chores off her list, Maude had more time to work the Barstow murder. She was in her office reading over what she had written the day before when Billy came in.

"Hey, mom, are you busy?"

"Just procrastinating. What do you need?"

He came further into the office and glanced at the ground to gather his thoughts before continuing. "I was wondering if you were working on your project, you know, the murder in our old house."

"I'm working on it right now. Why?"

"I just kinda wanted to see how it works, you know, to see you in action." His shy smile told Maude he still wasn't sure if what he was about to do was a good idea.

Maude tried to keep her expression neutral. If Billy was showing interest in developing his inner senses, she didn't want to scare him off. "Well, right now, I'm just reading what I wrote yesterday."

"Right, you told me that you can channel the past through your writing. So, how do you know where to focus?"

"Well, sometimes I feel drawn to a particular place or person. If I'm drawn to a place, I go there and try and focus on how it would have looked, say, during the 1920s, and who might have been there. If I'm drawn to a person, I try to find out more about them in the historic record or go to a place I know they had also been and try to connect with their energy. Basically, it's a combination of intuition, guessing and research. I also ask Spirit to guide me in the right direction."

Billy considered what she said before he spoke again. "I have an idea."

"I'm all ears."

"Well, what if we were to go to our old house to see whether I can connect with the woman who died there?"

Maude was stunned into silence. She thought he might ask to tag along on a trip to Lily Dale someday, but she never thought he would suggest trying to reach out to Eva Barstow. "Do you think you can do that? Did you encounter any spirits while we were living there?"

"Other than Aunt Mabel, no, but I think maybe I can do it." He shifted his weight and glanced at the ground again. "Last night I asked the old couple I had seen when I was a kid if they were still here. They are."

Maude could feel the weight of his stare. It was like he had just confessed something and was bracing himself for her reaction. "Did they actually appear to you?"

"I'm not really sure. I felt their presence, like literally. I got the sense they were in the room, but I couldn't see them. The lights were out, so maybe I would have seen them if I had turned the lights on. It was a little freaky, so I just stayed where I was."

"Did you communicate with them?"

"Yes." There was confidence in his answer. "They both kept saying the word 'family'. I got the sense they were glad we are here."

Maude thought about it and then her eyes got big. "You said they were elderly, and that they both died in the house, right?" He nodded, and she continued. "I wonder if it was the Nolans? Daniel and Katherine. They owned Nolan's Dry goods Emporium. They both died of cholera here in 1849."

"I don't know, but that makes sense. I got the sense they considered us family."

"Well, they would think that. They helped raise me, I mean Martha, who was me in that life. Boy, this is a really strange conversation."

"Ya think? Well, I was wondering, since I asked to connect with them, maybe I could do the same with the woman who died in our house."

"Her name is Eva Barstow. She didn't die in the house, though. She was shot in the house. She died in Sisters of Charity Hospital."

"Oh, does that matter?"

"I don't think so; my understanding is that her energy will be strongest where she was the happiest."

"How would we determine that? We can't just knock on the door and ask to speak to the woman who had been shot there." Billy laughed at his own remark. He had relaxed a bit when he discovered that his mother would take his suggestion seriously.

Maude smiled. "Good point. I don't think the house is the best idea. There isn't an explanation I can think of that would make sense to perfect strangers, if we were to ask to come in." She thought for a moment. "I remember reading in the newspaper that she loved Delaware Park, the rose garden particularly. We could try there."

"Okay. When do you want to do that?"

"How 'bout now?" Maude wasn't any further along in understanding why this mystery had been presented to her, so it made sense to see if any information could be gained by connecting directly with Eva Barstow.

"Okay, I'll just run upstairs and grab my wallet and a pair of shades."

Maude watched him go and wondered whether she should make a quick call to Charlotte for guidance. There wasn't even time to conclude the thought as Billy returned in seconds. Maude had participated in more than a few workshops on mediumship however, and felt confident she could at least guide him through the process without Charlotte's assistance. Whether they would be successful was another story.

During the short ride to the park, Maude angled a few surreptitious glances at her son, trying to gauge his mood. He seemed relaxed, so she decided a few questions wouldn't hurt. "So, your friend from Statistics, is she local?"

"Sheri? Yeah."

"Are you guys going to try and get together over the summer?"

"Yeah, we're going to the movies Saturday night. Can I borrow the car?

"Sure. What are you going to see?" Maude did her best to sound casual.

"I don't know. We'll figure it out when it gets closer to the weekend."

The conversation came to a stop as Maude pulled up to the park. The rose garden was on the Lincoln Parkway side of the park, across from the Albright Knox Art Gallery. They parked the car on the street and walked up the path.

It was a beautiful summer day, and the squeals of delighted children could be heard coming from the playground behind the garden. There were several rows of neatly pruned rose bushes still waking up from the long winter, and the only shock of color was from the tulips that lined the garden path. "Why don't we sit in the pergola," Maude suggested, pointing to the large wooden structure at the rear of the garden. "It's quiet and we won't be disturbed by anyone." Billy agreed, and they started up the gravel path that divided the beds.

Absent benches or seating, they made themselves comfortable on the stone steps, leaning against columns on either side of the entryway. "Okay, now what do I do?" Billy asked.

"What did you do last time?"

"I sat in my bedroom and asked if they were still around, and if they were, could they make their presence known."

"What I learned is that spirits on the other side need to sense love in your heart. They need to know that you are calling them with pure intentions," Maude told him.

"Okay, how do I do that?"

"Well, start by taking a few deep breaths to clear your mind." Billy nodded, and they closed their eyes and inhaled deeply, then exhaled slowly. "Okay, let's do a sort of prayer. Repeat after me: Spirit we are here today to connect with Eva Barstow. We come with love and light in our hearts. We ask that the information most needed come through with clarity."

Billy repeated those words and they both sat quietly. Finally, he said, "Is something supposed to happen?"

Maude opened her eyes to find him looking around. "Ideally, Eva Barstow will make her presence known." Maude took in his rigid posture and the uncertainty in his eyes. "Try and relax, like you are waiting for a friend to come along." She smiled as he shook like a wet dog before settling back against the column. "What were you doing when you connected with the couple in our apartment?"

"I was lying on my bed."

"Okay, so you said that you could feel when they were present. Take a few deep breaths and close your eyes. You don't necessarily have to speak out loud, but let her know that you welcome the connection, then reach out with your mind and wait for her to make her presence known." When Billy looked even more uncomfortable, she tried a different tack. "How about I take a short walk and leave you to try this alone."

He looked relieved. "Yeah, I think it's hard to relax with another person here. What do you want me to ask her?"

"Ask her to tell you about the night she was shot."

As Maude left, Billy took another deep breath and began mumbling the short prayer they had said together. Within a few minutes, he sensed a presence coming up from the casino, the direction toward which his mother had just departed. Had Mrs. Barstow been present physically, the two women would have crossed paths as Maude walked toward the lake and Eva walked from it.

The love that filled her heart was palpable, and Billy felt as if he knew her. "It's you," she said. She seemed very happy, and even relieved to see him.

"Do you know me?" He had spoken the words in his mind where he could clearly see her now. She was wearing a rose colored short sleeved dress. It hung loosely on her slight frame, just a few inches above her ankle. Her hat was a similar color and covered dark hair cropped at her jaw line. Its brim tapered at the front of her face, broadening at the back. When she looked into his eyes, Billy realized that he knew her, too. Remorse filled his heart as he recalled the last time they had met. "I'm so sorry," he said. "I never meant to hurt anyone." He closed his eyes tighter and when he opened them, he could feel that she had gone.

Billy looked around wide-eyed, relief flooding through him when his mother was nowhere in sight. He sat for a moment to catch his breath, considering what he wanted to tell her. Finally, he got up and headed in the direction of the lake. *What was I thinking?* He was pretty sure he said those words to himself as he looked around for Maude.

• • •

Maude hadn't thought to bring her laptop, so she headed toward the casino hoping to make the connection in her mind without it. The original building designed by Calvert Vaux in 1874 had burned down in 1899. A three-story limestone and white brick boathouse/casino was built in 1900 and finished in 1901 in time for the Pan American Exposition. It featured a loggia, a restaurant, a lounging room, amusement halls and boat storage. There was also an apartment and office on the third floor for the caretaker, which had been removed several decades ago.

The building was accessible from a pathway in the upper part of the park, or from a flight of stone steps on opposite sides of the stone building leading from the lake. Maude walked down the stone steps on the western side of the building to what was now called Hoyt Lake, but would have been known to Willy and Nina as Park Lake. It was constructed in the late nineteenth century by widening Scajaquada Creek, which flows westward through the park. A prominent feature during the Pan American Exposition, it served as a boat launch for gondolas, and provided entertainment thereafter for those who enjoyed boating, fishing, and even ice skating during the winter.

Maude asked Spirit to guide her to the place where Willy and Nina had met. As she shifted her focus, she could see in her mind's eye a young woman hurrying in the early morning light across the promenade and up the steps on the eastern side of the casino. Maude walked along the promenade in that direction. She got halfway up the stairs to the building entrance, just before the lower terrace overlooking the lake. It was nestled into the side of the building and surrounded by trees. It was the perfect place for a secret meeting. Maude sat down on the steps and closed her eyes, clearly seeing Willy move to greet Nina Barstow as she rushed up the stairs.

She ran directly into his arms. "Did anyone notice you leaving?" Willy asked her.

"No. You?"

"No, ma was still fast asleep. We don't have long, though. She'll be up soon."

The conversation between the two faded as Maude became aware of a darker presence on the upper terrace above them. Had she been writing, Maude would have described the same man that was in the cemetery, now pressed up against the wall, watching Willy and Nina. He must have followed Willy again.

For all that she was certain Willy would have recognized the man had he seen him, Maude could not see his face. Against the wall for cover, looking surreptitiously around the corner of the building, he turned his face downward. She had understood his feelings based on the energy around him, and his body language. He was no friend to either of them.

Willy had been sitting on the stone wall flanking the entrance to the building and hopped down as Nina approached. The man seemed to recognize her and seemed disappointed and a little annoyed. While his energy was dark, it also appeared ambivalent to the intimate conversation going on below him. In fact, he seemed impatient as the couple shared a passionate kiss, followed by a lingering embrace. Whatever he had hoped to observe, it hadn't been a lover's reunion.

Maude watched as the couple chatted for a while, all the while sharing sweet, lingering kisses. They were only together a short while before they parted and went their separate ways. Again, the man took time to pull his hat down and his collar up before he followed Willy out of the park.

"Billy was so quiet on the way home. I'm hoping the experience didn't scare him," Maude told Charlotte Lambert later that afternoon. "I'm not sure he even connected with her. Maybe that's why he didn't say much. Maybe he didn't want me to be disappointed that his effort to connect failed."

"I can't imagine that he had trouble making a connection. He's got a foot in each world, that boy."

Maude was silent for longer than was comfortable in a phone conversation. Finally, when she spoke there was accusation in her voice. "You've known he has this ability?" This wasn't the first time Charlotte had kept important information from Maude. She had known Maude and Don were soul mates but hadn't seen the need to tell Maude for nearly two years.

"I sensed it the first time I met him, and you would have, too, if you were ready to know." Charlotte would not apologize for holding back information Maude wasn't ready to hear. "Knowing young Billy had powerful inner senses would only have interfered with coming to terms with your own abilities."

Maude couldn't argue with Charlotte's reasoning. The old woman had been more than patient while Maude was trying to understand the changes in her own life. "You're right." Maude held back the words *as usual* but they were implied in her tone. "So, what should I do?"

"The temptation is to press him for details or to suggest he try to connect again, but you must resist doing either. Let him come to you. When he's ready, he'll tell you what you need to know."

When he's ready, he'll tell you what you need to know. Maude wasn't sure what Charlotte meant by those words, saying as much to Don while they were cleaning up after dinner that night. "Did she mean she knows what he is keeping from me?"

Don looked toward the hall to make sure Billy had left. "Maybe he isn't keeping anything from you.

Maybe he was just avoiding what might have been a lengthy conversation." Billy had gone just over the border to Canada with some of his old high school friends. The legal drinking age in Ontario was nineteen, and it was typical of college students from Buffalo to reunite to raise a pint in Canada after the completion of their semester. "He's been looking forward to tonight."

Maude reluctantly agreed that Billy wasn't inclined to be chatty when his mind was focused elsewhere. Still, she couldn't shake the feeling that both Charlotte and Billy were keeping something from her, and she had learned to trust her feelings. "Well, I've known Charlotte long enough to understand that I won't be able to pry something out of her that she doesn't want to tell me, and I agree that Billy shouldn't be pushed on the matter, so I guess there's nothing I can do but wait and see how it plays out."

Don smiled. "I'm proud of you, Maudie. I know this is hard for you."

Maude's own pride shown as she returned his grin. "You know what? It isn't as hard as it used to be."

"So, tell me about your experience at the park," Don prodded.

The prideful smile returned as Maude gathered her thoughts. "I was able to connect to Willy and Nina again, but I really don't know what transpired between them other than some smooching. It seemed more important that I focus on the man who was following Willy. He was there, on the upper porch of the casino." She had been loading the dishwasher while they spoke and closed the door before she continued. "It's weird, because I got a strong feeling that Willy would have known this man if he'd seen him."

"What's so weird about that?" Don grabbed a plate of cookies that had been set aside for dessert and ushered his wife into the living room.

"Well, I think I'd know him, too, but I can never see his face."

"Why not?"

"He's usually hiding behind something, and when he walks on the street, his hat is pulled down and his collar is turned up. I think that's so Willy won't recognize him."

"How would you recognizing him help you?"

"I think he's important in all of this."

Don offered her the plate of cookies. "Why don't you sleep on it? Maybe you'll have more insight tomorrow."

Maude nodded in agreement and took a cookie. She tried to stay focused as Don shared the details of his day, but her mind kept wandering back to the man at the Casino. Whoever he was, he meant Willy harm, and Maude began to wonder who else might be in jeopardy.

Part Two

Chapter Nine

Willy took his stroll around the zoo earlier these days, before Patrolman Brown began his shift. He was watching the alligators when the zookeeper approached, carefully pushing a wheelbarrow that had seen better days. Szymon Kowalczyk was not a young man anymore. He had been taking care of the zoo since it consisted of nothing but the Deer Paddock at the edge of Delaware Park. Willy had been coming there since he was a small boy, seeking out Mr. Kowalczyk during every major event in his life including the death of his father, his first day as a Buffalo Police officer, and the day Nina Barstow had agreed to go on a date with him. Now, when it seemed the rest of the neighborhood had turned against him, he came to visit the man every day. "Here again early, I see."

"Good morning, Mr. Kowalczyk. I just wanted a quiet place to think."

"You have much to think about these days," Mr. Kowalczyk replied, and Willy nodded in agreement. The keeper had heard the gossip, and Willy had confided in him what he could. "I don't believe a word of it. I told you already; you are a good boy, Willy."

The two men were quiet for a few minutes, watching the reptiles who laid perfectly still at the edge of their pond. Willy always thought of them as sly creatures. Laying so still, one might think they were dead, with eyes that never betrayed their thoughts. He once saw a large crow make the mistake of setting down on a log in the enclosure. The gators moved with brutal efficiency toward their prey. The fastest among them rose up on his hind legs, lunged forward and caught the bird in midair as it attempted to fly away. A vicious fight had ensued as several gators became frustrated at having missed out on a snack. Willy had run to find Mr. Kowalczyk only to find out that fights like that were common among the alligators, particularly at feeding time. There were far too many in the enclosure, and his requests for additional housing fell on deaf ears. Each time after that, when Willy passed their enclosure, he made sure it was well after feeding time.

Willy's expression must have betrayed thoughts of that horrific encounter. Mr. Kowalczyk placed a hand gently on his arm and said, "I've got some tea in my thermos. Why don't we go have a cup?"

Willy followed as the bent old man shuffled slowly in the direction of the keeper's office, leaving the wheelbarrow where it was. Neither spoke, and Willy was glad. The comfort between them was one of the reasons Willy loved the zoo so much. Lately it was one of the few places he was still welcome. The rumors surrounding his dismissal from the police department had only intensified since he was a person of interest in the Barstow murder.

A nice visit in the zookeeper's office was an unexpected gift and Willy hadn't realized the tension he was carrying in his gut until it began to unravel just a bit.

However, his relief was short-lived when Mr. Kowalczyk opened the door revealing Captain McNamara seated at the desk, waiting patiently.

Kowalczyk raised his hand to the captain. "Stay where you are. I'll stand." It would have looked strange for anyone watching if the keeper had deposited Willy in his office and left him there alone. Besides, McNamara had known the man since his days as a patrolman and trusted him to keep what he heard to himself.

The look on the captain's face confirmed Willy's fears, and he fell rather than sat in the chair opposite the desk. "What brings you here, sir?"

"We've got a problem, Willy."

Willy met the captain's eyes. "What's wrong?"

"Someone is following you."

Willy grimaced, thinking back to their last meeting at the cemetery. "I was afraid of that. I thought someone might have been tailing me when we met last week, but I didn't see anyone. There was someone at the park the other night, too, but I wasn't sure if he was following me, or just out walking."

The captain's smile was grim. "You have good instincts, lad. I've been concerned since we stashed Tocci, so I've been keeping a bit of an eye on you myself. I arrived at the cemetery early the other day and watched you approach. That's when I saw him."

"Saw who?"

"I don't know. He was far enough away that I couldn't tell."

"How long?"

"It's only been a few days, I think. I hadn't noticed anyone tailing you or me until the cemetery meeting."

"What do we do now?"

"Well, we need more time. It's hard to put a case together with all my detectives working on the Barstow murder."

"I'll lean on Tocci a little harder and see what I can get him to cough up."

"No, lad. You've got to stay away from him. I've got to believe if Saladino knew where Tocci was, he'd have made a move by now. So far, his spy has only seen what could have been a chance meeting between the two of us at your father's grave. If he thinks you know anything about Tocci, he'll snatch you right off the street and do what he needs to do to get you to talk."

Willy hadn't considered what he was doing could be dangerous. They had fixed it so that anyone interested would think Tocci had died in the Home. Now Saladino's thugs had been following him. They must know where he lived. Was his ma in danger? They must have seen Nina, too, if the man near the arch at the park was the same as the man in the cemetery. Could she be in danger as well? Concerned, Willy said, "What do I do?"

The captain grimaced. He knew what he was going to recommend to Willy would not go over well. "As soon as you leave here, lad, you should go straight home. Tell yer ma everything, then tell her to get on a train as soon as she can to visit her sister in Springfield."

Had he not already been seated, Willy's knees would have surely buckled underneath him. "Is she in real danger?"

"She might be, lad, once you are gone."

"Gone? Where am I going?"

McNamara blew out a long sigh, steeling himself to reveal the rest of the plan.

"You're not safe here, Willy. I'm going to take you into custody. There's enough suspicion surrounding your presence at the Barstow house the night of the shooting to bring you in. That just might redirect Saladino's men. At the least, it will keep you safe until we can build the case against him."

"But if it doesn't, you think they'll go after ma?"

"It's a possibility, but it will be more than any mother should bear, to have her son arrested under suspicion of murder. It would be better in either case if she left town until this has all blown over."

Willy took a few minutes to process what he'd heard. "You're going to arrest me?"

"It can't be me, Willy. It must look legitimate. Detective Malloy will come to the house this afternoon. He's been offering you up as a suspect every morning at the briefing. I'll tell him to bring you in. With luck, we'll only have to hold you for a few days. We're hunting down other suspects. We'll find the real killer and keep you safe in the meantime."

Willy ran a shaky hand through his hair. Arrested for suspicion of murder…how did it come to that? Willy doubted he'd ever regain the trust of his neighbors, regardless of what McNamara said or did to clear his name. "Only ma can know the truth?"

"I owe it to both you and your father to put her mind at ease. I know this hasn't been easy for her." He paused a moment, then added, "I've got no reason to

believe that Nina Barstow is in any danger and she'll stay that way if she doesn't know what you're up to." The captain's pointed look clearly communicated that he was aware that Willy had gone against his wishes and met with Nina.

Before the last week, Willy might have looked guilty or ashamed, but given all he was sacrificing for Captain McNamara and the case against the Saladino gang, Willy just met his eye. He would not apologize or even try and explain himself. "As long as she's safe."

Willy and the zookeeper left the office together, and Kowalczyk made himself busy fussing with the flowers planted by the East Meadow exit where Willy made his way out. There hadn't been any other visitors to the zoo that morning before the captain's arrival, about thirty minutes before Willy. Now there was a very tired looking woman pushing a baby carriage, an elderly couple that Kowalczyk knew well, and two men walking the grounds alone. The first man had stopped at the elephant house, and the other followed Willy out.

All the keeper could see of the man following Willy out of the zoo from his vantage point, crouched in the garden, was a pair of worn boots beneath plain wool trousers. He told Captain McNamara as much when he returned to his office. "Not to worry, Szymon, I appreciate your help this morning." McNamara assured him. "I've kept you from your work long enough."

"The boy has given up a lot for you," Kowalczyk replied, his voice lacking its usual accommodating cheer. "You will keep him safe."

"I will, Szymon."

• • •

Willy's meeting with his mother was not easy. He stumbled through an explanation of his current circumstances and stood with his head hung as she chastised him for having ever agreed to such a foolhardy plan. He made the mistake of trying to placate her when she directed her anger at Captain McNamara, which only made matters worse.

"He had no right to ask so much of you! Your father must be turning in his grave, bless his soul." Susan made the sign of the cross. "You've not been on the force more than two years. What was he thinking?"

Willy resisted the urge to insist that he did not lack the experience for such an assignment. "Ma, please try and understand. Joey Saladino is a terrible and ruthless man. You read the papers; you know the things he's been accused of. The captain is going to put him away for good and I'm proud to be a part of it."

"Ach, ye've got your father's sense of blind loyalty, for all you've got his big heart, too. Have you forgotten what he got for his trouble? Am I to lose you to a thug's bullet now? I can't bear it, Willy. I truly can't!" Susan Cooper sat down at the kitchen table, buried her face in her hands and cried.

"Ma, I'll be safe. The captain would have come and told you himself, but he can't risk being seen here."

Susan looked up, her tear streaked face dark with indignation. "He's got more to fear from me if he has the nerve to cross my threshold than he does from that lousy Guinea thug!" Susan wiped her eyes as anger once again took the upper hand. "I have to live in this neighborhood! There's already been talk, and now they'll come and haul you off to jail. I doubt either of us will survive the shame of it." She was pointing a shaking finger at him now. "You know well how fast bad news travels, but will they be so eager to spread the news when your name has been cleared?"

Willy took the seat next to his mother and then both of her hands in his. "Please, ma, please listen to me. I want you to go. Visit Aunt Lucille in Springfield. Leave today. By the time you come back from Massachusetts, this will all be over, and I'll be a hero. Then you can hold your head up high when you walk down the street."

"Do you think I shrink from such talk? Why, just the other day, Mrs. Orzo had the nerve to say something right to my face at Mrs. Cobb's millinery shop. Well, I told her just what she could do with her nasty rumors!" She stood up from the table and stood to face her son. "I told her and the other women in the place that my son was no drunk and he was certainly not a murderer, either!"

"Ma, nobody can know the truth, not right now, anyway. You must leave until this is over. Please, ma."

"Willy, I just can't leave while you go to jail." She repeated some version of that declaration a few more times, but Willy finally convinced her to go. Ultimately and thankfully, she departed for the train station before Detective Malloy came later that afternoon to arrest Willy. Her heart would have shattered to pieces to see him taken away in handcuffs, under the gawking eyes of the neighbors.

• • •

"They want Cooper for the Barstow murder. He's in custody right now. I saw when they brought him in," the informant told Saladino. The man had worn his hat low over his brow as he entered the men's room at the North Park Theater, not wanting to be recognized. The same hat was now in his hand, as he stood by the sink making his report to Joey Saladino.

Saladino laughed out loud. "That kid's no killer."

"A few of the detectives in the Fourteenth think he is. He was placed at the scene around the time of the shooting."

"That don't mean nothin', kid. McNamara could be up to something. He's a sly bastard. Stay on him and see what you can find out."

• • •

Nellie Finster knocked on the Barstow's door, forcing herself to slow the rhythm so her visit wouldn't appear urgent. It was a risk coming to the house, but it was urgent, and she promised Willy she'd deliver his message. She took a deep breath and blew it out just as the door opened.

"Hi, Jonathan," Nellie said as he stood aside to allow her to enter. Nothing more was said while she made her way to Nina's room, as she had a thousand times before. Pleasantries were always exchanged if Nina's mother or father answered the door, but the childhood practice of ignoring Jonathan's teasing had stuck with her, though the teasing had stopped years earlier. She took the stairs at a trot, as usual, forcing herself not to appear rushed. A single knock on the

door before entering, she was careful not to slam the door behind her.

"What are you doing here?" Nina asked. She had been crying, her eyes red and swollen.

Nellie motioned for Nina to move down then sat on the bed beside her. "I've brought word from Willy." She opened her purse and handed Nina a sealed envelope.

Shaking hands unfolded a single sheet of paper. Before she read the note, Nina glanced up at Nellie.

Nellie answered the question that hadn't been asked out loud, "No, I didn't read it. He gave it to me already sealed and told me to give it to you."

Nina took in the tidy handwriting as her eyes raced over the page. The note began 'My Darling Nina', which made her smile, but that warm and fuzzy feeling was soon replaced by anguish. "No!" The word came out as a strangled whisper. "Oh, no!"

"What?" Nellie caught the page as it fell out of her friend's hand.

My Darling Nina,

I won't be able to see you for a little while. I know it looks bad, but please believe that I am innocent. This will be over soon, and I'll explain everything, I promise.

Willy

"He's been arrested," Nellie said, and Nina nodded in agreement.

"Will they let you see him?" Nina asked.

"I don't know, but I can try."

Nina took the letter over to her desk and began writing on the back. "You'll take this to him?"

"Of course, if I can."

Nina was still writing when there was a gentle knock on the door before it opened. "Daddy, come in."

"Hello, Nellie. May I have a word with my daughter."

Nellie looked at the letter, half composed, and then at her friend, not sure what to do. Nina looked at her and said, "I'll see you tomorrow, Nellie." The girl smiled with relief and left.

"What is it, Daddy?"

Conrad bent down on his knees, so they were eye to eye and pulled an envelope out of his pocket. "These are train tickets to Cleveland. I want you to take your brother and sister to Aunt Grace."

Nina took the envelope and examined the tickets inside. "These are for tonight, and there are only three. What about Jonathan?"

"Jonathan has agreed to take over the jewelry shop for a while." The look of confusion and hurt on his daughter's face nearly brought Conrad to tears. "I need some time, honey, and I don't want the little ones to see me like this. They miss her terribly and I'm supposed to comfort them, but I can't right now." The tears started to flow, and he could do nothing to stop them. "I just can't. Can you understand? Can you forgive me?"

It broke Nina's heart to see her father prostrated by grief. "Oh, daddy, I don't want to leave you. You need us and we need you. Please don't send us away!"

Conrad wiped his own eyes with the backs of his hands then took out a handkerchief to gently wipe those of his daughter. "It's just for a little while. I need you to do this for me. Will you, please?"

She nodded, sniffing more tears away. "Who will take care of you while we are gone?"

Conrad wrapped her in his arms, his chin resting on the top of her head. "Don't worry, sweetheart. Jonathan and I will manage well enough." He closed his eyes while he held her, silently grateful that the conversation had gone as well as it did. Jonathan had heard that Willy Cooper had been arrested that afternoon and he wanted Nina and the children far away before it made the papers the next day. It was hard to believe that Willy could do such a thing, but maybe the police knew something he didn't. It was just as well to have his family away from the intrigue surrounding the investigation. The gossip was rampant and the children had become prisoners in their own house avoiding it. Ohio was far enough away to spare them the ugly headlines and whispers that followed.

"Hurry now and pack a bag, then help the children to do the same."

"Yes, Daddy." Nina rose from her chair, the letter to Willy forgotten, and opened the door to her room and called down the stairs. "Amelia, Matthew, hurry, we're to go on an adventure."

• • •

Nina glanced around her bedroom, making sure that she had everything packed when her eyes came to rest on the unfinished letter on her dresser. The children had put up a fuss when presented with the news of their departure and it had been an ordeal to calm them down and pack their bags. Nina felt a twinge of guilt that she had forgotten all about Willy. She picked up the half-composed letter and turned it over to read his original note. "Oh, Willy," she whispered, "I don't know what to do."

"Don't know what to do about what?" Startled, Nina turned to find her father standing in the doorway. "What have you got there, Nina?" He approached with his hand outstretched and she reluctantly handed him the page.

Nina stood with her eyes focused on the hardwood floor while her father examined both sides. "Did Nellie bring you this?"

Nina nodded, her eyes never leaving the floor.

Conrad said nothing, but the look of disappointment on his face was just as effective as any verbal scolding would have been. "Have you seen him?"

"Daddy, you know he isn't guilty of any of the things of which he's been accused." She couldn't lie to her father, but that didn't mean she would answer his question.

"Sweetheart, he was fired for drinking on the job. I don't want you spending time with a person of such low moral character."

"I don't believe it, Daddy, and I'm surprised you do. You've known Willy since he was a boy. All he ever wanted was to become a police officer like his father." Nina was careful not to divulge what little Willy had told her, but she felt compelled to defend him in some way.

"I didn't believe it, honey, so I asked Captain McNamara, and he confirmed that Willy came to work smelling of whiskey on the morning he was fired."

Nina looked surprised and could think of no counter to her father's statement. "Surely you don't think he was responsible for mother's death."

Conrad felt for the left pocket of his trousers, in search of his watch. He didn't pull it out but knew they would have to leave soon if his children were going to make the train. He was silent for a moment, searching for words that would end quickly what could easily turn into a long and unpleasant discussion. He did not want to part ways with his daughter after an argument. "No, Nina, I didn't think that when I was first told about his presence in our backyard that night, but the police are not in the habit of arresting people for no reason. They must know something we don't. I trust them to do their jobs. If he is innocent, he will not be held for long." Before she could speak in Willy's defense, her father continued, with more authority than understanding this time. "I know that Willy is your friend, but you must think of your family right now. I need you to take care of Matt and Amelia. I know it is a lot to ask, but you are the strong one, Nina, like your mother was. Please try to put aside your concerns about Willy Cooper and take your brother and sister to Cleveland. It won't be for long, I promise."

For the second time that afternoon, Nina nodded her head with tearful eyes, agreeing to ease her father's suffering while compounding her own. As she closed her bedroom door and headed for the stairs, she whispered a small prayer asking that Willy be safe while she was gone.

Chapter Ten

Miss Nellie Finster
23 Forest Avenue
Buffalo, New York
April 21, 1924

Dear Nellie

I am sitting on the train as I write this, the daylight fading to dusk. Daddy has sent Matthew, Amelia and I to Cleveland. None among us wishes to be away from home at this time, but we must trust that Daddy knows what is best. I have promised the children that there is a shop just like Parkside Candies within walking distance to Aunt Grace's house and that we can go there every afternoon if they like. That seems to have improved their spirits considerably. As for myself, it grieves me so to have left Buffalo while Willy suffers in jail. Please see that he gets the enclosed letter. There will be others to follow if you would be kind enough to deliver them for me. You are a wonderful friend and I am grateful for your help.

Your dearest friend,
Nina

William Cooper
Buffalo, New York
April 21, 1924

Dear Willy,

Can you ever forgive me for leaving when you needed me most? While my body is here in Cleveland be assured that my heart is with you in Buffalo. I think about you always and worry about how you are holding up during this most trying time. Matt and Amelia ask about you and insist I remind you that you promised them a special tour of the zoo and Matt is particularly excited to be able to meet the elephant face to face. I hope that this will give you something to look forward to when you are lonely, for the children adore you and are eager to see you again. I hope you know that I feel the exact same. We are apart, and that adds an additional layer to the grief I already carry for my dear mother, but I think of the day we will be reunited and free to enjoy each other's company. Until then, you are in my heart.

Fondly,
Nina

~

Nina Barstow
15 Beechwood Avenue
Cleveland, Ohio
May 1, 1924

Dear Nina,

I've been waiting nearly a week to send you this letter, although Willy gave me a note to include and I know you are desperate for news from him. The reason I have waited so long is because I have news that you must know, yet I have not been able to put the words to the page. I'll just get it over with, but please know that I wish with all my heart that I were telling you in person so that I could provide the comfort I know you will need after reading it.

Your father has put the house up for sale, and he and Jonathan are living in a flat on Hertel Avenue. I'm so sorry, Nina. I know your heart breaks to hear this news and it grieves me so to have to add yet more to your burden. Mother overheard Mrs. Lucchesi the other day in Mr. Donald's Dry Goods Store. She makes your father and Jonathan dinner most nights, as she says they would waste away if she didn't. Nina, she said that the flat they are living in above the bank is hardly big enough for the two of them, let alone you and the little ones. She also says that your poor father has let himself go so that she would not recognize him, were his name not on the mailbox. He's dreadfully thin, unshaven and in desperate need of a haircut.

Oh, Nina, I'm so sorry to have such dreadful news to tell you. I hope that the note included here from Willy will bring you better news. He does not say much to me during our visits, which are brief. He looks thinner and very tired. He is not well thought of among his former colleagues, and I fear they are doing little to catch the real killer. I also fear that one or more among them has misused him. The first day I saw him, to deliver your note, his face was bruised and his lip bloody. He told me he fell, but I don't believe him. When I handed him your note, it was as if he underwent a complete transformation, the misery replaced by relief and joy. You are very special to my cousin, Nina, and it will give him hope to continue to receive a few words from you. I eagerly await your reply to me so that I can know how best to help you, and to him so that I can play some part in keeping his spirits up.

Your very best friend,
Nellie

~

Dearest Nina,

It gave me great joy to receive your note, although I am very sorry to hear that you are in Cleveland. Please disregard whatever negative remarks Nellie might have made to you regarding my well-being. There is much I can't tell you, but everything happening here right now, regardless of how dreadful it might be, will benefit me in the long run. Please give my kind regards to Matt and Amelia (although I beg you do not tell them I am in jail). Thinking of all of you, and the great adventures we will have when all of this business is settled sustains me in this dark place.

We are apart, each of us in a place we do not want to be, all the while things are going on in our lives that we cannot control. I have had plenty of time to think and I hope it will come as no *surprise to you that my thoughts are often focused on us. I love you, Nina. I am more certain of my feelings for you than I have ever been about anything else. This is not the way I wanted to tell you, but I suspect that you also have a great deal of time to think. Please think about me and those three words that I have just written. I write my feelings here knowing in my heart that you feel the same, and that those three words will lift your spirits when you are down. Tonight, I will dream of the time when we are together again.*

All my love,
Willy

Maude was sitting at her desk, the chair pushed away to give room for her legs that were folded upon it tailor style. She was leaning forward, elbows propped on the desk and chin balanced on folded hands. Don recognized this as her thinking position. When some aspect of her writing or research eluded her, Maude tried to get her face as close to the computer screen as possible, as if to coax whatever clues it was hiding out in the open. Sometimes she was so engrossed in her thoughts, the precarious balance of her elbows on the desk gave way and she fell right off the chair. It looked as if she were close to that point, so he gently knocked on the office door. When that didn't get her attention, he came up behind her to steady the chair when he inevitably startled her with his voice.

"Jeez, you scared the daylights out of me!" Maude nearly jumped out of her seat when she felt two hands touch her shoulders.

"Well, I knocked on the door and you were too focused to hear me. I figured if I called out, I'd startle you and knock you off balance."

Maude sat up and tried to untangle her legs, only to find that they were stuck where they were. Don came around to the front and helped her by gently massaging some life back into her lower limbs. "Thanks. I guess I've been sitting that way for a while."

"A few hours at least. The shop closed a while ago and the rest of us already ate dinner. I figured I'd better come and check if you were ready to call it quits for the night." He pulled her out of the chair. "We made sandwiches. I took the liberty of making your favorite. It's in the fridge when you're ready, but it looks like you are no closer to solving your problem.

Maude looked at the clock on her laptop, first processing that she had been withdrawn into her thoughts for considerably longer than she realized. After that, she looked quizzically at her husband. "Problem?"

"Well, yeah. You only sit like a pretzel at your desk when something is really not making sense."

Maude scrolled back a few pages and pointed to the screen. "I wrote this earlier." She sat back and waited while Don scrolled through and read everything.

"Wow. You don't get a better tormented love story than this. Professing his devotion in a letter, from a jail cell." Don walked back around and took the chair on the opposite side of the desk. "So, what is bugging you about all this? Are you sure about the Aunt in Cleveland?" That was his way of asking if Maude was confident that what she had written had really happened. There wasn't much that could be verified in the historic record since the actual letters she had channeled were likely long gone.

"Yes. I wasn't able to look her up, because I don't know her last name, but I'm confident that the three of them went to see her in Cleveland. I just feel it."

That was good enough for Don. "Okay, so what's the problem?"

"I got a feeling when I was writing this, but I can't put my finger on it. I keep reading it over again, and I get the same feeling, but it's still elusive."

"Bad feeling or good feeling?"

"Both, I guess. There's something very final about these correspondences. I feel like Nina becomes separated from someone permanently, but I don't know who." Maude rose and motioned toward the stairs leading up to their apartment, deciding she'd think better after the turkey sandwich Don had made her. "At the same time, there's also a sense of comfort and familiarity. It's a bit more elusive, but definitely there."

"It's certainly a lot for a young woman to handle, all the while grieving her mother's death. Maybe she's relieved on some level to go and visit her aunt." Don commented as he reached into the refrigerator for the sandwich. "What do you want to drink?"

"Just water, thanks." She accepted the plate gratefully and savored the layers of roast turkey, crispy bacon, mayonnaise and hot sauce as she took the first bite. "The fact that I can't find her or the younger siblings in the historic record is troubling."

"Maybe the aunt took them in."

"I wondered that, but without knowing her last name, it's difficult to check." Maude took another bite of her sandwich. "You really know your way around bread and cold cuts, Don Travers!" For a while, they were quiet while Don considered the problem and Maude finished her sandwich.

"Well, if their father remained in the flat on Hertel, it stands to reason that Nina and her siblings didn't return to Buffalo," Don offered.

"Agreed, but I can't believe he never saw his three children again. I don't know, Don. Something is definitely bothering me about this family and I can't figure it out."

Their conversation was interrupted by the sound of flip-flops skipping down the third-floor stairs. "Where are you off to?" Don asked Billy.

"Sheri is here to pick me up."

"Is she here now? Why don't you ask her to come up for a minute?" Maude was careful to keep the question casual. She hadn't really seen or spoken to Billy since their afternoon in the rose garden. If not for the fact that he was spending all of his time with Sheri, Maude would have thought he was trying to avoid her.

"Yeah, sure, okay." Billy reached for his phone.

"Don't text her, you knucklehead," Don chastised. "Go down and invite her up like a gentleman."

"She can park in the alley behind my car." Maude called as Billy made for the front door.

Maude was putting her plate in the dishwasher when Billy and Sheri came in the kitchen.

"Mom, dad, this is Sheri."

Don stood and extended his hand. "Hi Sheri, I'm Don. This is Maude."

"It's very nice to meet you," Sheri told them, confidently shaking each of their hands in turn. She was as tall as Billy, with long, straight dark hair, like so many young women her age. Maude thought she would look much cuter with shorter hair but kept her thoughts to herself.

"Where are you guys off to?" Don asked.

"We're going to hang out with my friends from high school," Sheri answered. "It turns out Billy knows them from football."

"Oh, right, I forgot you are local. What high school did you go to?" Maude asked.

"Kenmore East."

"I don't remember you playing any public schools," Don remarked. Billy and Glen had received a Catholic education and competed with other schools in the Diocese when it came to sports.

"I know these guys from Pee Wees, haven't seen them in a while. I'm looking forward to it." Billy told him.

"Well, we don't want you to keep your friends waiting," Maude said. "It was very nice to meet you Sheri; I hope you'll come again for a longer visit."

Glen came down from their shared gaming room on the third floor just as the couple was leaving. He responded with a cool "Hey" when Billy introduced him to Sheri, which was reciprocated in kind as the two walked out the door.

"She's hot," Glen remarked with appreciation as he took a can of pop from the fridge and headed back upstairs.

"Well, his brother approves. What about his mother?" Don asked Maude.

"She seems nice," Maude said noncommittally.

"And?" Don knew she had more to say.

"And nothing, she seems like a nice girl and Billy likes her, so all is well." Maude's answer was defensive. She was determined not to be the mom who disapproved of every girl her sons brought home, even if that happened to be her current track record.

"She'd be cuter with shorter hair," Don commented. "I feel like it's the seventies again and all girls have to have long, straight hair."

Maude laughed out loud. "I was thinking the same thing!"

"Ha! I knew there was something. There's always something with you."

"That's not true, and you said it first. I just agreed." Maude went to grab a bottle of wine from the rack on the kitchen counter. "I'm just thrilled he brought her up. He hasn't said two words to me all week."

"Give him a break; he is obviously not thinking with his head at the moment."

Maude laughed. "I hope that's it, and that he's not brooding over whatever happened in the park."

Don shot her a knowing smirk. "I doubt he even remembers what happened in the park. He's nineteen, and a cute girl is paying attention to him. I'm pretty sure he has other things on his mind."

"Oh, great, that gives me a whole new set of worries. Do you think he needs a follow up to the safe sex talk?"

"Already on it!"

Maude looked up towards the sound of explosions coming from upstairs. "I haven't heard that one before. Did Glen get a new game?"

"Yes; he'll be busy for hours." Don drew her in and planted a kiss just behind her ear. "We should have plenty of time for a little safe sex if you can set aside your research for a while." He kissed her again with purpose, driving all coherent thoughts from her mind.

"Research! What research?"

CHAPTER ELEVEN

Willy paced in his cell for the rest of the evening and into the first hours of morning after sending his letter off with Nellie. It was a risk to tell Nina he loved her in a letter, with her so far away and preoccupied with her own family's problems. "You're an idiot for telling her that way," he hissed to himself.

There was a snicker from down the hall, just out of his line of sight. "Who's there?" Willy fought down an internal moment of panic, not sure how much of his worry had been articulated out loud.

He heard the footsteps move closer and scowled as he recognized the face. The panic took hold again. How much had Sergeant Wellesley heard? "Are you in the habit of spying on prisoners?"

Wellesley was in full view now and approached the cell with a cocky grin on his face. "Pouring out your heart while you're in the slammer, eh, Cooper?"

Willy just glared, unwilling to admit anything to Peter Wellesley.

"You might as well give up on her. You're going away for murder." Wellesley was now face to face with Willy, so close that Willy could actually smell the booze on his breath." He reached for the silver flask in the breast pocket inside his coat and brazenly took a swig.

"What are you gonna do about it, Cooper? Who's gonna believe a cold-blooded killer over an officer of the law?"

"You're drunk! I won't have to say a word." Willy countered calmly. He would not let the likes of Sergeant Wellesley get the better of him.

"The funny part is, Cooper, nobody had any trouble believing you were soused on the job, but they won't believe it of me. Even your own mother knows you're a boozehound. She had to leave town for the shame of it. You broke your mother's heart, Cooper."

Flask still in hand, Wellesley started pacing, slowly back and forth in front of the cell. "I gotta tell ya, though, I still can't believe it. Of all the guys here, you're the last one I would have expected to hit the hooch before work." He stopped and shook his head. "A good egg like you, no way." Standing in front of Willy again, he added, "The captain was pretty quick to give you the boot. I expected him to look the other way, being that he was tight with your old man." Willy looked surprised, and Wellesley snickered again. "You forget, Cooper, that I'm privy to things you are not. The captain's been lookin' out for you for a while now, although why he bothers is beyond me. Maybe he's stuck on your mother."

Willy ignored the comment about his mother, knowing Wellesley was deliberate in his provocation. The desk sergeant just kept talking and Willy found that the more his own anger grew, the more he was compelled to stay silent. The captain had reminded him before he left the zoo that there would be nothing he could do to help Willy once he was in custody.

Starting trouble now with the desk sergeant would only make matters worse for him, and Wellesley was right: nobody would believe that he had come down to the holding area drunk.

Willy continued his silence, hoping that the desk sergeant would just go away, but Wellesley would not be deterred. "I mean, if I didn't know better, I'd think you wanted to get fired." He looked Willy square in the eye. "Now why would a mama's boy like you want to get fired?"

Thus far Wellesley's attempts to get a rise out of Willy had been met with blank stares and then the back of his head. Wellesley's irritation was becoming evident as his voice dropped to a menacing whisper. "Oh, you're hiding something, alright. Know this, Cooper: I'm still watching you and I'll find out what it is."

Wellesley took one more healthy swig from the flask. He laughed as he took a peppermint candy from his pocket and waved it at Willy before he popped it in his mouth and left.

Willy let out an anguished sigh as he fell back against his cot. It took a few deep breaths before he was able to calm himself. The important thing was he hadn't let the desk sergeant get the better of him. He couldn't risk losing his visitor privileges. Nellie was his only link to the outside, his only link to Nina.

Wellesley had been sweet on Nina for years and they had come to blows a few times when Willy thought the desk sergeant's remarks about her were unbecoming of a gentleman. Wellesley wasn't past writing to Nina himself to fill her head with lies. She wouldn't believe them for a while, but if Willy were unable to get word to her… He couldn't even let himself think of what might happen.

He sat on the cot with his back against the wall and his knees folded up under his chin for so long that his legs began to cramp. At first, he was consumed with worry over the idea that Wellesley would make advances toward Nina; after all, he'd done so a few times already. Gradually, that worry wandered to the back of his mind as the overall strangeness of the desk sergeant's visit became evident. Wellesley hadn't come to interrogate him about the Barstow murder. He was more interested in the morning Willy had lost his job, the morning Wellesley had turned him in to the captain for drinking on the job.

Willy thought for sure Wellesley had been quick to turn him in that fateful morning to shame Willy and ruin his chances with Nina. He got what he wanted when Nina's father had forbidden her to see Willy, so why had Wellesley given the situation another moment's thought? Willy played the conversation in his head over and over. 'I expected him to look the other way.' 'You forget, Cooper, that I'm privy to things you are not.' '…I'm still watching you and I'll find out what it is.' 'I'm still watching you.'

"Oh no!" Willy sat bolt upright. 'I'm still watching you.' He'd been so focused on trying to keep his temper in check that he hadn't caught that one important word. Still. Wellesley was still watching him. Was it Wellesley who had been following him? If so, it meant he was the department rat!

Willy ran both hands through his hair, scrubbing his scalp vigorously, trying to wrap his head around what he was thinking. "Think, Cooper, think," he hissed at himself, closing his eyes to try and conjure the person he had seen walking away from them in the park the night he met Nina under the arch. It was getting dark, and the man's back was to them, but he could very well have been the same height and build as Wellesley.

"I've got to talk to the captain." Willy rose from the cot and began pacing again. "How can I get word to him?" He was careful to keep his voice low. Although he was alone in the holding area, it was evident that Wellesley had heard at least part of his nervous muttering before Willy had even known he was there.

Willy was close to pacing himself into a full-blown panic. He could think of no way to get word to the captain any time soon. Most of his former colleagues believed him guilty of murder and would never listen to any accusations against one of their own. There had been no sign of Captain McNamara since he'd been taken into custody. Even if Willy asked to see him, the request would be denied. His only hope was that Nellie would be back soon and that he could send word to the captain through her.

Maude was startled out of her writer's trance as if she had come up out of the ocean for air. It was hard to catch her breath and she took a minute to inhale deeply and exhale slowly until her heart slowed down.

"Damn!" she exclaimed, looking down at the screen to make sure she had captured all the details that were swimming in her mind.

"What's wrong?" Christine asked, poking her head into the office.

"Well, I'm not exactly sure." Maude had already explained that she could channel the past through her writing, a gift that Christine openly envied as she listened to what Maude had just written. "I guess I got caught up in Willy's anxiety about realizing that Sergeant Wellesley might be Saladino's informant. It actually startled me out of my thoughts, and just when I was learning some valuable information. Often these gifts are more frustrating than anything else."

"Can't you just work your way back into it? You know, start writing again and see where it leads you."

"Sadly, it doesn't work that way. I've tried before, but I never seem to be able to get back into it."

"So, what do you do now?"

Maude considered her options. "Well, you have things pretty well in hand here, so…" Her comment was cut off by the appearance of Billy in the doorway. "What do you need, Billy?"

Billy was shifting his weight from one foot to the other, eyes glancing everywhere but at his mother. "I wanted to know if I could borrow your car for the weekend."

Maude focused more closely on his body language, which clearly indicated that he would rather have died than asked her that question. "That depends: where are you going and who are you going with?"

He took a moment to regroup and seemed to have found his courage. Meeting her eyes directly, he said, "Sheri and I want to go to the Rock and Roll Hall of Fame."

"In Cleveland?"

"Yeah."

There were a million questions she wanted to ask but she settled on the most obvious two. "You plan on staying overnight?"

"Yeah."

"With Sheri?"

"Yeah."

At that point, Christine gave her an understanding smile and retreated from the room.

Maude had to give her younger son credit for not dropping eye contact when he answered. Billy was nineteen, going on twenty, a young man. Maude had longed for one of the boys to come to her with some issue before they went to Don. The saying 'be careful what you wish for' came to mind now.

"Mom?"

Maude hadn't realized she was staring at him, open mouthed. "Um, sorry." She took a deep breath and met the problem head on. "This isn't your typical request to borrow the car, Billy. I just need a minute."

"Fair enough. Do you want some time to think about it?"

Maude wanted to say "Yes, give me a few days", but that wasn't fair. It was Tuesday. If they were going away for the weekend, they'd have to make hotel reservations somewhere. The mere thought sent her mind reeling again, but she did her best to focus on her son. "You really like this girl."

"I do…a lot."

Maude took another deep breath. If Billy had gone away to school, she would have no idea what he was up to, something she worried about where his brother was concerned. She had grown used to the fact that Billy came home just about every night, no matter how late the hour. It wasn't realistic to assume his entire four years of college would follow suit. They had raised their sons to be level headed gentlemen. It was time to trust in that, but this wasn't a request she would grant without discussing it with Don. "You need to run it by your dad. If we are both in agreement, you can borrow the car."

She reacted better than he had hoped. No immediate refusal, no lengthy and embarrassing talk, and no reason to think his father would disapprove. After all, he'd been young once. "Thanks, mom," and then he was off before she could say another word.

Later, while her sons were engrossed in a video game on the third floor and she and Don were making dinner, they could hear them shouting at the monitor as they battled unknown beasts from another realm. "Listen to them. It doesn't sound any different than it did when they were kids. Remember? We'd climb the stairs to tuck them into bed and we could hear explosions and all sorts of yelling coming from their bedroom." Don smiled, recalling how much he used to enjoy listening to the boys when they thought nobody was around to hear them. It was the only time they truly got along. "You'd never know they are grown men."

Maude looked up and chuckled. One of them had just died, or, rather, their avatar, and there were howls of disappointment until the game restarted. She reached out, giving her husband an affectionate pat on the shoulder. "Well, one of them is about to embark on a very grown up adventure."

When Don looked confused, Maude led him over to the kitchen table, gently pushed him into the chair, and handed him the bottle of beer he had been working on. "Billy asked to borrow my car this weekend so that he and Sheri can go to the Rock and Roll Hall of Fame."

"In Cleveland?"

"Yeah."

"Where they will undoubtedly spend the night."

"Yeah."

"Together?"

"Yeah."

"And you told him that was okay? Why didn't you tell him you needed to discuss it with me?"

Maude was a little surprised to hear the irritation in Don's voice. "Because he is not a child anymore. I told him *he* needed to discuss it with you. I'm just giving you the heads up so you won't be blindsided, like I was."

"Well, I appreciate that, but now he will be pretty disappointed when we tell him no."

This was not the reaction she had anticipated. Maude figured Don would be surprised, and a little worried, but she never guessed he would decline Billy's request. "Well, if that is how you feel, you have to tell him, but don't drag me into it."

"C'mon, Maudie, we're a team. You can't be comfortable with your nineteen-year-old son taking a girl out of town for the weekend."

"Well, no, I'm not, but he's not a child anymore. He'll be twenty in a few months. Honestly, I don't think it is our place to give him permission."

"Not our place? It's our roof he lives under and our car he wants to drive there."

"Yes, and I gave him permission to use my car providing he discussed the matter with you and that you were in agreement."

"You said it was okay to take a girl to spend the night in a hotel in Cleveland?"

Maude didn't know whether to be amused by his outrage or annoyed that it was directed at her. "Honestly, Don, I'm surprised you have such a problem. Didn't you just go over the highlights of the safe sex talk with him? I mean, you and I discussed this when Glen went away. We knew he'd be having all kinds of new experiences in college, much like we did."

"Yeah, that's what has me worried. I was a lot more comfortable thinking that these experiences would occur without my knowledge." He looked up towards the game room as some victorious event in the battle had caused both boys to cheer rather loudly. "Glen had quite a few experiences during his freshman year, but it was easier not knowing when or where they occurred." He used air quotes around the word experiences with a cocky grin.

"What? Are you saying Glen slept around? How come I don't know that?"

"Well, I wouldn't say slept around, but he had a few girlfriends." Don laughed out loud as their roles reversed and it was Maude's turn to be shocked. "It's not easy, is it? You're his mother. Do you really want to know what he's doing when he is away?"

That was a loaded question. Of course, Maude wanted him to be safe, and to work hard, but she had already admitted to herself and to Don that she didn't want to know about their other 'experiences'. "Look, we raised good boys; we have to let them out there in the world."

"You're right, I know. Actually, I'm more concerned with him getting his heart broken than an unwanted pregnancy. Billy is a sensitive soul. I just think they're moving too fast."

Maude gave her husband a sympathetic hug. "Tell him that, but don't tell him he can't go. Broken hearts suck, but they happen a few times before you find the right person. Billy can handle it, with a little help from us."

• • •

Being away from her desk for an afternoon hadn't given Maude the perspective she had been hoping for and she sat in the office the next day wondering where to direct her efforts next.

Christine had popped her head into the office to announce her arrival. "Hey, I was thinking about your current research project and I have a suggestion."

Maude knew she was referring to the Barstow murder. "I'd be grateful for your help."

"Well, it occurred to me that Willy Cooper is connected to the thug named Tocci. This guy is responsible for Willy's forced separation from Nina and his estrangement from his mother. Have you considered doing a little research to find out what happened to Tocci? Maybe there's a connection there that will help you understand how all of this plays out."

It came as no surprise that Christine knew the entire cast of characters in a story she had only heard once. She was sharp and often saw things that Maude didn't. "That's a great idea!" She had done some basic genealogical research on Willy Cooper, but hadn't done any research on Tocci or Joey Saladino's gang. Perhaps a search of the period newspapers would help connect some of the dots.

As Maude opened up her search engine, the bell could be heard above the door of the shop. "Don't worry, I'll see who it is," Christine offered as she closed the door on her way out.

Maude heard the murmuring of voices and then the return of footsteps in the direction of her office as she prepared to search period newspapers. "I think you might want to come out here. Mrs. Houston is here."

The research was forgotten as Maude made her way toward the retail side of the shop. She invited Mrs. Houston up to the apartment to see the Tiffany lamp, which Don had hung above their dining room table.

"Your apartment is stunning," Alexandra said. "The lamp looks perfect here."

"Thanks." That was high praise indeed. Their house in North Buffalo had been decorated with two young, rough and tumble boys in mind, with simple, inexpensive furnishings that were easily cleaned or replaced. The downtown apartment reflected their appreciation for antiques. Maude was very proud of their home, which was warm and inviting, and had just enough period pieces to look authentic yet not museum-like.

"Thanks. I thought the lamp might look too elegant for the space, but it seemed to fit right in." She had made coffee and they both admired how the red and gold maple leaves of the lamp reflected in the glossy shine of the cherry wood table. Maude resisted the urge to confess that the gift was just too much and that Mrs. Houston should really take it back.

"I never could find the room in which it belonged," Alexandra confessed. "There hasn't been a card table in the billiard room for nearly fifty years, and the color scheme in that room now is all wrong for the lamp."

"What a shame. It was commissioned for that house."

"Perhaps, but that was a long time ago. It just seemed like the lamp had had its time on Chapin Parkway. When I brought it back, it didn't seem to fit."

It was nearly lunch time when Maude returned to the main floor of the shop.

"Are you meeting Sam for lunch?" she asked as Christine grabbed her purse and headed toward the door.

"Yes. We're just getting subs from around the corner. Do you want me to bring you something back?"

"No. The boys are supposed to make lunch for the three of us."

"You're a brave woman! I'll be back in an hour."

Maude brought her laptop to the front counter and once again attempted a search of period newspapers. She was able to identify several articles before she heard the sound of footsteps shuffling down the back stairs. "Hey, Bill. What's up?" She misread the expression on his face when she warned, "Don't even think of asking to order take out for lunch. You guys promised to make something."

Billy's sheepish smile clearly indicated he had forgotten all about lunch. "Glen left for a job interview about an hour ago, but I'll heat up the leftover chicken from last night for us if you want."

"That works for me, provided your dad didn't eat it for breakfast this morning." With each member of the household on a different schedule, they seldom shared a morning meal together. Left to their own devices, the Travers men all seemed to prefer leftovers as opposed to more conventional breakfast options, arguing that it was easier to just grab what was in the fridge than to prepare something new. More often than not, they didn't even bother to heat them up.

He was still standing in the doorway between the rear work area and the retail portion of the shop and Maude felt her stomach churn. It was less out of hunger and more from the anticipation that they might begin a discussion similar to the one they had yesterday. Maude wasn't sure she could take another discussion like that. "Do you need something else?"

Billy glanced at the door, not sure if he wanted to risk being interrupted by a potential customer. Finally, he took a deep breath and pulled up the stool next to his mother. "Well, I wasn't exactly honest about what happened in the park a few weeks ago."

Maude hoped her sigh of relief wasn't audible. She closed the laptop and shifted her position to look at Billy directly. "What happened?"

"She came. Mrs. Barstow came to me and, the thing is, she seemed to recognize me."

Having had some experience being recognized by someone from the other side, Maude could sympathize. She found out she had been Martha Sloane in a past life because a spirit from Lily Dale had recognized her. Did Eva Barstow know who Billy had been in his past life?

"How do you know? What did she say?"

"She said 'It's you!', and after a few seconds, I recognized her, too." He glanced quickly at the front door again. This was not the kind of conversation he wanted to be interrupted by a stranger.

"How did you know her, Bill?"

"She came to me when we lived in the house. I was really little, and I didn't even remember it until she spoke to me the other day. It freaked me out then and it freaked me out now. I'm sorry, mom. I know this is really important to you. I should have told you earlier, but I just needed to get away from the whole thing until I had a chance to think about it."

Maude gave his shoulder a comforting squeeze. "Billy, I know all of this is new to you and it's a lot to process. I'm still trying to make sense of it."

His shoulders slumped a bit in relief. "Anyway, I've been thinking about it, and what I remember makes me feel bad."

"How so?"

"Well, I vaguely remember her trying to say something to me, but I closed my eyes and told her to go away. I think I even hid under the covers. I don't remember what she was trying to tell me, but now I feel bad that I didn't listen to her. Maybe it was important, maybe it would have solved whatever problem you are working on back then."

It would have been wrong to gather him into her arms, but she wanted to anyway and resisting the urge was difficult. Too much sympathy or pity in her voice wasn't going to work either. How this conversation went would determine whether or not he would seek her counsel again as he continued to explore his gifts. No pressure. "Bill, you were just a little kid. Of course it freaked you out. Much of this still freaks me out."

"I know, but when she came to me in the park and I remembered her, that fear came right back and I'm afraid I chased her off again."

"Do you want to try to connect with her again?"

Billy's eyes shifted down toward the floor and Maude couldn't tell if he was avoiding her or thinking about his answer. "You don't have to. I appreciate that you wanted to try." He still couldn't bring himself to respond. "Listen, why don't you leave the supernatural sleuthing to me? I've got my own rhythm and I'm making steady progress."

He looked at her and smiled, and she thought her heart would burst. "You don't mind?"

"Of course not, and if you decide you have no interest in exploring your gifts, that is fine, too."

"Thanks, mom." He leaned in and gave her a peck on the cheek. "I'll go make lunch now."

He was about to turn and leave when Maude remembered something. "Hey, Bill?"

"Yeah?"

"You took the picture, remember? The picture of the Barstow family. It had to have been years after you chased Eva out of your room. Do you remember why you wanted to take it with us? Did you remember her?"

Billy thought about it for a moment, and then his brows rose as something obviously occurred to him. "No, I didn't recognize her. The odd thing is, I remember it was me who took it, but I don't remember actually taking it. I don't remember taking it from the basement or packing it so carefully. Isn't that weird? It was only a few years ago that we moved."

"I don't think so. You were still young then, and a lot has happened in your life since then." Actually, the idea that he had no conscious memory could have meant that it was his unconscious mind that had compelled him to take the picture, but Maude didn't think it wise to mention that. Billy had made his decision and she didn't want to give him anything else to worry about.

Maude resisted the urge once again to go and pull him in for a hug. "Ya know, now that I'm thinking about it, I kinda want Chinese." She took a twenty-dollar bill from her purse and handed it to Billy. "I'll buy, you fly."

Later, when she and Don were closing up the shop, Maude said, "I think the most surprising thing to me was that Eva had tried to contact Billy back then and not me."

"Really, I'm not surprised at all. Children are a lot more likely to be receptive to spiritual energy. Think back to when the kids were little, and you were still teaching."

"Yeah, I suppose I was pretty distracted. Even if she had tried to make contact, I likely wouldn't have noticed." Maude went to turn off her laptop, which had sat untouched after lunch when the shop became busy with grandmothers and great aunts in search of that special graduation gift. “I forgot all about this,” she said as she went to close out her search. “I guess it can wait another day.”

When she told Don about Christine’s idea to do some research on Luciano Tocci, he asked her, “Do you want me to handle dinner while you take a look at those articles?”

Maude shook her head. “It’s tempting, but I’ll need a solid chunk of time. They’ll keep until tomorrow.”

CHAPTER TWELVE

Four days passed before Nellie showed up to visit Willy, and then when she did come, she was escorted to the holding area by Wellesley. The desk sergeant would take no chance that Willy would tell Nellie about his habit to tipple on the job. Willy expected as much and also anticipated that Wellesley would stay just down the hall, where he could both see and hear them.

Although Wellesley had a clear view, he could only see Nellie's back as she stood facing her cousin. Willy made sure he stood directly in front of her, so that his arms and torso were obscured by hers. He wouldn't risk passing her a note which could get intercepted by Wellesley, however he knew one other way to communicate his important message. Nellie's older brother was deaf, and each of them knew sign language, a fact of which few people were aware because James Finster resided at St. Mary's School for the Deaf. Standing directly in front of Nellie, Willy spoke to her about mundane family matters, while he signed to her about getting a message to Captain McNamara.

All the while he asked her how his mother was doing, his hands were telling her to go and find Mr. Kowalczyk.

"We had a letter from her the other day," Nellie told him, signing the question 'why' in answer to his silent request.

Nellie went on to recite portions of Aunt Susan's letter, while Willy signed to her that Wellesley might follow her, so she could not contact the captain directly. Mr. Kowalczyk could get a message to him.

Willy was careful to remind her not to react when he told her that Wellesley was likely the informant Captain McNamara knew was supplying information to Saladino and his gang. To Nellie's credit she carried on her end of the conversation for another fifteen minutes as if they were only discussing his mother's habits while away in Springfield. However, the last information he signed to her was that it was no longer safe for him to pass information to Nina through her. He also asked that Nina not be told about Wellesley. Although she was in Ohio, he suspected that she was not beyond Saladino's reach. 'Tell her I love her,' he signed.

It was that comment that broke Nellie's stoic façade. "Oh, Willy, I just hate to see you locked up in here," she said as tears welled up in her eyes.

Before Willy could respond, Wellesley came up and told Nellie that her time was up. Unable to resist pressing his advantage, the desk sergeant gave Nellie a stern lecture as he escorted her out about the dangers of her being seen visiting a murder suspect. For the sake of her own reputation, he warned, she should stop doing so. He also made sure his next remarks were loud enough for Willy to hear. "I know you're in contact with Nina. Maybe you could pass along this little note from me."

Willy resisted the urge to laugh out loud when Nellie replied that she'd be happy to, providing Mr. Barstow allowed it.

She reached out to take the note, but he had changed his mind. "I'll just keep it and ask him myself, man to man."

Willy knew, as Nellie surely did, that Conrad Barstow was not receiving any callers. Even updates from the detectives working his wife's case were reported to Jonathan these days. Willy was fairly confident that Nina would never see whatever he had written in that note, and, he had to believe, she wouldn't credit it if she did.

Nellie could be trusted to get a message to Mr. Kowalczyk. Even if Wellesley followed her, Willy was confident that she would find a way to carry out his request without that snitch being any the wiser. Still, it would take a few days for the captain to be brought up to speed and come up with a plan.

Three days after Nellie's visit, Wellesley returned to the holding area accompanied by a tall, thin man who Willy recognized as his attorney, Mitch Finnegan. Wellesley looked none too pleased as he spoke. "Get up, Cooper."

Before Willy could even ask what was going on, Mr. Finnegan said, "You're going home, Willy."

"I am? Does that mean they caught the killer?"

"Yeah, we caught the killer, and now we're letting him go!" growled Wellesley.

"Sergeant Wellesley, the evidence clearly exonerates my client. Now release him and then go back to your post."

Wellesley opened the cell door and then stormed off, leaving Willy standing in the open doorway, hesitant to come out. "What is he talking about?" Willy asked.

"The evidence, Willy. One of the neighbors very clearly identified the get-away-car, and another clearly identified you hopping over the Barstow's fence before the car even pulled up. A third witness saw you walking up your driveway at the time of the shooting, so it couldn't have been you who shot Mrs. Barstow. You could not have been in two places at once."

Willy considered Finnegan's scenario. "What's this about a third witness?" He knew there could not have been a third witness who identified him coming up his driveway, because he had been on his way to the asylum with Captain McNamara when Mrs. Barstow was shot. Someone was lying for him.

"I've been re-interviewing all the witnesses who came forward initially trying to find anyone who can corroborate your story. I also decided to interview your neighbors, which the detectives hadn't bothered to do. Your neighbor across the street is the night watchman at Washburn Crosby. He was just heading to work that night and saw you come home."

Willy could think of nothing to say, and just nodded appreciatively. He knew the man across the street was a widower who was sweet on his mother. Likely he'd have said anything if he thought it would help her. Still, Willy figured that somehow Captain McNamara had something to do with this.

Willy signed for his belongings and took Mr. Finnegan up on the offer of a ride home. By the time he had cleaned himself up, he noted that Mr. Kowalczyk would be just getting ready to eat his lunch. Even if Willy was followed, he could visit the zookeeper in his office without raising suspicion.

On his walk to the zoo, Willy was so deep in thought that he did not notice the hushed whispers and hostile stares from those going about their business on Hertel Avenue. If he had, he'd have known it was some of the very same individuals who used to greet him cheerfully when he walked his beat.

He pondered the testimony of the third witness as he approached the keeper's office. Willy was convinced that Captain McNamara had orchestrated his release from jail and so was not surprised to see the man sitting once again behind the zookeeper's desk.

"You look like hell, lad." the captain told Willy as he entered the office.

"I'll manage." They were the only words that he could get out before Mr. Kowalczyk enveloped Willy in a hug the strength of which was at odds with the man's fragile appearance.

"You need to eat. Here, take this." The keeper said, passing a sandwich wrapped in wax paper to Willy. "You need it more than I do."

Willy smiled, relieved beyond measure to see his old friend, but politely refused the offer. "Grabbed something before I left the house." It wasn't exactly true. The ice box was empty and only a few stale slices were left in the breadbox, but Willy needed to hear what the captain had to say more than he needed to eat.

"You got my message from Nellie," Willy stated, in an effort to initiate the conversation.

"Yes, and it was good thinking to go through Szymon. She'd have been made if you had sent your cousin directly to me." The captain was proud of Willy and it was evident in his voice as he spoke. "I've done some discreet checking up on Wellesley and I think you're right. I've been so busy between this case and the Barstow murder that I haven't been really paying attention. I discovered that Sergeant McInerney had been filling in at the desk for a few hours each morning before you were taken into custody. Wellesley told him he'd been out doing business at my behest. Of course, since you were taken in, that's stopped."

"So, what's the plan?" There was a note of confidence in Willy's voice that hadn't been present before. The affable and diffident young man had undergone a profound metamorphosis since he had agreed to help the captain stash Tocci. He wanted this business over with so that Nina could return and they could be together. Finding out Wellesley was the rat was the first step in untangling the web of deception in which he'd become embroiled. Now Willy wanted that man behind the same set of bars from which he'd just been released.

"We have to be careful here; Wellesley is the Chief's nephew," McNamara told him.

Willy's eyes nearly popped out of his head not only at the revelation that Wellesley had connections in high places, which both McNamara and Chief of Police had kept secret, but also because of the possibility that somehow Wellesley's transgressions would go unpunished because of those connections.

"Oh, don't worry, son. Chief Kennedy will skin him alive once the truth comes out, but we have to catch him red-handed."

"How do you intend to do that?" This time the question came from Szymon. He looked at the captain as if he already knew the answer but wasn't willing to believe it.

"We already know he's been following you, so I want you to visit Tocci tomorrow. I'll tail Wellesley myself, and with any luck, straight back to Saladino. We get Wellesley and then when Saladino and his men make a move to get Tocci, we take them down, too."

"Much could go wrong with your plan, Captain." Szymon observed. He understood that once the desk sergeant knew where Tocci was, he would likely take that information straight back to Saladino. Could the captain keep himself, Willy and Mr. Tocci safe while apprehending Sergeant Wellesley and Saladino's gang?

"This is police work, Szymon. There's a risk every time we walk out the door," the captain told him.

"I would be sad, indeed, if this business were to put an end to either of you. Take care." Szymon said no more while McNamara explained the rest of the plan.

"Willy knows what we are up against." The captain held out a Smith and Wesson revolver. He wouldn't risk taking a service weapon from the precinct. The gun was old, but the captain had learned from the revolver's original owner, his father, to keep his guns in perfect working order. It would do the job if Willy needed it. "I'll need you to stay at the asylum and protect Tocci."

"You can count on me, sir, but I've got the easier end of this detail." Willy wouldn't come right out and say that he was worried about the captain confronting Wellesley, even with back up.

"I haven't been around this long without learning a thing or two about keeping my head down when the need arises. Just keep Tocci safe."

That night Willy laid in his own bed for the first time in weeks, unable to find the peace of mind needed to fall asleep. It wasn't the job that worried him. The plan was simple enough. He would allow himself to be followed to the asylum. Captain McNamara would then tail Wellesley back to Saladino. He insisted on confronting the Sergeant himself, to minimize the potential for violent confrontation, he said. The last thing the captain wanted was a shootout in the middle of the city. He would bring in backup when they went to the asylum to apprehend Saladino and his men. It was risky, but there was always risk in police work.

The problem was that he had never spent a night alone in this house, and the stillness of the night made him edgy. Absent was the comforting presence of another person, the predictable squeak of the mattress springs or the padding of footsteps across the floor in the wee hours. His thoughts strayed first toward his mother, probably because he felt her absence keenly in the dead of night. It was just as well she was not there. She would have been furious if she had learned of what he was about to do. He thought of her sleeping peacefully in the guest room at his aunt's house, unaware of the dangers he would face, and was able to leave her there and move on.

Nina came to mind next. God, how he missed her! He was still worried about the last letter he had sent. There would be no way to know her reaction to his profession of love until he saw her next. He thought of her, together with Matt and Amelia, so far away from their father and helpless to do anything to help them cope with their mother's death. He could appreciate the sense of powerlessness and frustration Nina must be feeling because he was feeling the same. Just as Nina was unable to help her father, Willy was unable to help her. She would put her own grief aside to help her brother and sister. While he couldn't put Nina in a peaceful place in his mind, like he had done for his mother, Willy put the matter to rest, at least for now, with the knowledge that the day would come when he would see her again. That day was drawing nearer. If tomorrow went well, he would have his job and his reputation back, and he would see punished the man who was largely responsible for his troubles.

Chapter Thirteen

Willy left the house the next morning with the loaded Smith and Wesson holstered beneath his coat. He was careful not to look over his shoulder, but he had the same feeling of being followed as he walked up Hertel Avenue. It was easier to ignore as he made his way along the busy street, as he was more focused on the folks who glared at him, or worse yet, looked away as he passed by. However, the feeling intensified after he turned on to Delaware Avenue and approached the section of the street that wound between the park and the cemetery. There were fewer people there, and Willy had to focus to keep his eyes forward and his feet moving along. It was hard not to quicken his pace and he felt as if the short distance from the corner of Forest Avenue to the asylum was twice its usual length. He passed through the front gates and made his way to the administrative building.

"C'mon, we're going to take a walk," he told Tocci when the attendant brought him in.

"Outside?" Tocci asked. The asylum was designed such that each wing was connected by a curved walkway. It allowed for easier access for staff and continued exercise during the cold winter months for patients. Tocci avoided the outside gardens, where the patients

were encouraged to stroll and take in the fresh air. The fewer people he encountered, the safer he felt.

"Outside, in the gardens."

Tocci looked uneasy but thought it best not to argue. He was more interested in the unscheduled disruption of Cooper's regular visits. "Where have you been, by the way?" He was immediately sorry he asked the question, as he could already tell from Cooper's expression that something was wrong.

"Outside!" Willy gave Tocci a shove in the direction of the door. Cooper was careful to walk closer to the building. He wanted Tocci to be seen by anyone who was looking, but he didn't want to run the risk of being too far afield in case there were more men than just Wellesley following him. "The captain caught someone tailing me." At the look of horror on Tocci's face, Willy added, "Relax, if he had followed me here before now, you'd be dead already."

"And if Saladino thought you knew anything, he'd have beaten it out of you himself."

"He might have, but not even Saladino has the nerve to walk into the Fourteenth."

Tocci looked at Cooper a bit more closely, noticing his gaunt face and the dark circles under his eyes. He looked like any one of the boys after some time in the joint. "They locked you up?"

"Yeah."

"That wouldn't have stopped him if he thought you had anything to do with my disappearance."

"The charge was murder. It had nothing to do with you."

"Murder? Whose murder?"

"Doesn't matter. I didn't do it, and now I'm here." Willy looked around. "I think we've been out long enough, let's go."

They hadn't taken more than twenty steps beyond the building. At first Tocci was confused, then his face went pale as he realized what this was about. "You wanted me to be seen, you son of a bitch! You think Saladino's rat followed you here. You just signed both of our death certificates!"

"Then you'd better get back inside," Willy told him as he turned and headed for the door.

Tocci hurried after him. Once inside the hall, he grabbed Willy by the arm and spun him around. "You'd better tell me what the hell is going on here."

One of the attendants had seen the move and rushed over to contain the patient if necessary. Willy waved him away, and he reluctantly stood a few feet away, ready just in case. "Get your damned hands off me!" Willy hissed. "The worst thing you can do now is draw attention to yourself." Tocci let go, and Willy gave the attendant a confident nod, ushering Tocci back into the reception room.

"We know who the rat is. Before I continue, is there anything you want to tell me?" Willy still did not believe that Tocci was unaware of the identity of Saladino's informant.

Tocci looked him square in the eye and said no. "I already told you: none of us know who it is."

"Well then, I've got something up on you. It's Wellesley, our desk sergeant."

The blank look on Tocci's face told Willy that the name wasn't familiar to him. "So, now you think this

Wellesley followed you here, and once he's got a look at me, he'll hightail it back to Saladino?" Cooper nodded and a slightly paler Tocci asked, "What are the odds that your man gets to him before he gets to Saladino?"

"Well, that's a question now, isn't it?"

"You dirty son of a bitch! You want him to come after me. You have no idea what you just invited here, kid."

A wave of nausea rolled over Willy as Szymon Kowalczak's words came back to him. 'Much could go wrong with your plan, Captain.'

Tocci read the panic in Willy's eyes. "You're in over your head, kid. Now, I figure it will take about an hour for your man to find Saladino, and another hour or two for him to get a crew together to send over here. We gotta get outta here now."

For all Willy knew, Captain McNamara was following Wellesley to his own execution. He couldn't be certain the confrontation wouldn't become violent. That left him to secure Tocci and defend the asylum until backup arrived...if backup arrived. "No, you're not leaving. You are still under arrest for your role in the Lemke murder." Willy looked around, his mind racing to formulate a plan. "This place is huge. We'll hide; they'll never be able to find us."

"They won't have to, knucklehead. They'll come in through the front door and shoot up the room until someone gives me up. Think about all the crazies you got wandering around here."

Willy wasn't fooled by Tocci's concern for the other patients. "If that's true, they're going to do that whether you're here or not." Looking around the room,

Willy counted twenty other patients, two attendants, and one person at the front desk. Although Tocci's concern for the other patients wasn't genuine, Willy couldn't put them in harm's way. He saw Dr. Detweiller approach the reception desk and stood up to get his attention. "Stay here, and don't even think of moving."

Tocci eyeballed the two formidable attendants at the door. "Where am I gonna go?"

Willy shot him a curt nod, confident that he wasn't going anywhere and went to meet the doctor. "We have a problem," Willy said, disregarding the usual pleasantries. If all went according to plan, there would not be time for the captain to call and explain matters himself. He went on to explain the situation, watching the doctor's expression grow darker as he did.

Before he responded to Willy, Detweiller went over to one of the attendants, motioning for the other to join them. He calmly whispered to clear the reception building of all patients, visitors and staff, and to close off the doors of the connectors to the male and female patient wards on either side. Each patient ward could be protected in case of fire by closing the doors of the connecting hallway. Detweiller hoped the doors would offer protection of a different kind now. With that done, he turned his attention back to Cooper, who had rejoined Tocci. "How many men are likely to come?"

"For a place this size, he'll have everyone. That's ten men all together, and all armed." It was Tocci who answered.

Detweiller passed a hand over his face, rubbing his chin with his thumb and first finger. "That's not many men when you consider all of the possible hiding places.

There are ten patient wards, kitchens, out buildings for laundry and maintenance, and the livestock barns, just to name a few. It would take ten men days to search the place."

"They won't bother to search the place, Doc. They'll come in here and demand what they want at gun point," Tocci warned.

"It's still a good idea for you to be someplace out of reach," Willy added. "So, what's our best hiding place, doctor?" He had no choice but to believe that Captain McNamara and the boys from the Fourteenth would come through in the end.

"If I were you, I'd head for the workshop. It's some distance from the main complex, but not as remote as some of the farm buildings."

Willy understood what he was getting at. If Saladino sent some men in from the back of the asylum, they would reach the more remote livestock buildings first. If his men started in the front of the asylum, they would be closest to the patient wards. The workshop gave them a safe place in the middle to hide while they were waiting for the captain and his men. "Okay, what about you?" Willy didn't like the idea of leaving the Superintendent to handle Saladino's men alone.

"Don't worry about me. My attendants are trained to manage violent patients. I'll try and deal with Saladino myself, but I'll have them close by and ready, just in case." Detweiller was confident he could manage the situation until help arrived. After all, he regularly dealt with difficult, even out of control patients, and their often unreasonable families.

Willy made sure any remaining visitors were escorted from the complex, the patient wards were secured and attendants in place before he ushered Tocci to the workshop. It was far enough away from the main complex that they would not have any way of knowing what was going on. Furthermore, the line of sight to the main buildings was obscured by some trees and a greenhouse. Willy did not care to be so isolated from the action, even if it was likely a safe spot to hide. He pulled out the revolver from his pocket and pointed it at Tocci. "Don't get any ideas out here."

Tocci put his hands up as if to surrender. "You're my ticket outta here, kid."

Willy knew better than to believe a two-bit thug and when they entered the empty workshop he shoved him in a chair and bound Tocci's hands and feet.

"Now I'm dead meat, you son of a bitch!"

"Then I suggest you keep your mouth shut and hope nobody comes in here," Willy told him.

• • •

Dr. Detweiller was standing behind the reception desk, five of his best attendants scattered close by, unseen. He took a deep breath as he heard several cars pull up. Oddly, he heard nothing else until the heavy doors of the administrative building opened. Within seconds he was surrounded by ten armed men.

He calmly met the eye of the man closest to him, Joey Saladino, he presumed, and said, "Can I help you?"

Saladino motioned for a handful of his men to spread out and search the place before he spoke.

Some headed toward the upper floors; others searched the reception room and lower offices. Two remained with him, weapons drawn. "You got someone I want. Bring him here now!"

Detweiller decided the best course of action was to treat Saladino like any family member of a patient. "Who are you here to visit, sir?"

"I ain't here to visit no one. You got Tocci and I want him, now!"

"Please lower your weapons. You'll get no trouble from me."

A man came from behind Saladino, waving his revolver at the Superintendent. "The Boss said he wants Tocci. Get him, or I'll put a bullet right between your eyes!"

Albert Detweiller had nerves of steel. He couldn't work with violent patients unrestrained otherwise. His eyes shifted to the man waving a gun in his face, but his calm expression never faltered. He returned his attention to Saladino and said, "As you can see, I'm the only one here. If you shoot me, you will have to find this Mr. Tocci yourself. There are over two thousand patients here, spread across the campus. It would take your men the better part of a day to find him yourselves."

Before Saladino could respond, muted sounds came from the reception room. He waved the two remaining men to go and check it out. "You try my patience doc. Now get me Tocci or this nut house is going to need a new doctor."

Detweiller maintained eye contact with Saladino. There didn't seem to be any benefit in pretending he didn't know who these men were and what they were after. "Shoot me if you must, Mr. Saladino, but know this: each of the patient wards is currently being guarded by several armed attendants who are trained to deal with violent patients. You are outnumbered and it's only a matter of time before my men overtake yours."

It was a hollow threat. There were attendants on each ward, but they were armed with chloral hydrate rather than guns, as were the attendants he had with him in the administrative building. He hadn't heard any shots fired, and Detweiller hoped that his men in the reception room had been able to overtake their assailants.

Saladino raised his own gun, then and cocked the hammer as he pointed it directly at Detweiller's chest.

"Drop your weapon!" Captain McNamara's voice boomed through the room and Saladino turned abruptly around.

Seizing the opportunity, Detweiller leapt across the desk and knocked the weapon to the floor as he tackled Saladino. Four of Saladino's men came running down the main staircase, weapons drawn.

"Drop 'em, boys!" McNamara shouted.

The four men were about to surrender, when a fifth came out of the office across from the reception area and shot at the captain, hitting him in the shoulder. Detective Malloy returned fire, fatally wounding the man from the office as McNamara fell. After that, shots rang out on all sides. The men on the staircase had clear shots at the police officers but hadn't counted on the ward attendants disarming the four thugs who had gone to search the reception room. Now armed with the weapons of the subdued men, the attendants were able to take out two of the staircase shooters. With all guns on them, the remaining gang members surrendered.

The police officers scattered, some heading upstairs to determine the well-being of the remaining hidden attendants, others to the reception room to find four of Saladino's men slumped up against the wall. Detective Malloy ran to secure Saladino, leaving Detweiller to help Captain McNamara. The captain had removed his own handkerchief and was pressing it to the wound. "It's nothing, Albert. Where are Willy and Tocci?"

Detweiller ignored the question and helped the captain out of his coat to get a better look at his wound. The bullet had passed through the fleshy part of his upper arm and was lodged in the bone. "It doesn't look bad, but I'll have to get the slug out. Can you walk?"

"Never mind me. Where is Cooper?" McNamara struggled to get to his feet and staggered slightly before finding his balance.

Seeing that the captain remained steady on his feet, Detweiller reluctantly answered the question. "They are hiding out in the workshop."

"Malloy, you're with me," McNamara called out before turning back to the Superintendent. "Can you take us there, Albert?" Detweiller agreed and the three men headed out the back door of the administrative building.

• • •

"It's been about an hour. Whatadaya think is happening over there?" Tocci asked Willy.

"You'd know better than I would. Detweiller won't give you up. Will Saladino just shoot the man and search the grounds himself?"

Tocci shrugged. "I doubt it. Not much can make Joey Saladino flinch, but thousands of nut jobs all under one roof would do it. He'll try and get the doc to bring me to him."

Willy had a plan in the event that Saladino's men got close. The workshop was large, including a boiler room, coal shed, plumbing shop and a blacksmith shop. There were several entrances, so they could easily sneak out and make their way to the chapel or the laundry. From there they could hide out in other nearby outbuildings. If they stayed on the move, they had a good chance of avoiding Saladino's men. If not, he had the Smith and Wesson.

"So, they picked you up for murder?"

Willy figured that Tocci would not have forgotten that. "What of it?"

"I gotta wonder what you were doing that landed you as a suspect."

Willy considered just ignoring him, but as Tocci was to blame, he decided to give him an ear full. "I nearly lost my best girl because of you!" He went on to explain that he had to give the appearance that he had been fired and that he had gone to Nina's to find a way to assure her that all was not how it currently appeared. "In the end, I couldn't figure out a way to tell her without telling her, so I hopped the back fence and left.

It was only a few minutes after that that some men entered the house and shot her mother."

Tocci was quiet for a long time, looking at Willy as he considered his story. "You say the rat is the desk sergeant?"

"Yeah, what of it?"

"I hate to tell you this kid, but the men who went into your girlfriends house were probably looking for you."

Willy was shocked at the possibility. "Who would be looking for me? Nobody even knew I was going there."

"You said it yourself, kid. Wellesley was following you. He likely saw you go in there and then tipped off Saladino's men. They'd have thought you lived there and wouldn't have seen you hop the back fence, so they'd have broken into the house." Willy was stunned into silence as Tocci continued. "There was four of them, right?"

"Yeah, that's what the captain told me."

"I got a pretty good idea who it was. You can bet they're long gone from here, though. Joey would have sent them to Chicago until things cooled down a bit."

"How would you know who it was? You were still at the county home."

"It don't matter, kid. Joey always sends the same four guys for that kind of thing."

"What kind of thing?" Willy thought he knew, but he wanted to be sure because it would be the first concrete tip they'd had in the Barstow case.

"He'd have sent them to beat it out of you."

"Your sure, the same guys?"

"Yeah."

"You can identify them?"

"Yeah, but I wanna renegotiate my deal."

Willy lunged at him, grabbing him by the front of his shirt and rocking the chair backward. "Listen, you bastard, this is all on you! I'd have never been over there if I hadn't agreed to help protect you. If that poor woman died because…because of me… Oh God!" Willy let go and the chair came down with a thud, throwing Tocci forward. Willy slumped against the work table and buried his face in his hands. "Jesus, they'd have never gone there if I hadn't wanted to talk to Nina!"

Willy looked at Tocci with such rage in his eyes. "You son of a bitch!" He punched him square on the jaw with a force that sent him flying back again. Willy was landing another punch when the captain and Detective Malloy came in.

The two men took in the scene: Tocci bound in the chair and Cooper giving his face a pounding. "Hold on there, son," McNamara said. "Tell me what this is all about. If you've got good reason, I'll let you back at him."

Tocci looked horrified. "You keep this crazy bastard away from me!"

McNamara ignored Tocci and ushered Willy across the room. "What's this all about, Willy?"

Willy looked at Malloy, who had thought him guilty of all he'd been accused of, then back at the captain. "Am I free to speak of matters previously confidential, sir?"

"Yes, of course. We've got Saladino and his men. Between Tocci's testimony and attempting to shoot the Superintendent of the asylum, he'll go away for a long time."

"I think I've got a solid lead in the Barstow case," Willy told them, and proceeded to relay what Tocci had told him. "This dirty rat won't give up the names of the four intruders unless he can renegotiate his deal."

Malloy approached, rubbing his hands together. "Why don't you leave it to me, Captain? I can handle the negotiation." As he said it, he cracked his knuckles, and Tocci visibly flinched.

PART THREE

Chapter Fourteen

Billy sat bolt upright in bed, staring around wildly trying to get his bearings. Gradually his own possessions became familiar to him and he realized that he was in his own room. "What the hell was that?" He said it out loud, although there was nobody else to hear him, and thank God for that.

It had been a dream, a vivid dream. It wasn't real, or was it? The details were so clear: Willy Cooper conspiring with Captain McNamara to expose an informant and arrest a gang of thugs. It wasn't just the details, it was the emotions too. He felt Tocci's anger and fear when he realized he was no longer safe in the asylum, and Dr. Detweiller's calm resolve when facing down a gang of armed men. Willy had experienced a roller coaster ride of emotions, determination, anger, profound sadness and regret. The regret was an ache in his heart that hadn't gone away when Billy woke up.

What did it all mean? His mother had told him she had dreams like this. Billy grabbed his phone off the nightstand. It was after two o'clock in the morning. He knew he'd not get any more sleep, and regretted having to wake up his parents, but this was too important to keep to himself. It would be important, he realized, to record the details while they were still fresh in his mind.

That would take a while and allow his parents to sleep for a bit longer.

It ended up being a family affair when Glen woke to the animated conversation coming from his parents' bedroom. "What's going on?" he asked as he came in and took a seat on the bed next to Billy. It reminded Don of when the boys were little and one of them would have a bad dream. It was only a matter of time before the other one wandered in to their bedroom behind his brother and they'd both crawl into bed. Maude must have had a similar memory because she caught his smile and returned it.

"Billy seems to have inherited my ability to dream about the past," Maude told Glen.

"Cool." Glen's one-word response was a relief to both his parents and his brother. He could see that Billy was shaken and knew better than to give him a hard time about it.

"Why don't we move this discussion into the kitchen," Don suggested. "I'll put some coffee on and Billy can bring Glen up to speed." They were all coffee drinkers now that the boys were in college, and Don enjoyed those rare occasions when one or the other of them would wake up early and enjoy a cup with their dad before they started their day. It was a different sort of rite of passage than sharing their first beer, but just as important in the Travers' household.

When they all had cups fixed to their satisfaction, Glen asked, "How do you really know what you dreamed happened?"

Billy raised his eyebrows and cocked his head, acknowledging the point. "I guess I don't."

"That's not entirely true," Maude interjected. When they all looked at her, she said, "I have some period newspaper articles on Luciano Tocci. I haven't had a chance to actually look at them yet. Maybe they will help to verify some of the parts of your dream. I left my laptop down in my office."

"I'll go and get it," Don offered.

He came back to find Billy typing feverishly on his own tablet, adding details he'd learned from his mother that helped him to understand some parts of his dream better. Maude and Glen had taken their coffee into the living room and were chatting quietly about Glen's new job. "Let's wait for Billy to finish," he suggested.

"No." The answer came from the kitchen as Billy picked up his tablet and coffee and moved to join them. "I'm just about done."

"There aren't too many," Maude said as she opened and turned the computer on.

"Well, I'd say this is confirmation," Don said as he read the headline of the first article. "*Shoot out at the State Hospital, Police capture notorious crime gang.*" He read the headline for the rest of them to hear.

Maude turned the laptop toward Billy. "Take a look."

Glen rose to stand behind his brother as they both read the article. In a matter of seconds both parents were also crowded around the computer, nobody wanting to wait for the details. "Well, other than the specifics of the individual conversations, which I heard in my dream, that's pretty much what happened," Billy told them.

"It says here that the captain's wound was superficial," Don noted. They had interviewed Dr. Detweiller who had stitched up McNamara in the asylum infirmary.

"Yeah, and they listed the names of Saladino's men who died in the confrontation," Maude added. "Do you recognize any of them, Bill?"

Billy shook his head, telling them none of the men were referred to by name except Saladino.

"Wow, bro, it looks like you got it right. That's freakin' amazing!" There was pride in Glen's voice, and a bit of envy too as he gave a congratulatory slap on the shoulder to his brother before taking a seat.

Billy was very quiet. He was re-reading the short interview with Willy Cooper, who seemed to be vindicated when news of his undercover work and participation in the take down at the asylum became public. "What's wrong, Bill?" his mother asked.

Billy took a moment before answering. "I'm just getting the same feeling that I did during my dream. Cooper should be on top of the world. The whole city thinks he's a hero, but the grief he felt is still so…so…heavy, I guess."

"From what you've told us, he suspects that the men who killed Nina's mother had been following him. He must feel responsible for her death," Don suggested.

"I wonder if he ever found out for sure, or told the girlfriend about it?" Glen asked.

"I think the only way he'd know for sure is if the men were apprehended, and according to the newspaper, they were never captured." Maude answered.

"This has got to drive you nuts, mom," Billy told her. "Dreams that hold so much detail, but don't tell you the entire story."

"Yeah, what do you do now?" Glen asked. Clearly, the entire family was becoming invested in the story.

"Well, it was frustrating before I really understood the extent of my abilities. I've had some success trying to guide my focus to specific people or situations so I can learn more." Pointing to the computer screen, she added, "Stuff like this is a real gift because it helps to validate what we are seeing in dreams, or guided meditations."

"You should teach Billy how to do what you are doing, that way you guys could divide and conquer," Glen suggested.

Billy got a look of panic, which both of his parents noticed while his brother was completely oblivious. It took only seconds for Maude and Don to exchange a look and formulate an unspoken plan.

"Anybody hungry?" Don asked, knowing Glen would be the first to answer in the affirmative. "Why don't you and I see if we can pull together some breakfast while these two formulate a plan?" He was already hauling his eldest son up off the chair and leading him toward the kitchen.

"I don't know about all this, mom," Billy said when the two of them were alone.

"I know you don't, and you have already told me that you are not interested in pursuing these gifts right now." Maude shifted on the couch so that they were now face to face. "I can tell you from experience that you are in this whether you want to be or not.

You made your wishes very clear to me, and yet you've had this very vivid dream" *A dream which just so happened to be easily validated with documentary evidence already in hand.* There was no point, Maude thought, in saying that last part out loud, but it wasn't lost on her and she'd thought to call Charlotte when the hour approached reasonable to see if she would make anything of it. It seemed to Maude as if Spirit was either trying to lure Billy into accepting his gifts, or that he was somehow important to understanding this particular story.

Billy blew out a frustrated sigh. He was tired despite the coffee he'd had. "I really don't have time for this right now, mom. Sheri and I are supposed to be leaving for Cleveland tomorrow morning. Why can't these people just leave me alone?" It was as close as he could come to saying to his mother that he didn't want to have any unusual dreams while he was with Sheri.

Maude gave him an understanding smile. "There is something unresolved in all of this. Given that you are feeling Willy's regret so strongly, I'd say it has to do with him."

Part of her wanted to suggest that he reschedule his big weekend until this whole thing was resolved, but she didn't have the heart to when she knew the information they sought was available through different channels. "There's another way to approach this if you are interested." Billy seemed receptive, so she continued. "We can do a guided meditation. I can talk you through how to connect with Willy's energy and hopefully pick up somewhere close to where your dream left off."

"Do you think I could really do that?"

"With some help, yeah."

"Do you think that if I do this, I won't have any more dreams?"

"That I don't know, Billy. This whole thing involves you, and Spirit will find a way to guide you to the information you need to understand your place in it."

The poor guy looked exhausted and Maude was sorry she couldn't give him a more definitive answer. "Why don't you go back to bed and see if you can sleep for a few hours. You can decide when you wake up."

Billy looked reluctant. "What are the chances I'll have another dream?"

"I can't say for sure, but I'd be surprised if you did. You need time to process this one first. Spirit doesn't usually bombard you with information."

As her son exhaled a sigh of relief, Maude realized just how much the experience had shaken him, as it had her in the beginning. Again, she found she had to resist the urge to pull him in for a hug. She settled for a pat on the shoulder. "Go take a nap, you'll feel better after." She followed that up with a confident smile and thought she had done all she could to try and ease his mind.

It was close to noon when Billy woke up again. He looked refreshed when he poked his head in her office door, and in a better frame of mind. Maude felt a pang of sympathy for Glen, who didn't have the option to sleep in as long since he was to start training for his new job at one of the new Canalside restaurants.

"Hey, mom."

"Hi, Bill. Your dad put the leftover bacon in the fridge before he left."

"Yeah, I just ate." He hesitated for just a moment, but then seemed to find his courage. "I'm interested in trying that guided meditation if you are still willing to help me out."

Maude was careful to keep her expression neutral. She was glad, even relieved that he was willing. It was her hope that by helping Billy to control the flow of information, it might make him less uneasy about what was happening to him. "Yes, of course I'm willing. Just let me tell Christine I need her to cover for me."

It was interesting to note how relaxed and accepting Christine was about all of this now that she knew what was really going on. She seemed to take Billy's newfound ability in stride and didn't find it at all unusual that he and his mother were going to park in front of a house on Commonwealth Avenue in the hopes of connecting with the energy of the young man who lived there in 1924, Maude told Billy that as they drove to North Buffalo, to Willy Cooper's old house.

"I hope everyone is as receptive as she is," Billy said.

"Well, I really haven't told anyone other than you guys. There's nothing wrong with keeping it to yourself for a while."

"Yeah, that's the plan."

They pulled up in front of the Arts and Crafts house that had been Willy Cooper's home. Maude turned the car off and turned to her son. "Are you ready?"

Billy looked around. There was no foot traffic on the street, but plenty of parked cars, as much of the street consisted of doubles where the tenants were not allowed to park in the driveway. "Doesn't look like we will be noticed."

"I think you're right. So far, I haven't had anyone call the police on me while I've been parked on various streets around the neighborhood channeling spirits!" She laughed in an effort to make him feel more comfortable but saw right away her joke had the opposite effect. "Oh, c'mon. Everything will be fine." He smiled, took a deep breath and shook himself as he blew it out like a dog climbing out of a pond.

"Okay, I'm ready."

"Great. Just take a few more deep breaths and try to focus on Willy Cooper. Try to engage as many senses as you can. What is he wearing, the timbre and tone of his voice? Were there any smells in the air that you noticed?"

Billy closed his eyes and tried to recall what he had observed in his dream, but a different scene popped into his mind. "I'm picturing him at home, after the bust at the asylum. He's in bed."

"Tell me what you see, what you feel." Maude leaned back and closed her eyes as she listened to Billy speak. He was able to create a very vivid picture, and as Maude relaxed, she realized that she was actually connecting to the same energy and was able to see Willy for herself, tossing and turning.

Willy was back in his own bed and still unable to sleep. The operation had been a success, in fact more so than they expected. Saladino and the six surviving members of his gang were all behind bars, as was Peter Wellesley. Connections in high places, or not, the former desk sergeant would spend the next several years in jail. As Captain McNamara came to understand the depth of Wellesley's role in Joey Saladino's gang, he also obtained further evidence to keep the gangster where he was for a very long time.

As if that wasn't enough, they had a solid lead in the Barstow murder. Malloy had spent a few minutes alone with Tocci and didn't even need to raise a fist to get the man to talk. Assurances that they'd see him locked away in the asylum in the violent patient's ward were motivation to keep Tocci talking.

Four young men related to Joey Saladino in one way or another had likely been sent to lay low in Chicago. They were hiding out with a cousin, who had also been identified by Tocci. McNamara placed a call to the Chicago Police Department and requested the men be taken into custody. Later that evening he had dispatched Detectives Malloy and Schneider to escort the four men back to Buffalo. With any luck, the case would be resolved over the next few weeks.

Sleep eluded Willy because, if Tocci's lead panned out, he would have to accept the idea that Mrs. Barstow lost her life because of his selfish need to stay in Nina's good graces. His insecurities had cost a woman her life and all he could think about was whether or not Nina would forgive him.

Willy had been given some time off by the captain. He wanted to go straight to Nina in Cleveland but felt compelled to wait it out for Malloy and Schneider to determine if the four men who had invaded the Barstow house had done so in search of him. It was not something he felt he could keep from Nina if it turned out to be true. The fact that he could not foresee her reaction was what was keeping much needed sleep at bay. He'd professed his love and was reasonably certain that she felt the same way, although he had not received confirmation of that. Would that love be strong enough to forgive him?

The hours until morning were spent pacing the dark house, wanting to go to Nina, and yet afraid to leave without all of the facts. There was also a different kind of guilt gnawing at him. He'd received a telegram from his mother two days after the bust at the asylum. In those few words, she was still able to convey the hurt she felt that she had to hear of his exoneration from her sister, Nellie's mother. She also announced that she would be home as soon as transportation to Buffalo could be arranged. Willy immediately sent a response telling her that he still had work to do and that she was better off where she was for the time being. Susan Cooper fussing over him while he still had important issues to resolve was the last thing he needed.

Willy had been given a full month off by Captain McNamara and he was only a week into it. He wanted to be certain about any part he may have played in bringing four gangsters to the Barstow home before he saw his mother. She wouldn't judge him - he knew that. In fact, she'd go to great lengths to convince him that he could not fairly be blamed for any of it. If he was being honest, he didn't deserve such kindness.

The darkness had faded while Willy was lost in his thoughts and he was brought out of them by a knock on his door. It was Blake Hallard, a young patrolman who had just recently joined the BPD. "Hallard, come in." Willy stepped aside so the young man could enter. "What brings you here so early?"

"The captain sent me straight away. Malloy and Schneider are back. The four suspects got away sometime before the train stopped in Cincinnati. There's a manhunt already under way."

"What? Damn it! How did they let that happen?"

"Malloy said they jumped right off the train. It had to have been planned; there was a car waiting. Before either officer knew what had happened, the men were speeding off into the night."

"You mean to tell me that four shackled men managed to get the better of two armed detectives and jump off a moving train?"

Willy repeated the question to himself long after Hallard had left. The four thugs had maintained no knowledge of Saladino or the Barstow shooting during the preliminary interrogation. Yet, someone made sure they never arrived in Buffalo. Jumping off a moving train in the middle of nowhere in the dead of night was brilliant. It was likely hours before the detectives had been able to get word to the surrounding police departments, plenty of time for the men to get away, never to be found. They were no closer to finding Mrs. Barstow's killer. Now what?

How to proceed from there was the question that dominated his thoughts when Willy was satisfied he'd brooded long enough on the escape of the prisoners. The capture of Saladino and his men had sent the precinct into a whirlwind of activity so that the

Saladino case could be brought to trial as soon as possible. Wellesley had also provided additional testimony that would surely put the gangster and his band of thugs behind bars for a very long time.

Wellesley, that snake. It took him no time at all to flip on Saladino in an effort to shorten his own prison sentence. The man had been given every opportunity to succeed in life in an honorable profession, but he chose instead to aid and abet the lowliest of criminals. Willy still couldn't understand what had motivated the man to betray his profession, his fellow officers, and his own uncle, the Chief of Police.

"Wait a minute!" Willy hadn't realized he was pacing until he stopped, nearly tripping over the hassock at the foot of his mother's favorite chair. "Tocci had said it was probably Wellesley who had followed him and then tipped Saladino off."

There had been certainty that the apprehension of the men in Chicago would hold the solution to the Barstow case and Captain McNamara hadn't given it much more thought. He had all his available officers working on the Saladino case and hadn't spared Wellesley any further consideration after he had been locked up.

Glancing at the clock on the mantel, Willy saw it was not yet eight o'clock. If he showered quickly and passed on breakfast, he could get to the correctional facility in time for visiting hours. In a little more than an hour, he was sitting in a small room, across the table from a shackled Peter Wellesley.

The prisoner's face remained neutral as the guard placed him in the seat opposite Willy. "Miss me, Cooper?"

The comment was dripping in sarcasm, clearly an attempt to mask Wellesley's surprise.

"Did you think nobody would remember what you did?" Willy could barely contain the anger in his voice. He leaned across the table, almost nose to nose with his enemy, daring the man to lean back. The guard started to move forward, but then Willy raised a hand to assure him there was no need to intervene. He moved his chair back, a gesture of assurance that he would keep his distance. "You rotten bastard! She was killed because of you!"

The fury in Willy's eyes was unnerving, but Wellesley did his best to look calm. "I don't know what you're going on about."

"You were following me. You tipped off Saladino and he sent his thugs to Nina's house. Her mother was shot because of you, killed because of you, you dirty rat bastard!"

Wellesley hadn't allowed himself to think about that night. He'd been paid to keep an eye on Willy, which is what he had done. He'd thought Willy lived in that house. All Saladino's men were supposed to do is rough him up a little until he coughed up what he knew about Tocci. Although he didn't like to dwell on it, Wellesley knew it was likely to go further than that. They'd have threatened Willy and his mother, at gunpoint if necessary, to get what they wanted. Wellesley had done a good job of convincing himself that it wasn't his problem. Any guilt over the consequences of his efforts for Saladino were offset by the regular supply of cocaine and whiskey Wellesley was able to obtain and the cash that lined his pockets.

To deny it seemed pointless, Wellesley was already in jail and likely to stay there for the duration of his sentence, but he'd be damned if he'd feel bad about it. People died all the time without warning, and it's not like he pulled the trigger. He wasn't even there. "It wasn't supposed to go down that way." That was all he was willing to say.

The ambivalent response infuriated Willy and he lunged across the table and grabbed Wellesley by the collar of his shirt. To both of their surprise, the guard did nothing. "You really are the lowest form of filth! That woman left babies behind and now they will grow up without a mother. Mr. Barstow has shipped them off and is now drinking himself senseless, and all you can say is that it wasn't supposed to go down that way?" Willy shoved the man back into the chair. Had he not been consumed by frustration, anger and grief, he might have seen Wellesley's composure falter for just a second.

That fleeting acknowledgement of the consequences of Wellesley's role in the tragedy was so immediately painful, like a blow to the chest. He had so carefully avoided thinking of such things, and it took him by surprise. Like all thugs, he immediately struck back. "I don't know, Cooper. Sounds like you're looking for someone else to blame." His response was as cold as ice. "It was you that went to that house. How was I supposed to know you didn't live there? How would I know you were in the habit of snooping around other people's houses in the middle of the night? You brought those men to her doorstep."

Now it was Willy's turn to absorb the blow and for a moment he was speechless. Finally, he looked Wellesley square in the eye, and in a voice so deadly quiet said, "This is on you. She's dead because of you, and if I can find a way to keep you here longer because of it, you can be certain I will." He glanced up at the guard and mumbled "We're done," as he walked out.

Sheer exhaustion hit when Willy got home and while he only sat down to get his bearings, sleep overtook him almost immediately. He slept fitfully and dreams stopped and started without warning. First Nina sobbing 'How could you?' Then his mother, hanging her head in shame as she sat in the very back pew at St. Mark's. He could hear her sniffling, holding back tears as she endured yet more whispers from neighbors she had once called friends. His mind wandered back to Nina, crying again over the unconscious body of her father, whiskey bottle clutched to his chest. Jonathan had the younger children, one in each hand, telling Nina they had to go. They couldn't stay there. The scene shifted abruptly again to Wellesley, sitting across the table. 'It wasn't supposed to go down that way.' Willy could feel the anger building in his chest. He thought it would burst, and the force of it woke him up.

The pounding in his chest was indistinguishable from the pounding on his front door, and it took him a few moments to separate the two. "Willy, it's me. Are you there? Open up!"

Chapter Fifteen

He recognized Nellie's voice and bolted out of the chair. "What's wrong? Is Nina okay?"

"She's back in town." Nellie was out of breath, her bicycle thrown carelessly in the driveway. She had rushed straight to Willy the minute she got the news. "Jonathan found their father unconscious yesterday. He was taken to Sister's Hospital. Nina was on the first train this morning."

Willy was brought back to his dream, seeing Conrad Barstow passed out with a bottle in his hand. "What happened?"

"Oh, Willy, he's been drinking so much. He must have passed out. He has a fractured skull. They're not sure if he'll make it."

Just like in his dream. Did that mean the rest of his dreams were also true? "What about Matt and Amelia?"

"Still in Cleveland. Everyone thought it best given the change in their circumstances. There'd be no room in that tiny little flat and nobody to watch over them while Nina was at the hospital." She looked at her cousin, who was making no overtures to leave the house. "C'mon. I'll leave my bike here and we can take the street car together."

A part of Willy wanted to go as fast as he could to Nina's side, but he hadn't expected to see her so soon, and under such dire circumstances. "A lot has happened since I saw her last."

Nellie's eyes narrowed, unsure how recent events could be problematic. He had been exonerated after all. Seeing her confusion, Willy blew out an anxious sigh. "Can you sit down for a minute?"

As efficiently as he could, Willy told her of his most recent letter to Nina, in which he professed his love for her and when she tried to assure him, he said, "Wait, there's more." He went on to tell her of his brief discussion with Luciano Tocci and his visit to Peter Wellesley. "Can you believe the bastard actually said that?" He could feel the anger taking hold again as he explained how Wellesley tried to shift the blame back onto him. "The thing is, he's not wrong. If I hadn't gone there, Mrs. Barstow would still be alive, the family would still be together, and Mr. Barstow wouldn't be lying in a hospital bed fighting for his life."

Regret was radiating off him in waves so strongly, Nellie felt she might choke on it. Words seemed hollow, but they were all she had. "I don't think Nina will see it that way. You had no way of knowing an informant from your own precinct was following you."

Nellie knew her opinion would not change the way he felt, so she tried a different approach. "Willy, I don't think anyone would fault you if you didn't tell her this. She's just lost her mother and is about to lose her father. What she needs now is love and support. You can give her both of those things in a way no one else can. Just let it go."

Willy shook his head. "I could never keep something like this from her."

"Don't you see that you have to, at least for right now? She can't take one more thing. Help get her through this nightmare. I'm not sure she can do it without you."

Maude could feel the connection growing weak and it seemed as though they both lost it at the same time and came back to the present together. "Were you able to see everything I saw?" Billy asked, amazed that he felt his mother's energy directly connected to what he had just experienced.

"Yes. I can't believe it. I've never experienced that before. I did a past life regression with Charlotte once and she was able to be with me during the journey, but I never thought I was capable of doing something like that myself."

Billy's smile was contagious. "That's really awesome, mom. You're really amazing."

"Apparently!" Maude was thrilled to have discovered this new gift and over the moon that it seemed to have increased the admiration of her son.

"Why did it end? I could feel the connection fading."

"I'd say the intensity of the emotion was too much for us. I see why Willy's feelings of regret affected you. I could feel them, too, and it lingers." She cleared her throat in an effort to shake off the feeling.

"So, what happens now?"

"Well, we should go home. I'd like to take some notes while it's all still fresh in my mind and study them in the context of the other details we've learned. You should do the same."

"I will," Billy promised, "but I still have to pack for my trip."

"Make sure you pack condoms." Maude said it half under her breath, mostly because she was not sure she had the nerve to say it out loud.

"Mom!" The muscles of the human face, when partnered with the human voice, were truly amazing as Billy managed to express surprise, mortification and disdain using just his eyes and a single word. The radio kept them company on the way home, as Maude was satisfied she'd made her point and Billy had no intentions of discussing it.

"What do you think they're doing right now?" Maude asked Don the following evening as they were walking down Hertel Avenue. With Billy gone and Glen at work, they had decided to check out some of the new restaurants in their old neighborhood.

"Billy and Sheri? I have no idea and I don't even want to think about it." He stopped and turned to her. "We have to decide. I'm starving." They had walked up and down the main drag debating the merits of the many dining options the neighborhood now had to offer. There were exotic tacos, burgers made from every herd animal imaginable, and mountains of French fries smothered in everything from gravy to hot sauce and blue cheese.

"Everything sounds great; I can't decide." She hadn't been aware until she stopped walking that they were standing in front of the Wellington Pub, their old favorite. Maude looked at the sign and smiled at Don. "Were you planning this all along?"

Don laughed out loud as he led the way to the door. "No, really I wasn't. It's just divine intervention. C'mon, let's eat."

When they were seated with menus, Don asked her, "Aren't you a little bit curious to continue connecting with Willy Cooper while Billy's gone?"

"Maybe a little, but I'm not sure I'd be able to do it without him." She held up her hand to forestall the inevitable comment about how she was underestimating herself. "Okay, maybe I'm not sure I *should* do it without him." In her mind, she added *assuming I'd be able to.*

I have to admit, I'm jealous." Don told her. "I wish I'd been able to see what you were seeing when we were in Ireland a few years ago." Without telling his wife, Don had done some training on his own in Lily Dale prior to their trip abroad to learn how to guide Maude into a meditation that allowed her to connect with the memories of her past life. Without his help, she never would have learned that she could access spiritual energy outside of her dreams. She had actually been able to visit the cottage where Martha Sloane was born, so in a sense observed her own birth. It always gave Maude a lump in her throat when she thought of the lengths to which Don had gone in order to help her understand these emerging gifts.

Before she could say anything, Maude's phone began the first twinkling notes of Hedwig's Song, the theme from Harry Potter. "It's Billy."

"Well, things can't be going well if he's texting you."

With a dramatic eye roll at her smirking husband, Maude opened the text. It was a picture of Sheri and another girl with chin length platinum blond hair. With the exception of the length and color of her hair, the other girl looked nearly identical to Sheri. The first line of the text read 'Sheri found her twin!' She showed the screen to Don.

"Who's that?"

Maude scrolled down and read the message. Evidently, she was just a girl Sheri met in the restroom at the Rock and Roll Hall of Fame. They were both looking in the mirror and couldn't believe how much they looked alike.

"Let me see again." Don took the phone. "Yeah, I see it now. Are they related?"

"He didn't say, hang on a minute." Maude's fingers flew over the keyboard and within a few minutes of her hitting send, there was a response. "He says that Sheri's family is all from Buffalo, so I guess that's a no."

"Well, they say everyone has a doppelganger." Don took a look at the picture again. "I told you she'd be cute with short hair."

Maude laughed. "I was just thinking the same thing!" She took the phone and glanced at the picture before she put it back in her purse. "The other girl looks familiar."

"That's because she looks very similar to the girl who is sleeping with your son." Don couldn't resist teasing her.

"Very funny." The familiar chords of the Celeste chimed again, and Maude opened her phone. This time there was a picture of Billy and Sheri, hand in hand.

They both had big smiles, and Billy's head was angled just slightly toward Sheri. The look in his eyes made Maude's heart flutter. She showed the picture to Don.

He took one look and sighed. "Ah, to be young and in love."

That comment nearly made Maude's heart stop. "Who said anything about love?"

Don laughed out loud, which only made the situation worse. "Sooner or later both of your sons are going to leave you for another woman. Better start preparing yourself now."

Maude hoped it would be later - much later. "I need a drink. Where's our waitress?"

Much to Don's chagrin, they spent their dinner conversation discussing their youngest son and his current relationship. Maude was worried that things were becoming serious too quickly. Don assured her that Billy was levelheaded and would place his education at the top of the list of his priorities as soon as school started. There was nothing wrong with a summer crush, he told her. It was not lost on Maude that they had already had a similar discussion in which their feelings had been reversed, but she saw no need to point that out. Thankfully, neither did Don.

Don's confidence in their son's maturity didn't ease Maude's mind and she spent the better half of Sunday waiting for Billy to come home. More than once, she opened her phone and stared at the picture of the two of them. Without thinking, she scrolled up to the picture of Sheri's lookalike. The resemblance really was uncanny, and damn it if she didn't look familiar.

Maude sat in the living room, trying to place the girl's face, all the while wondering why she hadn't felt that same sense of familiarity when she met Sheri. "It's the hair," she said out loud.

"What hair, whose hair?" Don asked as he brought two cups of tea toward the couch and handed one to her.

"Oh, thank you." She sniffed the tea appreciatively before answering. "Sheri's hair. It's long and straight."

"Yes, and we both agree it should be shorter. What of it?"

"Well, I can't shake the idea that the other girl looks familiar. I was wondering why I didn't think that of Sheri when I first saw her, but it's because of the hair. The long, straight hair was enough to throw me off."

"Still no idea who it is?" Don took a tentative sip of his tea, decided it was still too hot and put it on the end-table.

"Not a clue."

Their conversation was cut short when they heard the front door unlock and the first footsteps on the stairs. "Quick, into the kitchen," Maude hissed.

Don laughed, but Maude was already up, her tea sloshing onto the saucer as she rushed out of the room.

"What are you doing?" Don asked, knowing full well what she was about.

"You don't want him to think we were waiting for him, do you?" She was still whispering as she could hear Billy at the top of the stairs.

"Well, we were waiting for him…at least you were. I was just keeping you company."

"Don! Sit down and act casual, or he'll know."

Don laughed at the desperation in her voice. "No way. You can stay here if you want, but I'm going back in." Don took a few long strides and was back in the living room before the door was fully open. He was sitting there, tea in hand, as if he'd never left. "Hey, buddy. How was the weekend?"

Billy tried and failed miserably to suppress a sly grin. "Great."

Looking at his son, Don found he was unable to as well. "Good to hear. Sheri get home alright?"

"Yeah, I just dropped her off." The two of them continued to stare at each other like idiots. When the silence became uncomfortable, Billy said, "Well, I'm just gonna go unpack, and maybe take a quick nap before I meet her for dinner later."

"Yeah, you must be tired. Get some rest, pal." The comment was followed by a knowing chuckle that sent Maude out of the kitchen when she was certain Billy was out of sight.

"What are you laughing at?"

"Oh, nothing. I have to admit, you were right. That was definitely a father and son moment."

"I agree, there are just some things a mother doesn't want to know."

A looked of feigned shock came over her husband's face. "Hey, I didn't ask for details. I just asked how the weekend went and if Sheri got home okay, like any concerned parent would."

"Judging by the smirk on your face when I came in here, I'd say you found out what you wanted to know."

"Hey, a dad needs to be there at the milestones in life to offer pearls of wisdom."

"'Get some rest'? That's genius. You're just full of… pearls, aren't you?"

It was only about an hour after he had gone to lay down that Billy was up again. His parents were still seated on the couch, well into a lazy Sunday afternoon with tea, newspapers and crossword puzzles. They hadn't even heard him go downstairs to Maude's office. When he came back up looking pale, Maude knew immediately he had had another dream.

"What is it, Bill?" She asked.

"It was her this time, the woman from the picture, the one who got shot."

"Sit down, pal, and tell us about it." Don moved to the seat across from the couch so that Billy could sit next to his mother.

"It wasn't a long and detailed dream like before. I just kept seeing her face. She didn't even say anything." He turned around the framed photograph that he'd been clutching to his chest. "Genevieve, that's the girl we met in Cleveland, the one who looked so much like Sheri, she's Mrs. Barstow with blond hair. Take a look for yourself."

Don moved behind the couch to look over their shoulder. "Wow, you're not kidding."

Maude pulled out her phone to compare the two. The two women had very similar haircuts that showed off their refined features to their best advantage. Maude scrolled to the picture of Billy and Sheri. She did have the same face; it was just not as evident because of her long hair. "Wow, a haircut really can make a huge difference. It's been bugging me since you sent this picture last night. I knew I'd seen that face before, but I couldn't place it."

Don looked at the pictures and then at Billy. "These two young women are sure they are not related?"

"Not that they're aware of. Sheri's family is from Buffalo, and she doesn't know of any family outside of the area. Genevieve's family is from Ohio."

"Did they hit it off, or exchange contact information?" Maude was hoping there would be some way of contacting this woman.

"They only talked for a few minutes. I have Genevieve's cell number, though, because I sent her a copy of the picture I took," Billy told her.

"What do you think this means?" Don directed the question to his son.

"I have no idea. I was hoping you guys could tell me." He shifted to face his mother directly. "I mean, Sheri and Genevieve look like they could be twins. The two of them look like this woman who died almost a hundred years ago, who has haunted me both in my dreams and in my actual bedroom!"

"Calm down, Billy, we'll figure it out." Of course, it was his father who said the words, because his mother was just as unnerved as her son.

"I really like this girl, Dad. How am I supposed to tell her about all this?"

"You might not have to tell her anything. Maybe you could just encourage Sheri to do a bit of genealogical research to see if they are related through Eva Barstow." Again, it was Don's suggestion.

"How would I do that? The research, I mean?"

"Your mother does that type of research all the time. I'm sure she would help if both women were interested."

Maude had been silent while father and son were formulating a plan, her eyes skipping between the three pictures. She looked up to find both of them staring at her, expecting an answer. "What?" She obviously hadn't heard the question.

"Will you help me figure out how Sheri, Genevieve and Mrs. Barstow are related? You know, using records and stuff?"

"They are related. I'm certain of it, not because they look so much alike. I can just feel it. You probably can, too, Billy. I'd just never seen them all together before. Only Eva seems to know they are related. I think that's why she keeps making contact with you."

Billy stood up and began pacing the floor. "So, are you telling me that this woman started haunting me as a child on the off chance that years later I'd start dating her relative and help that person connect with her other relative? You've gotta be kidding me!"

Don looked at his wife, and then at his son. They were so much alike. Maude had similar moments of incredulity when her gifts began to emerge. He had done his best to help her through a very confusing and often unnerving time. Now it was time to do the same for Billy. "The gifts you and your mother have, they form the basis of a belief system, a religion. An important part of that religion is the belief that there is something beyond life as we know it and the beings on the other side can connect with those of us on this side. Before you decide what to do next, I suggest that you think about what has happened to you throughout your life and what is happening now. Decide how you can best make sense of that…decide what you believe.

When you have figured it out, come and talk with us. We can help you move forward from there."

Billy seemed relieved for a moment, but then his face clouded with worry. "Do you think I'm only with Sheri to help her find her family? What will happen to us when this is over?"

It was Maude who spoke this time. "I'm sorry, buddy, but we don't have an answer for you. I can tell you that everything happens for a reason. You and Sheri will be together as long as you are supposed to be. You'll know if and when that changes."

Those were not the words he wanted to hear. "What ever happened to 'It'll be alright, you'll see'?"

"Spoken like your mother! She's says some version of that to me every time she finds herself in the middle of one of these supernatural mysteries. The truth is, Bill, grown up life is full of uncertainty. Just know that we have your back while you're trying to figure it all out."

"Speaking from experience, there is no one better to have at your back while you are trying to understand all of this than your dad. I don't know what I would have done without him."

Billy smiled, looking much more relieved. "Thanks, mom; thanks, dad."

When he left, Don returned to his place on the couch next to Maude. "Thanks for that," he said, pulling her into his arms.

"Thanks for having my back."

"Always, my love!"

Chapter Sixteen

Maude was in the kitchen deep in conversation with Glen when Billy awoke the next day. Glen had been lobbying for a car since he started college, and now that he was making some money of his own, had announced his plans to use whatever he made by summer's end as a down payment on a used one.

"We've been over this before, Glen. You really don't need a car at school and you can take the train to work while you are home during the summer. Besides, you can use my car when you need to."

"Yeah, that was fine until Billy got a girlfriend. Now he has your car all the time." It wasn't exactly true, but he was using it more than usual these days. "If he were to actually get a job, we'd need a third car."

"You're talking about saving for a down payment. How would you be able to make car payments during the school year when you're not working?"

Glen hadn't even considered that. He thought if he could come up with the down payment, his parents would pay for the rest. "I'm not talking about a brand-new car. I'm talking about something used. It would be way cheaper."

"Well, maybe you should keep what you make this summer in the bank and then add to it next summer. By then you should be able to afford it yourself."

His mother's suggestion did not go over well, and Glen responded with an exasperated sigh. "I gotta go to work."

Billy had heard the discussion as he made his way into the kitchen, where Glen nearly plowed into him on his way out. "Better hurry, you don't want to miss the train. Then mom would have to drive you."

The smart-ass remark was met with a hard shove against the wall as Glen walked by, muttering to himself that he'd have better luck convincing his father, the nicer parent.

"Yeah, good luck with that!" Billy shouted as Glen slammed the front door behind him.

"Why are you two always picking at each other?" Maude asked him as she filled a coffee mug and handed it to her youngest son.

"What?" He really didn't know what she was talking about.

Maude decided to ignore the comment and move on. "How'd you sleep last night?"

"No more dreams, if that's what you mean, but I was up until about two thinking and reading."

"And?"

"Well, you and Dad were never very religious."

"No, we weren't. I guess because we hadn't found the right religion."

"Yet Glen and I went to Catholic school. I guess I just considered myself Roman Catholic. I mean it's not perfect, but I like a lot of the basic teachings of Christianity."

"Billy, Modern Spiritualism isn't asking you to give up your beliefs for them. They embrace the idea of God, and the basic foundations of many of the world religions. They also believe in the direct communication with beings on the other side."

"I know. I did some reading last night. I believe what is happening to me is real, obviously. It really helps that you have the same… gifts, I guess."

"They are gifts, Billy, they really are. I know it doesn't seem like that now. What's that line from Spiderman?"

"With great power comes great responsibility?" His mother nodded, and Billy smiled. "Yeah, that's the problem. I'm not sure I really want the responsibility. I mean this Spirit you keep talking about has a strange way of going about things. The first real test of these gifts just happens to involve a girl I really like. I have no idea how even to try to explain all of this to her. I mean, you had Dad. You knew he wouldn't call you crazy and break up with you."

Maude gave him an understanding smile. "You really like Sheri, and if she really likes you, too, she won't call you crazy and break up with you."

Billy didn't look convinced, but he was willing to move carefully forward. "I hope you're right, but first we have to figure out what all this means."

"Agreed." She guessed that while he was up thinking and reading he'd formulated a plan, so she waited for him to explain it.

"Are you willing to do what we did the other day?"

"Of course. When?"

"Can you get away from the shop this morning?

"Yeah. I asked Christine to open for me just in case." Maude looked at her watch. "She should be here in about an hour, but I still have to shower."

"Cool. Me, too. Let me know when you're out, and I'll hop in. It won't take me long to get ready after that."

Maude could hear the familiar clicking of light switches and door locks as she came down the back stairs and so was not at all surprised that Christine had come in about twenty minutes early. "Good morn…" All of the joy of her greeting faded quickly away when Maude saw Christine's face. "What happened?"

Christine was dressed meticulously as always, though minus any makeup. She'd obviously been crying. "It's over."

"Oh, Christine, I'm so sorry." They had been down this road so many times before, but Maude had never seen her friend looking so devastated. Most of her break-ups had been on her terms, so she had only the regret that the guy wasn't quite as perfect - or wealthy - as she had been led to believe. She had been cheated on a few times, and Maude had witnessed her furiously plotting revenge against those few men who were foolish enough to think they could shop around while they dated her. This time was different. "What happened? You seemed fine when I spoke with you last night."

"I was, then. Sam came over last night. Can you believe an old girlfriend has recently come back into the picture? He's not sure if he still has feelings for her and wanted to be totally honest with me."

"What did you tell him?" Maude expected to hear that she told him to go straight to hell and was momentarily speechless when Christine answered.

"I told him to go and figure it out and to let me know when he did." She could see the look of shock on her friend's face and felt compelled to defend her answer. "What was I supposed to say? I love him, and he said he loves me."

For the first time in their friendship, Maude really wasn't sure what to say. "He was honest with you. That should tell you that he holds you in high regard." The minute the words were out of her mouth she wanted to suck them back in. High regard? What was she thinking? "I mean, a total creep wouldn't have bothered to tell you."

"I know, that almost makes it worse." She looked so vulnerable, Christine, who considered dating a recreational sport. "What if he picks her instead?"

"Then he's a complete idiot." Maude could hear Billy coming down the stairs. She was conflicted about leaving Christine without a shoulder to cry on, but knew Billy needed to take the next step on his journey.

Christine seemed to be able to read Maude's mind, or at least her expression. "Hey, don't worry about me. Go do your thing and tell me all about it when you get back." She did her best to put on a confident smile and shooed Maude out the door.

"What was that all about?" Billy asked when they got in the car.

"Oh, Christine's new boyfriend broke up with her."

"Why?" It wasn't a question Billy would have normally asked, and Maude thought it had more to do with his insecurities about his own relationship than concern for Christine.

"Oh, it's a long story, and nothing you need to worry about." She was relieved he was content to let it go.

"I think we should go to the cemetery," Billy told her. When he saw the confused look on his mother's face, he went on to explain. "The father's accident is what brought Nina back to town. I feel like whatever happened to him is important. He had a fractured skull, so I don't think it's likely that he survived, do you?"

Maude couldn't help being impressed with her son's ability to analyze the situation using both his gifts and his common sense. "No, I know he didn't survive. He died only a few months after Eva. I remembered it after going through my notes last night. Going to the cemetery is a great idea."

They were silent on the drive over to Forest Lawn Cemetery. When they arrived, Maude went about the task of trying to find where Conrad Barstow was buried by accessing the cemetery's website. With the click of a few buttons, she had the location. "Why don't we park and walk over? It's not far, but it's up on a hill."

Billy looked uneasy. "What if people see us?"

Maude had grown accustomed to loitering in unusual places to make her connections but could understand why her son felt self-conscious. "I don't think that will be a problem in a place like this. People come to pray, or even talk to a departed loved one. I can't imagine we will draw any attention."

They walked along the curved pathway and then up a small hill where Conrad Barstow was buried next to his beloved wife. There wasn't much space between the graves, but they managed to sit down just in front of the headstone. "Given how he deteriorated mentally after his wife's death, there wasn't much written in his death notice," Maude told Billy.

"What do you know about the day he was buried?" Billy asked. He knew he needed to form an image in his mind and needed some details to help him to picture the scene.

"Well, he died in June, and was buried on a Monday morning. It would have been warm in June, even in the morning. There would have been the smells and sounds of summer, like mowed grass and chirping birds." She noted as she spoke that Billy already had his eyes closed, trying to connect.

"His children would have been at the funeral, even the little ones, and the neighbors," Maude went on. "He owned a jewelry shop, and knew a lot of people, so I think his funeral would have been well attended."

"Yeah, but the grief is overwhelming, mostly because the children lost both parents so close together, I think." Billy could clearly see the people in attendance and went on to describe them to his mother. When he told her of Matt and Amelia, so stoic, but with tear streaked faces, Maude was able to connect and see what he saw.

The children had gotten through the service. Nina was so proud and told them so. They had been informed by Aunt Grace of their father's death and whisked off to the train station to come to Buffalo almost immediately thereafter. Nina had wanted to go back to Cleveland and tell the children herself, so that she could be with them as they traveled back to Buffalo, but she couldn't leave Jonathan. He was devastated, and unable to even accomplish simple tasks of daily life, like dressing and eating. The funeral arrangements had been left to Nina.

Aunt Grace had come with Matt and Amelia just the day before and were staying with Nina at Nellie's house. The Finsters had been gracious enough to also offer their home for the calling hours, since the tiny flat on Hertel Avenue wouldn't do. Jonathan had been absent during the wake and he hadn't joined the rest of his family for the interment at the cemetery.

People were starting to file down the small hill and toward the exit when Willy put a hand on Nina's shoulder. "He's not here, Nina." Willy had looked carefully among the many mourners and could not see Jonathan among them.

"I want to wait. I know he'll come. He wouldn't miss Daddy's funeral."

Willy glanced down at Matt and Amelia, who were sad, confused and above all, exhausted. "Let me bring the children to Nellie. She can take them back to the house. After that, I'll wait with you."

Nina nodded absently, scanning the dwindling crowd in search of her brother. Willy swung Amelia effortlessly into his arms and took Matt by the hand, but Nina hadn't even noticed when they walked away.

Nellie's family had come in their car, so Willy walked down the hill to meet them, leaving Nina alone at her father's grave. He had to take his time on the incline with the children in tow and he forced himself to slow down, although he was anxious to return to her side.

Nina sat watching as the men began to shovel dirt on to her father's casket. The brown patch of earth would stretch out next to the green fuzz of newly grown grass that marked her mother's grave. She didn't hear someone coming up behind and started when her brother laid a hand on her shoulder. "Oh! It's you. I knew you would come."

Jonathan looked ragged. He was wearing street clothes that looked as if he'd slept in them, his hair was unkempt and his face in need of a shave. "I waited for the little wonders to leave."

The use of his father's endearment for their younger brother and sister brought fresh tears to her eyes. "Oh, Jonathan, whatever will we do for them?"

"You have to take them back to Cleveland. I can't help you with them, Nina, I just can't. I'll send money, but I just can't be around them. It's too painful."

Nina felt her heart shatter in pieces. She'd had the same conversation with her father just weeks ago. At that time, she thought their separation would be temporary, but she could see in her brother's eyes and hear in his voice that it would be permanent. "Jonathan, you can't mean that." Her own words were calm. It was as if she made the transition from young lady to grown woman in an instant. So much had been thrusted upon her recently, but this conversation with her brother made her feel old and tired.

"I do, Nina. I'm sorry, but I do. You didn't see father at the end. He was a broken man. I feel the same

way now, and I won't put you through what I had to endure."

Willy came up the hill and saw brother and sister talking. The anguish on both of their faces broke his heart. He considered waiting until they were through, but he knew Nina would need him and Jonathan had been a close friend at one time. Things had improved between them since Willy's name had been cleared, but there was a distance between them. Willy attributed it to the hardships Jonathan had endured since his mother died. To honor the friendship they once had, Willy felt he should offer support now.

He approached the pair, arm in arm, each trying to hold back more tears. Jonathan was facing Willy and saw him first. His face grew dark and he pushed his sister aside. "You! This is all your fault. None of this would have happened if it were not for you!"

Willy's heart leapt into his throat. Jonathan knew. Somehow, he knew that the men who shot his mother had been chasing Willy.

Nina had been knocked off balance, more emotionally than physically, but she did stumble when her brother released her. "What's this about? Jonathan, you know Willy's been working undercover. He had nothing to do with father's death."

"That's not what he means, darling." Willy's voice was quiet, and he kept his eyes locked on Jonathan's.

"Did you think you could keep such a thing from her?" Jonathan was shouting, and Nina's confusion was gradually shifting to panic.

"What's all this about?" she asked.

"Tell her! Tell her you son of a bitch!"

Willy took a deep breath and turned to face Nina. "The men who shot your mother, they weren't random thieves. They were Saladino's men. They followed me to your house, thought it was my house. They came in looking for me, hoping to get me to give up Luciano Tocci's location."

Nina just stood there, speechless, but her brother still had plenty to say. "Don't you see, sister? If Willy hadn't come looking for you that night, mother would have never been killed! Father would still be alive, and we would all be together!" He grabbed her by the shoulders, his eyes wild with grief. "This is all his fault."

In the face of Jonathon's hysteria Nina became calm. She pulled her attention from her brother and turned to Willy. Her face gave away nothing. "How long have you known this?"

Jonathan interjected before Willy could answer. "Long enough, Nina, long enough. Maybe from the beginning."

There was panic in Willy's voice as he tried to explain. "No, no, I only just found out for sure a few days ago. Nina, I'm so sorry. I'd never do anything to cause your family harm. I don't know what to do to make it right. Please tell me. I'll do anything."

"You can never make this right!" Jonathan answered while his sister stood in stunned silence. "Our parents are both dead, you can't bring them back so that Matt and Amelia can grow up like normal children. Our family will never be the same again." He grabbed Nina and began pulling her away. Looking over his shoulder as he stormed off, his sister numbly following, Jonathan shouted, "You stay away from us!"

Willy just stood there. He wanted to go after her, to make her understand, but the look of betrayal on her face as she turned to look back at him kept him riveted to the spot. He couldn't have said how long he stood there, hoping against all odds she'd climb back up the hill and forgive him. The gravediggers had left, though he hadn't noticed when. Willy was all alone, and he feared that he'd remain that way for the rest of his life.

Maude thought she had come back to the present before Billy, but then realized that he was just struck silent by the tragedy he's just witnessed. She gently laid a hand on his shoulder. "You okay, pal?"

He took another moment to compose himself before answering. "Yeah." He heaved out a sigh that said more about his state of mind than his single word. "That was really intense."

Maude arched her back. They'd been sitting for a while and she was getting stiff. "Yes, it was."

"I really feel bad for Nina," Billy told her. "First her father deserted her and now her brother. He abandoned the younger ones too. I'd call him a jerk, but I could feel how broken up he was."

"I felt strong emotions coming from Nina, too, but it was hard to tell what was there beyond profound grief," Maude added. She would have continued along the same train of thought, but something in Billy's body language changed. His shoulders slumped just a little bit and Maude couldn't tell whether he was still feeling connected to the emotions of the people they had been observing, or if something else was troubling him. "You've got more to say. Why don't we walk for a bit?"

Billy nodded and sprung up, extending an arm to help his mother up. They walked under the cool shade of the trees, in no particular hurry. "We didn't really learn anything that might help me to understand Sheri's relationship to Genevieve."

"No, I guess not. We might have to try again."

That's what he'd been afraid of and he told her as much. "I don't know if I can handle that again. It's really intense, and I'm beat."

"That doesn't surprise me. You sort of jumped into the deep end of the pool, so to speak. You're able to do things that I wasn't able to do when I first realized I had special gifts. It's a lot to process and it's draining both physically and mentally."

"So how many more times do we have to do this before we find the answers we are looking for?"

"That's a great question and I wish I had a solid answer for you. Your instincts were spot on so far. Do you have any thoughts about how to move forward from here?"

"Not right now, but I'll think about it and go over both of our notes again." He was silent for long enough that Maude knew something else was on his mind. She was about to ask when he spoke up again. "Mom, I don't think it is a good idea for me to see Sheri until I work all this out. I feel like I'm keeping something important from her and I know I'll be weird around her, which will cause problems."

"That makes sense. What will you tell her?"

"I don't know. I don't want to lie or anything."

"You're right, just be honest. Tell her you are helping me with a project and it's going to take up a lot of your time over the next week or so."

The idea that this could take a week or more didn't go over well with Billy. "Do you really think it will take that long?"

"I really don't know, Bill. I can tell you what Charlotte tells me, and I suspect it will make you as frustrated as it makes me. These things have their own time table, and there's no rushing them." He rolled his eyes, and Maude laughed.

Billy would not admit to his mother, or even to himself, that he did not want to be separated from Sheri for that long, so he adopted what he thought was an agreeable smile. Maude wasn't fooled, but wisely kept her comments to herself.

Later, when she and Don were getting ready for bed, she said, "I think he's way too attached to this girl if he can't go a week without seeing her."

Don was eyeballing the paperbacks on his night stand, trying to decide which one he'd pick up until he was relaxed enough to go to sleep. "Give the guy a break, Maudie. You remember what it was like when we were dating. You couldn't keep your hands off me!"

Maude rolled her eyes but smiled as she remembered their college years. "I think that was the other way around. Besides, we were older and we'd both dated other people."

"You are making too big a deal out of this. This relationship might not even last the summer. Who knows? Maybe not seeing each other for a week or more will make one or both of them lose interest."

"No, I can promise you that their meeting wasn't by chance. Sheri is caught up in this and she'll be around at least until it gets resolved."

Don abandoned the idea of a book and sat on the bed next to his wife, pulling her into his arms. "What are you really worried about?"

Maude just sat there for a few minutes in the comforting presence of her husband and tried to put some order to her concerns before she spoke them out loud. She was sitting with her back against Don's chest, his chin gently resting on her head. It felt too good to move so she could see his face, so she directed her comments to the wall. "I'm worried about our son. He's caught up in something he doesn't want to be involved in. The connections to the past are hard on him. Now this girl he has very strong feelings for is part of it, too. What if we find out something about her family she's better off not knowing?" Now she did twist so that she could meet his eyes. "Or what if the pursuit of this puts Billy in danger? I don't want him hurt." She was thinking of how Don almost died trying to recover Mrs. Houston's jewels.

As he listened, Don felt a twinge of guilt that he had suggested Maude was making too big a deal of the situation. "I stand corrected," he told her. "I guess I just want you to try not to worry about things over which you have no control. We've been through enough of these experiences to know that whatever comes out of this needs to see the light of day. The parties involved are always better off knowing. Even if there is some family scandal, there is a need for some form of resolution or it wouldn't have been put in your path." He carefully avoided bringing up the dangers his son might encounter during this pursuit. That idea hadn't occurred to Don, and he needed a bit more time to think about it.

"I agree, but most of what you and I have experienced really only affected us. We are dealing with people we don't even know. Billy may be very attracted to this girl, but he doesn't really know her. We are meddling in the lives of strangers. I'm not comfortable with that and I don't think Billy is either."

"Have you considered just walking away and suggesting to Bill that he do the same?"

"If I thought we could walk away, I might, but I think you're right. Something here is unresolved, and we are meant to help resolve it, whatever it is."

"Well, you know I've got your back, no matter what."

"You always have, and I love you dearly for that." Maude knew just how fortunate she was, even if she didn't mention it often enough. Don supported her in this as he did in all things. Over the past few years, he took on more of the household responsibilities, and spent more time in the shop so that Maude could explore her new abilities. Just a few weeks ago, they had celebrated the return of normalcy to their lives and in doing so, opened the door and allowed the normalcy to escape yet again. Don adjusted, as he always did, without complaint. Perhaps she didn't tell him how much she appreciated him often enough, but she could show him. "You are a good man, Don Travers, and I don't deserve you." She reached up and met his lips, with the intent of showing him what he meant to her for the rest of the evening.

Chapter Seventeen

Billy
Hey, I have to cancel for tomorrow.
Helping my mom with some stuff.
I think it will take a while, so can we reschedule for next week?

Sheri
Yeah, no problem. What are you doing for your mom? Anything I can help with?

"Son of a…" Billy didn't have time to finish his curse before Glen was in his face.

"What's up? Trouble in paradise?"

"Don't worry about it." Billy tried to put his phone away, as if whatever conversation he had going on could wait, but he couldn't hide the worry on his face, and his brother noticed.

"D'she break up with you in a text? That's harsh, dude."

"What part of don't worry about it did you not get?"

Glen held his hands up in surrender. "Whatever."

Billy shot his brother his best look of disdain. "It's easier to go through life like a clueless moron, right?"

"At least I don't have voices in my head." Glen was actually envious of his brother's gifts, but it was his duty as the bullying older brother to keep that to himself.

"They're not voices, asshole."

"Oh, right, you see shit that's not there, too." Glen knew as soon as he said it, he'd gone too far.

Billy only glared at his older brother and then pulled out his phone again. He read the text from Sheri, muttered the same curse, this time in its entirety, and put the phone away.

"So, what'd you do to piss her off?" Glen asked, his tone a little less antagonistic this time.

"She's not pissed at me."

"Then why do you keep pulling out your phone?"

"It's complicated."

"Does it have to do with whatever you and mom are up to?"

"Yeah." Billy studied his brother, trying to determine if he could actually have a serious conversation with him. Glen was a safer option than confiding in one of his friends, because although his older brother would give him shit about it unmercifully, he would also keep it between them. So, before Billy could change his mind, he told Glen of the recent developments.

"Dude, this is some seriously intense shit."

"Yeah."

"So, she wants to know what you're doing, just tell her no big deal, just some stuff."

"I told her I wouldn't be able to see her all week. She wants more of an answer than 'some stuff'.

"So, tell her family stuff."

"Good idea."

Billy
Just family stuff.

Sheri
Will you be busy all day? Can't we hang out at night or something?

"Shit!" Billy handed Glen the phone. He read the text, rolled his eyes and began typing a reply. "Hey, what are you doing?"

Glen finished what he was typing and handed the phone back to his brother. "You're welcome."

Billy looked down nervously to see his brother's reply.

Billy
You know how it is, moms…
Gotta go now. C ya!

The room was totally silent while they awaited her reply. When the phone chirped, Glen grabbed it.

Sheri
K

"What does that mean?" Billy asked.

"It's all good, Dude."

"You better be right."

"Trust me; I know what I'm doing."

"Yeah, you're so wise. That must be why I have Sheri and you have Xbox."

The moment of brotherly bonding had ended with the typical pushing and shoving. When furniture started to fall on the floor, Don came upstairs to make sure no limbs were broken in the mix.

"Would you two knuckleheads give it a rest? Some of us are trying to sleep."

"He started it!" They both spoke at once and their father just shook his head and chuckled as he descended the stairs.

The next morning Maude came in the kitchen and Billy quickly put his phone in his pocket, as if he'd been caught looking at something he wasn't supposed to. "Hey, mom."

"Good morning, Billy." She narrowed her eyes as she looked from his face to his hand, which was still in his pocket. "Did you need to make a call or something? I can take my coffee in the other room."

"No, I'm good."

Maude knew better than to push the issue and so poured her coffee and began rummaging around in the refrigerator for breakfast options. "Sleep okay?"

"Yeah."

There was left over macaroni and cheese from two days ago and Maude pulled the container out and waived it at Billy in invitation.

"Nah, not right now."

It was unusual for either of her sons to turn down a meal, particularly homemade mac and cheese with breadcrumbs on top. "You feeling alright?"

"Yeah, I just sometimes feel a little sick to my stomach when we, you now, tap into the past. I'll just wait until we're done."

"Really? Why haven't you said something before now?"

"It's no big deal, mom. It's just really intense sometimes. I seem to pick up on Willy's emotions. I get the feeling that he was the kind of guy who had a nervous stomach. Things weren't exactly going well for him…"

Maude considered giving him an out, but she knew at this point he wouldn't take it. Billy wouldn't feel comfortable around Sheri until her connection to Genevieve and Eva Barstow was understood. He'd just want to get on with it. "Okay, we'll get started after breakfast unless you've got something else to do."

"I've got nothing all day." *And every day after that until this thing is resolved.* The look on his face clearly communicated the unspoken, although he didn't say it out loud.

"Any thoughts about where we should go?" Maude portioned out some mac and cheese and put it in the microwave as she spoke.

"Yeah, I was thinking that we should follow Nina. I know that the father and older brother had moved out of the house, but I wonder if it had been sold yet. When Nina took her brother and sister to Cleveland, they would have packed for a short-term trip. If they were leaving Buffalo permanently, Nina would need to pack of the rest of their things."

"So, you think we should go to the Barstow house?"

"Possibly. The other option was Nellie's house. Nina was staying there, right?"

Maude pulled her breakfast from the microwave and sat down across from Billy. "Yes, but that house would have been pretty crowded with all of the people staying there in addition to Nellie and her family. I can't see Nina discussing any of this in front of Matt and Amelia, or any of the others, with the exception of Nellie, of course."

"So, we'll go to the old house?" Billy asked.

"Sure, we can always think of something else if we don't make a useful connection."

"The house was for sale," Maude said as they pulled up in front of their former home. "They'd have covered all the furniture in sheets to keep it clean. That's what people did back then."

"I think Nina would have gone alone," Billy added. His eyes were already closed, and he was trying to picture her coming into the closed-up house after being away for so long. "I don't think she'd have wanted anyone else around." He could see her standing in the front hall, looking into the parlor. It didn't look or feel like the house she grew up in. The drapes were drawn, the furniture shrouded. The air was hot and thick. Gone were the familiar smells of oil soap and lemon polish.

She was glad she came alone. It would have made Matt and Amelia sad to see the house looking so lonely. They had both been born in this house, and it became a more joyous place with them in it. Better to remember it as it was. She tried to shake off that feeling of regret; there was work to do.

Pressing the button of the light switch, she climbed the stairs toward the bedrooms. Stopping on the landing, she collapsed to her knees. The image of her mother struggling to pull herself upright, blood pooling onto the runner, was so clear she could almost see it in the reflection on the floor boards. She'd thrown it out, the carpet. There was no saving it. The oak flooring had been scrubbed and polished to glossy perfection. Nina had done it herself that same night. She didn't want the children to be reminded of what they had seen.

Nina sobbed for all that they had lost, she, Matt and Amelia. They'd go on without a mother and a father, without their brother. Jonathan had disappeared after the funeral without a word. She knew he wouldn't come back until they had left town. She was left alone to see to packing up the house and the final details of its sale. It was overwhelming, and she lost her composure with the enormity of it right there, where her mother had lost her life. She was on her knees, sobbing, for some time and she was startled to feel a hand on her shoulder. She leaned back to find Aunt Grace crouched beside her.

"I thought you could use some help." Grace Nolan was a truly formidable woman, and if she had stayed in Buffalo, never would have allowed her brother-in-law to fall to pieces. She had the same quiet dignity as her sister Eva, but where Eva was graceful and elegant, Grace was hard as nails. She never married, having lost her beloved George to tuberculosis about a year after they'd met. She understood the need to get away from everything that reminded Conrad of her sister; she'd done the same after George was buried. She realized all it had cost her and should have prevented her sister's husband from doing the same. He had so much more to lose, but she'd never dreamed his life would be among them.

Grace collected Nina into her arms and held her while she cried uncontrollable tears, completely convulsed with grief. They sat there on the landing until Nina felt able to speak. "Oh, Auntie, everything is ruined. I don't know how we'll go on."

"Oh, you'll go on, darling. Women always find a way." She pulled a handkerchief from her sleeve and handed it to Nina with an understanding smile. It would have been wrong to tell Nina that everything would be alright soon enough. She knew from experience that it wasn't true. Nina would move from one task to the next and, in time, would find that it became easier. "Here, dry your eyes; we have much work to do. With any hope, we'll find our purpose as we complete each task." It was all she could think to say.

Nina went about the business of putting herself to right, while Grace proceeded to the bedroom Matt and Amelia had shared. When Nina joined her, she said, "You look so much like your mother. Jonathan, too, but not quite in the same way, he being a man and all. Matthew is the image of his grandfather, my pa, and Amelia seems a perfect blend of my mother and yours. It would have pleased Ma and Pa had they lived to see the younger two."

"Daddy called them his little wonders." As an afterthought, she added, "I'm sure it broke his heart to send them away."

Grace had suspected that it was Nina he really wanted to send away. She was so like Eva. Conrad loved his daughter so much, but he couldn't look at Nina without thinking of her mother, and that, more than anything, likely killed him before the drunken fall. "Nina, I want to take the children back with me."

Nina looked at her aunt, confusion and anxiety etched on her face. "I thought we were all going back together."

"You have a lot to sort out before you come back. Let me take the children so you can focus on matters here."

Anxiety took the upper hand as she began to understand. All of her siblings needed her. The younger two needed love, understanding and patience, all things Nina was able and willing to provide. She didn't know how to help Jonathan. He was so angry; she thought it might consume him. "I don't even know where Jonathan is or when he's coming back, or even if he's coming back. I might be here for weeks waiting."

"Jonathan will come back. He is hurting now, but he will not let your father's business fail. Besides, there are other matters you can sort out while you wait."

"Well, the house is already sold, and the new owners are taking some of the furniture, so all I have to do is pack our things and arrange for the rest to be shipped. That won't take very long. I'm not sure what else will require my attention." Nina tried to keep the uncertainty out of her voice. She feared that there would be more to handle regarding her parents' affairs but had hoped that whatever legal details remained could wait until Jonathan was feeling well enough to help her.

Grace smiled and smoothed back the hair from Nina's face. "My sweet girl, your parents' affairs will keep for the time being. I am talking about your young man."

Nina became very still, eyes focused on the floor. Grace placed a finger under her chin, lifting it so they were eye to eye. Nina didn't know what to say, and so said nothing.

"It's unfair to hold him responsible for what happened." Grace told her, and Nina tried to look away, but her aunt wouldn't allow it. "Do you blame Nellie for having a birthday party? For if she hadn't, you'd have been home and there would have been no need to leave the door open for you." Nina shook her head and Grace continued. "Do you blame your own mother for leaving the door unlocked, when she could have given you a key? If it had been locked, someone might have heard the prowlers trying to get in and warned them off or called the police."

"Of course not."

"No, I didn't think so. Those who are truly at fault are the men who took aim and shot your mother."

Nina struggled to hold back the tears. "Why would Willy keep such a secret from me?"

"I don't think he intended to forever, but the weight of these losses is so heavy just now. I think he did not want to add to your burden."

"Have you spoken to him?" There was a mixture of accusation and hope in her voice.

"No, darling, but I saw how you were together in the days before the funeral. It is obvious he loves you very much."

Nina knew she was right, but it wasn't that simple. Grace hadn't been at the cemetery at the time and seen Jonathan so furious. "Jonathan will never forgive Willy for coming to the house that night."

"It's not your brother's forgiveness he seeks." She paused for a moment before asking, "Do you love Willy?"

"Yes, I do, but I love my brother, too."

Grace took in a breath to steady her nerves and blew it out slowly. This was shaky ground, and she wasn't sure she had the right to share this particular piece of advice, but she had failed to intervene with Conrad and the consequences of that failure had been catastrophic. Nina and her siblings were all the family she had left, and she would do what she must to see them recover from this. "Nina, my love was lost to me, and I miss him every day. In my grief, I withdrew from the world. I left Buffalo; I left my family. In time, I reconnected with family, and you all were a comfort to me, but I would have given anything to have George back."

"Your brother is consumed with grief and anger right now, but he will move on eventually, and where will you be? It is unreasonable to expect that Willy will be waiting, should you decide in the future to forgive him. His heart is broken, too, and you have seen what is possible when a man is bereft of love."

Nina looked up at her aunt, whose expression was filled with understanding, and love and warning. It wasn't that she had decided she couldn't forgive Willy. There just hadn't been time for her to process how she felt about what he had done. Jonathan had reacted for both of them with shock and outrage and her feelings matched his in the moment. Then Jonathan took off, leaving her to manage everything. She felt so hurt and betrayed but couldn't really sort out the source of those feelings. "Oh, Auntie, I feel like I've been pushed down a hill, and every time I find something to grab on to, it comes up at the root."

Grace looked around the children's room and then back at her niece. Nina was once again holding back tears. She was so young to have so much thrust upon her. Grace held her once again, so she could let it all out. After a while, she said, "Darling, you need a break from all of this. Let me finish packing the children's things. Go and take some time for yourself; think about what it is you need for a change."

Nina put up an argument but, in the end, left with the intention of heading back to Nellie's house for some rest. She made her way to Forest Avenue on autopilot, barely looking when she needed to cross the street. Before she realized it, she found herself in Rumsey woods, near the arch where she had met Willy that day, which seemed so long ago. She sat underneath the arch, thinking about that encounter. Willy had been in her thoughts often in the days before her mother had passed. Never for a minute did she believe the rumors that had begun circulating around the neighborhood, rumors that were fueled by Peter Wellesley. It had been the letter from Wellesley that had sent Jonathan into such rage the day of their father's funeral. Peter had tried to sully Willy's name before and he was trying to do it again.

Nina knew in her heart that Willy could not be blamed for what happened to her mother, and eventually her father, but neither would forgiving him bring them back. Would she be able to look at him and not be reminded of that fateful night and all that went wrong subsequently?

• • •

Willy had seen her turn from the road into the woods, but he was afraid to call out to her. Nellie had told him that Nina was at the house packing and he'd gone straight there, only to be told by her aunt that she was on her way back to Nellie's house. He followed at a discreet distance until she came to the arch. Now he watched, unsure of what to do. She looked depleted, thinner than the last time he saw her, if it was possible, and exhausted, if the slump of her shoulders was any indication. She looked like she might doze off right there under the arch. He could let her sleep and stand watch until she woke. Perhaps what he had to say would go over better if she were rested. He was still arguing silently to himself, when she turned as if she heard someone call her name. It made Willy look around too, but they were alone.

"Willy, is that you?"

He was standing mostly behind a tree a few yards away, not exactly hiding but hoping to be unnoticed until he had decided what to do. "Yes, it's me. May I come talk to you?"

She nodded reluctantly, and he approached with caution. They both stood there for a moment, neither of them knowing what to say. Finally, Willy spoke. "I'd say I'm sorry, but it hardly seems enough."

The fact that she wasn't eager to forgive him surprised her. "I know you're sorry, Willy. I also know you did not come to my house that night with the intent to cause anyone harm."

He should have been relieved, but the tone of her voice was not encouraging. He was searching for the right words when he heard footsteps approaching behind him.

"What are you doing with him, Nina?"

"Jonathan, you're back!" She had thought to rush towards him, to welcome him home, but the cold darkness in his eyes stopped her in her tracks.

"I was coming to find you. We have business to discuss." That part was true, but as he drove up Delaware Avenue, he saw Willy walking along the road making his way into the woods. Jonathan pulled the car to the side of the road intending to catch up to Willy and pound the daylights out of him. The rotten bastard had it coming for all he had cost the Barstows, but Jonathan hadn't expected to find his sister with him. "Have I interrupted a secret meeting? Have you learned nothing from our losses, sister? How could you be so foolish as to request the company of this…this villain?"

Desperate for the outcome of this conversation to take a better end from the last time they spoke, Willy felt compelled to explain himself. "Jonathan, with all due respect for your loss, you've got it all wrong. This is no secret meeting. I wanted to talk to Nina and found her here on her way back to Nellie's."

"She's got nothing to say to you!"

"Jonathan! Please don't speak for me."

Jonathan turned to face his sister, radiating hurt and betrayal. "You can't possibly forgive him." His voice lowered in disbelief. "Nina, we have lost everything because of him. Matt and Amelia will grow up without parents because of him!"

Her brother's words brought all of the grief, anger and confusion to a boil such that she might burst. "Yes, well, they'll grow up without an older brother, too, won't they, and I'm left dealing with all of it! Father pushed us away, now you're pushing us away. Did you ever stop for a minute and think that we are grieving, too?" She faced her brother so that the full force of her words was upon him. "I'm devastated, too, brother. I don't have the luxury of running away as you did or drinking myself into a stupor as father did. Someone had to plan Daddy's funeral. Someone had to see to his estate and the sale of the house. Where were you when that was happening? Do you not think I would love to just run away for a little while? Who is left for Matt and Amelia if I do? Certainly not you. You've made that clear!"

"Nina…" Willy didn't get a chance to finish before she turned to face him.

The rage had left Nina when she met his eyes, but the hurt and confusion were still there. She started to say something, but stopped and just looked at him again, trying to find the words. When they refused to come, she simply said, "I have to go." She turned and walked away from them both.

As Nina headed toward the street, she heard the sound of fist meeting flesh and the accompanying crack of bones. This was followed by cursing, grunting, and more punching. She didn't care to stop them, or to even look back to see who had the upper hand. She just kept walking and was relieved to find no one at home when she reached the Finster residence. Climbing the stairs to her room on the third floor seemed a herculean effort, and entering, she collapsed onto her bed into a deep sleep.

Chapter Eighteen

The knock on her bedroom door shook Nina out of her fitful dreams. "Come in."

Grace came in with a covered tray. "You slept through dinner." She placed the tray on the nightstand and helped Nina to sit up. "Eat, darling. You need to keep up your strength."

Nina uncovered the tray and absentmindedly swirled her fork around in the pile of mashed potatoes. "I'm not very hungry."

"You will be once you have a taste of Mrs. Finster's meatloaf. It is delicious."

Nina took a small bite of meatloaf and conceded that it was very good, but she placed her fork on the tray and looked at her aunt. "Can we be ready to leave tomorrow? There is no more business keeping me here."

Grace looked at her and took a seat at the edge of the bed. "Does this have anything to do with your confrontation in the park?" When Nina looked surprised that she knew about the events earlier that afternoon, Grace shook her head in mild disgust. "Oh, yes, I know all about it. Your brother came to the house looking much the worse for wear."

"They were fighting when I left, he and Willy."

"Yes, I learned that, too. Your brother has a great deal of anger, but also a great deal of remorse. He spoke to me of his regret over leaving so much for you to manage by yourself." Nina had no response to that, and Grace went on. "He is very sorry and has assured me that he will handle the remaining details, so we are free to leave tomorrow if that's what you wish."

Nina looked up at her aunt, her eyes dry and her face resolute. "You'll forgive me, aunt, if your words bring me no comfort. I would be surprised if he did not feel some remorse, for he is a decent human being, and as such, would eventually come to regret any pain he caused me and the children. However, that does not make up for his actions, or rather his refusal to act, and the consequences it has had on the rest of us."

Grace knew there was more to say and remained quiet until Nina found the right words.

"Men… good intentions and apologies can't take away the consequences of their actions. I don't blame my brother any more than I blame Willy, and I don't love either of them any less, but I can't say I forgive them either."

Grace put her arm around Nina and pulled her in close. "I don't know how to advise you, darling, but I am here to help however I can. If you want to leave tomorrow, we will."

After Grace left, Nina picked at her dinner. It was nearly time to tuck the younger children in and that was excuse enough to leave the rest of the plate untouched. She hadn't seen Matt and Amelia all day, and she needed to discuss their travel plans for the next day.

Grace had seen to the children's baths and they were climbing into bed when Nina made her way to the second floor. Matt looked very put out. "Aunt Grace says we're going back to Cleveland tomorrow. I thought we were back home to stay."

Nina couldn't bring herself to lie to the children or give them false hope. "I think under the circumstances, we would be better off staying with Aunt Grace."

"But what about Jonathan?" Amelia asked.

"Jonathan has to stay here and run Daddy's store. Anyway, he lives in a tiny flat and there is no room for us."

"Why can't we all just live together back home?"

"Oh, Matt, do you think you could? Wouldn't you be sad, knowing what happened to mother?"

"Maybe...but couldn't we find another house?"

Nina searched for the words they would understand. "It's all very complicated right now, and I'm very sad and tired after everything that has happened. I need Aunt Grace to take care of me for a while, to take care of us. Can you understand?"

"She tells good bedtime stories," Amelia conceded.

"And she bakes cookies on Sunday," Matt added.

"Yes, Aunt Grace will give us a very loving home and if we try very hard, we might come to a place where we don't feel so sad anymore," Nina suggested. "Wouldn't that be nice?"

They both nodded, but Matt added, "I'll worry about Jonathan, here all alone. Who will help him not to be sad?"

The little boy's face was so sincere, as was Amelia's, who echoed his concern. Nina had to compose herself before she spoke again. "You are right to be concerned for our brother, as I am. Jonathan will be kept busy running the shop and having lots to do will help to occupy his mind and keep the sad thoughts away. We will write to him as well, and even call him on the telephone sometimes. I think that will help, don't you?"

"Can we come to visit him?" Amelia asked.

Again, it was important not to give them false hope, and it broke Nina's heart to answer the question honestly. "Someday, I hope."

That seemed to be enough for them and they were quiet for a time while they settled under the covers. Amelia yawned sleepily and as an afterthought said, "We'll have to say goodbye to Willy."

That comment brought Matthew upright. "Oh, but we can't leave just yet. Willy promised me a special tour of the zoo!"

The mention of Willy's name brought distress to Nina's face that her sister picked up on immediately. "Is something wrong with Willy?"

"No, Amelia, nothing is wrong with Willy," Nina assured her.

"Then why can't we ask Willy to take us to the zoo tomorrow? We could leave the next day." Matthew suggested.

"Can't we please go to the zoo tomorrow?" Amelia begged. "We have to say goodbye to Mr. Kowalczyk, too."

There were plenty of people who Nina felt she should visit before she left, but her need to be away was stronger than her sense of propriety. "I'm afraid not. We must leave tomorrow," Nina told them.

"Nina, you can't leave without saying goodbye to Willy," It was Matt who spoke, but Amelia who again noticed the stress those words caused her sister .

"Did you and Willy have a fight?"

Here Nina felt she did not owe her siblings complete honesty. "It's nothing for you to worry about. Now go to sleep, both of you. We've got a long day tomorrow."

When Nina turned out the light and left the room, Amelia turned to her brother. "Do you know the way to the zoo from here?" she whispered.

"Of course I do!" Matt sounded indignant that she could ask such a thing until he realized why she did. "I bet Willy still goes there every morning."

"Yeah, I bet he does."

• • •

The next morning, Nina came down to the kitchen feeling a little bit more herself after a decent night's sleep. "Have the little ones finished their breakfast already?" she asked Nellie, who was chatting with her father and Grace over coffee while Mrs. Finster fussed over sizzling bacon and eggs.

"I don't think they're up yet," Lawrence Finster answered as he watched with interest as his wife spooned scrambled eggs into a large ceramic bowl.

"They must be up; they're not in their room," Nina argued.

"That's odd," Alice Finster commented. "I was the first one up and I haven't seen them."

"Maybe they're out in the yard," Grace suggested.

Nellie went to the window that looked out onto the spacious and well-manicured backyard. "They're not out back." She went to take a peek out the front door and came back to report that they were not out front either.

"Where could they have gone off to?" Grace asked.

"They can't have gone far," Lawrence assured them.

"I wonder how long they have been gone?" Nina asked, concerned but not ready to panic.

"I've been up for a little over an hour and haven't seen hide nor hair of them," Alice told her.

"Mother, I doubt they could have crept down the stairs without you knowing. They creak terribly." Nellie knew this from experience.

"So, you think they have been gone more than an hour?" Now Nina was starting to get worried.

"Now, let's all keep level heads," Lawrence insisted. "They know the neighborhood well, and everyone knows them. They'll not come to any harm." He didn't want to say it out loud, but an hour was plenty of time for them to go beyond the neighborhood, even on foot. "Where are they likely to have gone?"

"At six o'clock in the morning, who knows?" Grace was starting to get worried too. "I'll bet they're hiding, although God only knows where. They were not keen on leaving today."

"They were terribly worried about Jonathan. Maybe they went to his flat," Nina suggested.

"Knowing those two, they are probably huddled outside of the candy store waiting for it to open," Nellie said, trying to lighten the mood.

"Now you're thinking," Lawrence agreed. "Why don't I drive you there, dear?"

"I'll head over to Jonathan's flat," Grace offered.

"I should stay here just in case they come back," Alice suggested. "You can wait here with me, Nina, unless you can think where else they might have gone."

Nina thought back to the conversation she'd had with the children the night before. Her expression changed from recognition to wariness in an instant, but fortunately they were all too preoccupied with their plans to notice. "Actually, there is one more place I can look." She noticed that all the bowls and platters had been filled and were waiting to be placed on the table. To Mrs. Finster she said, "I'm sorry they've ruined your wonderful breakfast."

"Don't worry dear; it will keep."

Nina set out on foot to the zoo slower than she might have given her concern about the children. If they had gone to the zoo, they'd most certainly gone to see if Willy was there. She found herself hoping they had found him. Nina had spent her time before sleep thinking about Willy and trying to find a place in her heart to forgive him. She hadn't quite gotten there when sleep beckoned, so she was nervous at the likely possibility of seeing him again. With the hope that the right words would come to her when they met, she continued on her way.

When Nina walked across the park meadow toward the zoo, she saw Mr. Kowalczyk, alone and pushing his rickety wheel barrow. A wave of panic fluttered through her and she wondered if she'd gotten it wrong, and perhaps the children weren't there.

"Mr. Kowlaczyk!" she called as she ran toward him.

"Miss Nina, good morning to you."

"Good morning, Mr. Kowalczyk. I wonder if you've seen Matthew and Amelia this morning."

"Yes, yes. No need to fret. They are with Willy at the elephant house."

"Oh, thank God. I woke up this morning to find them gone. I was trying not to fear the worst."

Mr. Kowalczyk smiled, patting her gently on the shoulder. "Willy has already scolded them for leaving the house without permission this morning."

"I'm sure they just wanted to say goodbye, to both of you. They do love you so and they love the zoo."

"Yes, they told young Willy that they were leaving and would like to meet the elephant before they go. The bears were getting hungry for their breakfast, so I left Willy to it. Shh, don't tell anyone." He gave her a conspiratorial wink. "That old pachyderm always did like Willy better than me."

"Thank you so much, Mr. Kowalczyk. That will mean so much to them."

He waved it off, and then gave her a questioning look. "You have decided to go back to Cleveland with your aunt?"

Nina cleared her throat, unwilling to meet his eye. "Yes, I thought it best under the circumstances."

"Many of us will miss you." His smile was warm and understanding and she found she was able to smile back. "I know Willy will miss you most of all." He turned and saw the young man heading toward them with Matt and Amelia in tow. Willy's pace slowed when he saw her. "Here he comes now. I'm off to feed the

deer next. I'll take the children to help me so that you can say your goodbyes."

Mr. Kowalczyk moved faster than she thought him capable in order to intercept the approaching trio and redirect the children towards the deer paddock. Willy watched them go for longer than was necessary. Finally, when he turned and saw Nina was still there, he moved cautiously in her direction. "I'm sorry. Did the children give you a fright?"

"They did, until I realized they were probably here. They didn't want to leave without saying goodbye to Mr. Kowalczyk." She thought about not finishing her sentence, but she couldn't hurt him that way. "And to you."

"Were you going to leave without saying goodbye to me, Nina?"

"I..." The way he was looking at her stalled the words in her mouth. The idea that she would leave town without saying goodbye cut him most of all, more than the entire neighborhood thinking him a drunk and a murderer, more than Jonathan's fists, which had left cuts and bruises on his face. Nina almost couldn't finish her sentence, but then she thought of her mother on the landing. "I thought it would be best under the circumstances."

She couldn't meet his eye but the certainty in his voice as he spoke got her attention. "No. It is not for the best. None of this is for the best. I would give anything to go back in time and tell Captain McNamara I would not work undercover, but I can't do that." He moved closer and took her hand. A jolt of relief shot through him when she didn't pull away.

"Nina, you and I have been a part of each other's lives since we were children. Will you let one bad decision sully what we had, or what we could have?"

She was struggling to answer the question and that gave him hope. Without giving it a second thought, he closed the distance between them and slowly, giving her the opportunity to pull away, pressed his lips to her. When she didn't recoil, he cradled her face in his hands, pouring all of his love into the kiss. What he offered in love, she matched with forgiveness, pulling him closer still. When they parted, she was able to answer his question. "No, I won't, I can't…"

"Get your hands off of my sister!" Jonathan grabbed Willy by the back of his shirt and pulled him away.

"Jonathan, leave us alone this instant!" Nina was furious when she got a good look at her brother, battered and bruised.

Jonathan gave Willy a hard shove back before addressing her. "You've forgiven him! How could you? Our family has fallen to pieces because of him, and you stand here necking with him like some kind of quiff!"

"Hey, you watch your mouth!" Willy raised his clenched fist, prepared to connect with Jonathan's already bruised jaw, but he saw it coming and landed a solid punch to Willy's gut instead, sending him to the ground. Jonathan pounced on him, prepared to finish what they had started the day before.

"Stop it, the two of you. The children are coming," Nina hissed.

"Jonathan, what are you doing?" Matt asked as he ran towards the two men.

"Leave Willy alone!" Amelia shouted as she struggled to keep up with her brother.

The two men were rolling around the ground by the time Mr. Kowalczyk and the children reached them. The zookeeper grabbed for Jonathan and Nina grabbed for Willy. Over the grunts of the two fighting men were the terrified shrieks of the children begging them to stop. Willy gave in easier, not wanting to hurt Nina, and embarrassed that the children had witnessed his behavior, but Jonathan continued to lunge after his enemy even after Mr. Kowalczyk had pulled him off. Not for the first time, Willy was amazed by the strength of the old man.

"That's enough! You behave like animals, both of you." The Keeper's reprimand was enough to settle them both, and they kept their distance, eyeing each other warily.

"Jonathan, why would you hurt Willy? He is our friend!" Amelia asked.

"He's no friend of ours," Jonathan replied. The words came out in a harsh breath, his chest heaving with anger and exhaustion, and Amelia cautiously took a step back.

"Stop it, Jonathan, you're scaring her," Nina warned.

"You haven't told them, have you? Of course not, you've clearly taken his side." Jonathan turned toward the children, but Nina placed a hand on his shoulder.

"Don't," she begged.

"Why not? They have a right to know what he did and that you have apparently forgiven him for it!"

"Jonathan, please..." Nina did not get a chance to finish before he cut her off.

"Oh no, sister, I will not spare them his treachery or your betrayal." He turned back to his younger siblings. "This man, who you call friend, is responsible for mother's death! That makes him responsible for father's as well, for he died of a broken heart."

"No!" Matt cried. "It's not true!"

"But it is true, little brother." Stabbing his finger toward Willy, Jonathan continued. "The men who murdered our mother followed him to our house. He had come into the yard to talk to Nina, and they followed him. The men who shot mother were really after Willy!"

The children stood numbly processing what had been told to them. Amelia was shocked by her brother's accusations and she turned to Willy with tears in her eyes. "Did you know those bad men?" It was a simple question Jonathan hadn't bothered to ask, but it was important to her.

Willy bent down to wipe her tears gently with his thumb. "No, I did not know they were bad; I did not know them at all, or even that they were following me. I'm very sorry, Amelia. Can you forgive me?"

She looked up at him, her face still damp, and nodded. In her child's mind, it was very clear. Here was a man she had known all her life and she knew him to be a good man, a man who would never knowingly cause harm to those he cared about. "You didn't know. If you had known bad men were following you, you would have arrested them because you are a policeman."

Nina knelt down to her sister, her own eyes welling up. "That's exactly right, Amelia." Her little sister had cut to the heart of the matter. Nina had allowed Jonathan's anger to cloud her own emotions, creating anguish that she now realized she didn't really feel.

Jonathan took Amelia's arm and jerked her towards him. "No, don't you see? Mother is dead, and father, too, all because of him. It doesn't matter if he knew the men or not!"

"Hey, leave her be!" Matt had never seen his brother in such a state and the more he listened, the more he saw, the angrier he became.

Jonathan let go of Amelia and abruptly turned toward Matthew such that Amelia stumbled forward until Willy reached out and broke her fall. Jonathan stood staring at his little brother, eyes blazing, but Matt didn't flinch. "You, too? You would side with this murderer?"

"He said he didn't know they were following him. He'd never let anyone hurt mother!"

"You all disgust me! How could you betray our parents?"

Until now, the zookeeper had thought to simply stand by in case the conversation took another violent turn, but he could not watch a family who had already lost so much splinter into more pieces. He moved between Jonathan and the others, so that he was eye to eye with the man. "Surely you do not mean such harsh words. This is your family; they are all you have left."

"I have no family; all of my family is dead." With that, he turned and walked away while the others watched in stunned silence.

"I should go after him," Nina said.

"Let him go for now," Mr. Kowalczak said. "He is too angry to hear you just now."

Nina and Willy walked Matt and Amelia back to the Finsters. The children were tired after the events of the morning and willingly went down for a nap after their breakfast. After Nina got them settled, she said to Willy, "Would you take a walk with me?"

They strolled down Forest Avenue, close enough that his shoulder nearly brushed up against hers as they moved along. No words had been spoken since they left the Finster home, each more comfortable with the chirping birds and the chug of the occasional motorcar than what needed to be said. Finally, Willy felt he had to ask her what was weighing on his mind. "What will you do now?"

Nina took a deep breath and let it out. "I think I have to try and make amends with Jonathan before I leave town."

"You are determined to go?" There was a note of distress in Willy's voice that he couldn't hide.

"Determined is not the right word. I don't see that I have a choice. Even if things were not strained with Jonathan, we can't all live in his flat. Besides, I think it would be better for the children to be away from Buffalo. People are talking about father's death. I don't want Matthew and Amelia to know what it was like for him at the end."

Willy was silent for longer than was comfortable for either of them, but he was working up to something and he wasn't sure if it was too soon. "What will you do in Cleveland?"

"I don't know, to be honest." There wasn't much else she could say. While she truly forgave Willy, she hadn't had time to think about what that meant for their relationship. It would have been easier to leave thinking she'd never see him again. Now that thought stuck in her chest, making it difficult to breath. "I suppose I'll have to get Matt and Amelia settled and in school. Now that the house is sold, there's money enough so I don't have to get a job right away if I feel the children need me more."

"I'd come with you." He blurted it out before he could talk himself out of it. "There's really nothing for me here now. Peter's seen to that." Willy realized that it had been Peter Wellesley who had written to Jonathan. He was the only other person who knew the truth about the intruders who entered the Barstow house that night. Talk in the neighborhood would start up again, he was sure of it. It really hadn't stopped, truth spreading slower than lies. He was fairly certain that when he found the courage to tell his mother, she'd likely stay in Springfield.

Nina looked unsure, but that only gave Willy the confidence to keep going. "Nina, please don't give up on us. Things are very confusing right now, but there is one thing I know for sure, and that is that I love you. Do you love me?" They hadn't discussed the letter he'd written from jail; there hadn't been time after Conrad Barstow's accident. It seemed selfish to ask Nina to focus on anything other than her family, but now she was leaving and he had to know.

"Of course I do, but…"

"Say it, Nina; I need to hear the words, please." There was nothing of desperation in his voice, just a wish for her to articulate what he already knew. It was important for her to say it out loud so that it could not be something she could dismiss while making important decisions about her future.

Nina understood this and did not hesitate. "I love you, Willy. I truly do."

He pulled her in, at the same time exhaling the breath he had been holding. For a while, they just stood there, neither willing to give up the comfort of the other. When they parted, Willy took her hands into his own and brought them to his lips. "I want to move to Cleveland. I'll get a job, and we can get married. Nina, we can raise Matt and Amelia. We can be a family."

As young girls often do, Nina had dared to think about being Mrs. William Cooper early on when she had first realized her feelings for him had grown beyond that of friendship, and while his offer made her heart soar, it also terrified her. So much of becoming Mrs. William Cooper would have involved her parents. Her mother would have helped to plan the wedding, offered advice on marriage, housekeeping, and childrearing. They would have had Nina's father to help when it came to the purchase and maintenance of a home. Now it would just be the two of them making their way in a strange city with two children right at the outset. Nina would have Aunt Grace, but all Willy's social and family connections were here in Buffalo. He'd be giving up a lot. "You would do that for us? What about your mother?"

"I can't think of doing anything else. I love all of you and I want us to be a family. I can't see my mother returning to Buffalo with things the way they are, though I think she would be thrilled to come and see us in Cleveland once in a while."

"I would like that, too."

Nina's eyes were full of hope for the first time in a long time and he didn't want to take that from her, but there was more that needed to be said. "Your brother won't approve. In time he might have forgiven you for what he now sees as disloyalty, but if we marry and raise your brother and sister, I fear he will turn his back on all of you forever."

It was a sobering thought, and the change in her expression indicated that Nina felt the weight of his warning. She would not look away, but her eyes began to glisten as she realized the truth of it. When she finally spoke, her words were measured. "I could not allow myself to go through with it, if that were the case, so I have to believe that you are wrong. Jonathan is our brother. He loves us, and I must have faith that in time he will forgive us."

Chapter Nineteen

There was a knock on the car window that brought both Maude and Billy back to the present with a jolt. Maude regained her composure and rolled down the window while Billy was blinking his eyes and looking around trying to get his bearings. "Mrs. Rosalini, how are you?" It was the woman who lived across the street, walking a rather ancient pug.

"I thought it was you! I was just passing by on the other side of the street and I noticed you, but it was too far away to tell for sure, but here I am on my way back, and you are still parked here, so I just thought I'd come and take a closer look."

"Is that Norman?" Maude asked pointing to the dog, who was wheezing and snorting from the exertion of his daily constitutional. She was hoping to deflect any questions about why they were sitting in a parked car outside of their old house.

"It is. He's fourteen and still goes on his walk every day. Of course, it's not easy for either of us at our age, but we get up anyway, don't we, Norman?" Mrs. Rosalini smiled affectionately down at the dog.

"I'll bet you don't even recognize Billy," Maude continued.

"Is that you, Billy? Why you were just a boy the last time I saw you!"

Billy leaned forward to be seen out the driver's side window. "Hi, Mrs. Rosalini. Hi, Norman."

"Billy's in college now, can you believe it?" Maude beamed at her son, who looked away, embarrassed over the attention.

"Oh, my, is that right? Well, you've turned into a handsome young man, haven't you?"

A gentle nudge from his mother prompted Billy to say, "Thanks, Mrs. Rosalini."

There was a moment of uncomfortable silence as Mrs. Rosalini tried to find the right words to tactfully ask what they were doing in a parked car, staring into space, but Maude saw it coming and spoke first. "Oh, it's getting late! I have to get this guy home. Well, it was really nice talking to you, Mrs. Rosalini. Take care." Without further comment, she rolled up the window, started the car and pulled away as the old woman waved cheerfully, if a bit confused.

"Well, that was close!" Billy said.

"Yeah, I wonder how long she was knocking on the window before I noticed?"

Billy laughed. "You handled that well, mom. I thought for sure she'd ask us what we were doing there."

"She would have if we'd stayed any longer. No worries. I had a plan if anyone asked." Maude shot him a sly smile as she turned toward the expressway.

Billy pulled out his notebook and began writing as she drove, wanting to record the highlights of what he had learned while they were fresh in his mind. He finished quickly and to his mother's raised brows said,

"Well, the take away here is that Nina made up with Willy and that seemed to piss off her brother."

She couldn't deny those were the salient points but would write down more detail of her own once she got home. "True, but we don't know if the falling out was permanent."

Billy nodded, glancing back at his notes and then closing the notebook. "What do we do now?"

Maude noticed the genuine interest in his voice. "Well, we can try this again, but not today because I'm exhausted and I'm guessing you are, too. What do you know about Sheri's family?"

"Not much. Why?"

"Well, we had talked last week about doing some genealogical research, so I called my friend, Abby." Abby Stevens was a genealogist Maude had met years earlier when she won a certificate for family tree research at a fundraiser. They had become friends and Maude called on Abby occasionally when she needed her specialized skills, which went way beyond the typical genealogical search engine. Abby could find people hiding in the historic record.

"Oh, yeah, I remember her. What can she do to help?"

"Well, my working theory was that Genevieve and Sheri are cousins. Based on what we learned today, I wonder if Sheri's ancestor is Jonathan Barstow, who remained in Buffalo. Genevieve's might be directly related to Nina, or possibly one of the younger siblings, who likely went to Cleveland. I was hoping Abby could figure it out. I'll give her a call after we eat lunch and see if she has made any progress."

"Lunch? Have you looked at the time? It's closer to dinner, and by the way, I'm starving."

"What?" Maude looked at the clock on her dashboard, it was nearly five o'clock. "How did it get to be that late?" she asked as she pulled the car to the curb and reached for her phone.

"I don't know, but I wonder how many people passed while we were just sitting there, staring at the windshield?"

Maude shrugged her shoulders, unconcerned with any potential passersby, while she turned on her phone and waited for all the notifications to stop chirping and whining. "There are three texts from your father wondering if we will be home for dinner."

Billy had been doing the same. "Yeah, I've got a few from Glen. He must be off tonight." There was also a text from Sheri, but that was private.

"Why don't you give them a call and ask if they want to order something for us to pick up on the way home?"

"Drive through would be faster." The comment was punctuated by a large stomach growl.

"Okay, Mighty Taco it is. Text them and let them know we'll be home in twenty."

Billy's finger moved deftly over the keyboard until he pressed send, then he was quiet for a moment while he considered how best to ask his question. Finally, he just said, "Can we not talk about this when we get home?"

Maude was surprised at the request. "I don't know how we are going to avoid it. Your dad knows what we were trying to do. He'll be interested in finding out how it went. Truth be told, I think he is a little envious of our gifts."

"He can have mine," Billy said. He noticed disappointment pass quickly over her features, although she tried to hide it. "It's just that if we all talk about it, we'll end up analyzing it to death."

That comment stung just a bit. All the men in her family, but Billy in particular, were men of few words. The answer to 'How was your day?' was usually 'Fine.' He resented further probing - they all did. It was frustrating to be the only woman in a house full of strong silent types.

Maude could admit to herself that it was a bit disappointing. Any spirited family discussion was a treasure, particularly since her sons were now young men with interesting opinions and points of view. Sharing this part of her life was its own special gift, but it was still so new to Billy, and he was still making up his mind about his own abilities. He deserved some time for private reflection. "Okay, we'll be done with it for tonight, but I'll give Abby a call when we get home." She started the car again and pulled back into traffic.

Just because he wanted to avoid a lengthy family discussion didn't mean he had no questions at all. "So, you think Nina and Willy stayed in Cleveland?" It was a cautious inquiry, like Billy was weighing her answer against something in his own mind.

"I don't know, but it looks that way. It's odd, though, because there is no record of Willy leaving the Buffalo Police Department in their annual reports.

There would have been a record if he'd been fired, resigned or died."

"He resigned." Billy said with calm certainty. It did not occur to Maude to question how he might know that; however she was curious as to why there was no record of it in the annual reports. When she asked, he said, "He didn't accept it, Captain McNamara. He ripped it up."

"Can you see that? I mean actually see him ripping up the letter?" Maude was intensely curious about Billy's gifts. He seemed able to do things with ease that it had taken her years to learn.

"It's not so much that I can see it, more that I feel it. I think it's because I'm still tuned into Willy's life. I felt that he wrote a resignation letter, but that the captain didn't want to accept it, like really didn't want to. Maybe I just guessed at the ripping up part, I don't know, but it felt like he would have done that. Does that make sense?"

"Yeah, actually, it does."

"That's why I don't want to talk about this with anyone else. I just know things sometimes. I didn't realize before, that it was all part of this thing." He gestured between the two of them and she took 'this thing' to mean the gifts that they possessed. "I can't explain it any better than that, and I certainly can't prove that what I know about Willy's resignation is true."

Maude considered his comments carefully before addressing them out loud. "The historic truth of what I dream, or see, or write has always troubled me. Some people or events are easily verifiable with research, but so much of it isn't. That doesn't make it any less important. I write fiction as a way of recording it all because I feel that since I experienced it, it was important and shouldn't be forgotten. I don't feel the need to defend it to anyone, though."

"But you still keep it a secret, for the most part."

It wasn't really an accusation, but Maude couldn't help but take it that way. "I choose not to tell others because it is a very personal thing for me." To her surprise, Billy seemed relieved by her response.

"I think I would like to keep it private, too."

"Well, I don't think you have to worry about the small circle of people who know spilling the beans, and if you prefer not to discuss this project we are working on, they will just have to respect that."

That seemed to ease Billy's mind, and they retreated into their own thoughts until they arrived at Mighty Taco. With the order stowed safely in the back seat, Maude turned to her son and asked, "Are you still worried about telling Sheri?"

"Yes and no."

Maude was surprised that he answered so easily. "Okay, let's go with no first."

Billy smiled. "Well, after I did some reading and thought about what Dad told me, about it being part of a religion, it didn't seem so weird to me. If I just had to tell her that I have gifts that allow me to talk to dead people, and see into the past, she'd think that was pretty cool."

"Well, that's a big plus. So, what are you worried about?"

It was harder to articulate what he had been wrestling with privately, and he wasn't sure saying it out loud would help, but Billy knew his mother and the easiest way to end the conversation would be to just get it out. "Well, I mean, c'mon, mom. Listen to how this actually sounds out loud to other people. 'Sheri, it turns out that I can talk to dead people. Anyway, the ghost of this woman, who was murdered in my old house, and who I think is your great grandmother, has haunted me several times throughout my life so that my mother and I could discover that you have relatives you didn't even know you had.'" Before his mother could comment, Billy continued. "Once that sinks in, I think she will be upset that I didn't tell her sooner." Hunger had finally gotten the better of Billy, and he reached behind him and grabbed a taco out of the bag while he waited for his mother's reply.

"I don't know her, so I'm afraid I can't offer much in the way of advice. If it were me, I'd be clear that I didn't want to raise the possibility that the two women were related until I was sure. Beyond that, you have to believe that if she really cares for you, she will get over it."

Maude didn't say another word, which came as a surprise to her son. When they got home, Don asked how their day went. She simply said fine and gave him one of those 'I'll tell you later' looks and that was the end of it. Glen gave the rapid consumption of his dinner all of his attention. By the time all the paper bags and wrappers made it to the trash can, he had left to meet some friends at the movies.

"I'm whipped," Billy said after his brother left.

"Go get some rest," Maude told him. "You did great today, by the way." Billy smiled, and then left the room, pulling his phone out as he went.

"So?" Don asked as he rose to grab a bottle of wine from the rack in the dining room.

"We learned a lot," Maude told him as she reached for the two wine glasses she had set out on the kitchen counter. She told him about their experience, and their plans to move forward.

"Sounds like you have everything under control." There was just a hint of envy in his voice.

Maude smiled. "Yes, for a change and I must say, it feels kinda nice." Don looked very pleased for her, which also felt kinda nice.

"Have you heard from Abby?"

"I left her a voice mail, so I'm hoping to hear back tomorrow."

"Okay, how 'bout we take this bottle, get comfortable on the couch and watch an old movie?"

It sounded like the perfect end to the day, although Maude was reasonably sure she'd be asleep long before the credits rolled. Still, the thought of snuggling up on the couch with Don was too much to resist. "That's a great idea."

The next morning Billy was in and out of her office wondering if there had been any word from Abby. When she told him for the fourth time that she'd let him know as soon as she heard, he stopped showing up, but still texted every hour. She turned the volume down just before lunch time and rolled her eyes when the phone vibrated on top of her desk. The latest message sat unread for about another twenty minutes while she finished filing the invoices she had spent the morning paying. "Oh, finally," she said out loud as she realized the message had come from Abby instead of Billy.

> Sorry, Jenny's getting a tooth. I finished up the work you requested and sent you an email just now. How do you manage to keep finding these people? Let me know if you need anything else.
> A

Jenny was the latest addition to the Stevens family, and Maude felt a pang of guilt for asking Abby to help. Life was pretty hectic with a toddler and an infant, and Maude thought she'd make it a point to offer to babysit next week in thanks for Abby's help. She shot Billy a quick text before she opened her e-mail, and by the time she had the file opened, he was sitting in her office.

"What'd she find out?"

"Gimme a minute." Maude looked at the files Abby had sent. There was a family tree and a bunch of supporting documents that had been consulted to construct said tree. There was no need to examine the supporting data yet, so she opened the first file, which showed the Barstow family tree.

"Ha! I was right. Sheri is Jonathan's great granddaughter. See?" She pointed to the bracket that contained Jonathan's name. He had married a woman named Agnes in 1927. They had three daughters, among them, Rose Mary. Rose Mary married a man named Edgar in 1952 and a few years later gave birth to a daughter named Michelle. Michelle and her husband David are Sheri's parents."

"That's odd, though; there is no mention of Genevieve anywhere in this genealogy."

"But how could that be? They look identical."

"I don't know, they could be related to Matt or Amelia, but there is no indication that either ever married."

Billy studied the tree carefully, hoping that his mother missed something. "Wow, would you look at that!" He pointed further up the tree to Grace and Eva.

"Holy shit! I didn't even catch the name."

"Yeah, that's really freaky that Grace Nolan was one of your Nolans."

Maude looked at the screen, speechless. Grace Nolan: the unmarried sister of Eva Barstow… They were both the great granddaughters of Ciara and Michael Nolan. Ciara was the oldest sister of Martha. Maude had learned a few years ago that she was Martha Sloane Quinn in a past life.

Billy spoke as he traced the brackets back. "It looks like their father Ian was one of Daniel's sons." Daniel Nolan was Ciara and Michael's surviving son, they had lost their eldest son Ian, their grandson's namesake, during the Civil War.

"Yeah, it looks like it." Maude continued to stare at the family tree, which could not confirm tracing the family back beyond the generation of Ciara and her two younger sisters. However, Maude knew the three sisters had another younger sister named Katie, who died on the ship from Ireland to America in 1835. She knew the four girls were the daughters of Ian and Mary Sloane, who had come from Inis Mór, the largest of the Aran Islands off the west coast of Ireland. She knew that Ciara's older son, Ian, named for the grandfather he never knew, died in the American Civil War. Her other son, Daniel, had lived with his wife and sons in Lily Dale. Ciara's middle sister, Patricia, had left Buffalo for Albany towards the end of the nineteenth century to be with her daughter's family, and Martha had lived in Lily Dale for a time after the death of her husband, but ultimately had returned to Ireland. Maude had visited Martha's grave on Inis Oírr. She knew all this not from records, but from her dreams and visions of the past, some of which had been substantiated by historic records. She had pieced together the lives of this family, a family she had been a part of, and here they were again, in Buffalo during the 1920s. "I can't believe it."

"Definitely freaky," Billy repeated. "What do you suppose it means?"

"Hell if I know." She shrugged in response to his raised brows. "I mean I thought it was weird when there was a death at the old poorhouse mixed up in all of this, but I'm thinking now that it was a coincidence."

Maude was quiet for a moment, trying to settle some things in her mind first. "I guess it shouldn't come as a surprise that there is a descendent of Ciara Sloane caught up in all of this. I'm connected to that family, and, so far, all of my explorations into the past have been linked to them." She wanted to say that Billy was now connected to them, too, at least by virtue of his current relationship to Sheri, but that would likely not sit well with him. They were young, and just starting school. It was possible, even likely, that their romance would fizzle out by the start of the fall semester. Instead, she redirected the discussion. "So, it looks like there are some interesting files here in the way of supporting evidence, more than just your typical census data, so I think you should wait until we go through it before you talk to Sheri."

"What do you think we'll find?"

"Well, Abby has a way of finding things nobody else seems to be able to find. There may be more to the story of Nina and her brother's falling out than we are aware, or there might be something that substantiates what we have already seen. My gut is telling me that the answer to where Genevieve fits into this is in these documents."

"When can we get started?"

"How about now? Christine can handle things in the shop, so why don't you bring down your tablet and I'll e-mail you these files and we can divide and conquer?"

"Yeah, I'll go get it."

Mother and son hunkered down for an afternoon of archival research. Once they eliminated the census, birth and death records from the list, there were a few .PDF files containing period newspaper articles and other documents.

"This looks interesting," Billy commented, looking up from the screen.

"What did you find?"

"Court documents, I think." Billy enlarged the print and studied the screen. "Yeah, it's full of legalese, but it looks like Jonathan was trying to get legal custody of Matthew and Amelia." He reached over to show his mother the file so she could open it on her laptop.

They spent the next half hour combing through the documents in the file. "He claimed their current home to be unfit." Maude couldn't believe what she was reading. "But the case didn't seem to go anywhere. This was in 1925. By then Nina and Willy were married, but Jonathan wasn't. He wouldn't have been able to care for the children."

"Yeah…but take a look at this." Billy had already opened the next document. "He tried again in 1927. By that time he was married."

Although it went against the grain for her, Maude closed out the file she was examining before she had looked at all of the documents and opened the one Billy was looking at. "It looks like a judge never heard the case."

"Oh my god! They ran away," Billy exclaimed as his eyes raced over the screen. "That's why the judge never heard the case. Matthew and Amelia ran away. Why would they do that?"

"I'm not sure I can answer that, Bill, but maybe you can." When he looked skeptical, she continued, "You seemed to know that Willy had resigned from the BPD and that Captain McNamara refused to accept his resignation. Take a deep breath and focus on Matt and Amelia. Close your eyes and see them in your mind and ask why they ran away."

Billy did what his mother asked. She saw his whole body relax and his mind turn inward. He hesitated when he spoke, trying to put into words the images and feelings he was getting through his mind's eye.

"When Willy and Nina married, they moved out of Aunt Grace's and took the children with them. Jonathan was furious, but his legal action went nowhere because he was a single man with a business to run." He stopped for a moment to focus his attention further inward. "I think the only reason he married was so he could take Matt and Amelia from Nina and Willy. He was obsessed. I feel so much... hatred is not the right word, disgust, maybe, and I think it's directed at Nina. He never forgave her for marrying Willy." Another pause. His face wrinkled in concentration. "The second attempt must have been more serious, because it frightened the children. By then they were frightened of Jonathan in general. He seems to have really gone off the deep end. He had resources, though. Somehow, he managed to keep the jewelry store profitable. I can feel the power he was trying to exert over Nina and Willy, using his money and his influence. They were frightened, too." He opened his eyes before he spoke again. "They must have thought that Jonathan had a chance of winning his case, so Matt and Amelia ran off. I don't think they were ever found." Without warning, Billy lurched forward with such pain in his eyes.

Maude was at his side in an instant. "What is it? What's wrong?"

"He died, mom. Little Matthew died while they were on the run. I don't know how, but it feels like the force of an impact, like he got hit, or fell."

Maude was overtaken with grief for Matthew, but also with dread for his little sister. "What happened to Amelia?"

"I'm not sure. She was there when it happened. I'm feeling shock, and fear. She's terrified." It was almost an instantaneous shift for Billy; once he felt the impact of whatever had killed her brother, his focus immediately switched to Amelia. "There's a person approaching, a man. There's something about him. He has kind eyes, and Amelia isn't afraid of him. The man helps Amelia."

"Do you know who he is?"

Billy screwed his eyes shut in an effort to sharpen his focus. "They are at a train station. The kids must have snuck onto a train. The man came out of a small building. He looks like he works there."

"What train station?"

"It's hard to tell. It looks pretty old-fashioned. Just a platform and a little ticket office. It could be anywhere." Billy came fully back to the present to find his mother staring at him. It was hard to read her expression. Don would have recognized it right away, having seen that combination of shock, confusion and disbelief a few times since she had discovered her own gifts.

Maude was blown away by what Billy had been able to learn. "That was really amazing, Bill."

It was relatively effortless, and he felt guilty taking the compliment. "But we still don't know how Genevieve fits into the family."

"Well, we know she wasn't Nina's direct descendent, or Matthew's, because he died in 1927."

"Another death.' His words were full of shock and disbelief. "That was some serious shit happening to that family."

"Yeah, you're not kidding." Maude chose to ignore the profanity under the circumstances. "It would have been devastating to lose any family member, but two parents and a brother all within a few years is… I don't even know. I can't even imagine."

There was nothing Billy felt he could add, so he tried to refocus on the original problem. "Do you think that Genevieve is somehow related to Amelia?"

"That sounds like a reasonable assumption based on what we know. I have to admit, Bill, I'm not sure how to proceed from here."

Billy was silent for a few minutes as he considered the dilemma. "I suppose I have no choice but to tell Sheri what I know and ask if she wants to contact Genevieve. Maybe Genevieve knows enough of her family's history to fill in some of the blanks."

"What will you tell her?" Maude was thinking back on their earlier conversation, and Billy's mixed feelings about telling Sheri what they have been up to.

"Sheri? The truth, but I think it's up to her to decide what we say to Genevieve."

Maude smiled. When had her baby boy grown up? "I'm not sure how to help you here. I'd offer to be around when you tell her, but that feels weird to me."

Billy laughed out loud at the offer and his mother's honesty about it. "Yeah, that would definitely be weird."

"When will you tell her?"

"I'm gonna call her now and see if we can meet today. Don't worry, mom, I'll let you know how it all ends."

Maude smiled, but it occurred to her that she would not be party to the resolution of this mystery. Billy would see this through to the end without her, and she wasn't sure how she felt about that.

Chapter Twenty

Billy found himself standing by his car as he waited for Sheri to get out of work. Since she hadn't counted on seeing him for a few days, she had taken a few extra shifts at the ice cream shop in her neighborhood. He really didn't know what prompted him to get out of the car until he saw her and was able to take her into his arms and show her how much he missed her. There were a few whistles from the people in line waiting for ice cream, as well as a few envious stares from her female coworkers.

"This is a nice surprise," Sheri told him when they finally parted. "What do you wanna do now?" She had a few ideas of her own, but they would have to wait for a more private setting.

They had made plans over the phone to hang out, destination to be determined, which had given Billy the chance to figure out the best place for what was sure to be an interesting conversation. He had decided on the park. It was warm but breezy, a nice evening for a walk, and Billy liked to keep moving when he was nervous. There were also plenty of quiet places for a private conversation when they got into the thick of the discussion.

They parked near the rose garden and headed into Rumsey Woods. The sun was still high in the sky and they walked with purpose toward the shade of the trees. Sheri reached out for his hand and gave it a squeeze. She had missed him during these few days more than she had thought possible. It wasn't just that they hadn't seen each other, but that Billy wasn't particularly chatty the few times they had exchanged texts. Sheri wondered when he finally called if this meeting was so that he could break up with her. That worry was put to rest quickly, thankfully. No one who kissed a girl like that planned to end the relationship. She was careful not to sound too needy, but really wanted to know why he dropped off the planet for a few days. "So, what have you and your mom been up to?"

The playground was full of children running off their last bursts of energy before bed and Billy waited until they were beyond it before he answered. He shot her a hopeful smile, not really sure how to begin. "I want to tell you all about that, in fact, I have to tell you all about that, but first let me ask you something." She nodded and he continued. "When we met that girl, Genevieve, in Cleveland, did you think it was odd that you looked so much alike?"

"I mean, it was kinda freaky, but I really haven't given it much thought. They say everyone has a twin somewhere in the world. Besides, there are other parts of that weekend that stand out in my mind." A sly smile slid across her face as she leaned in to kiss him.

He kissed her back, and for a minute it was tempting to just forget about the Barstow family, but he stepped away, and cleared his throat in an attempt to regain his focus. "Do you think you could be related to her?"

She would have been happy to just stand there in his arms, madly kissing him until they both couldn't breathe, but he pulled away. It was hard not to feel a bit of a sting, but he clearly had something on his mind, so she would see it through in the hopes that they could have a pleasant reunion under a secluded tree after. "I don't know, but I doubt it. I've never heard that I have any relatives in Cleveland."

Billy stopped, held her eye, and took both of her hands in his. She looked nervous, so he raised one hand to his lips, brushed them across the tops of her knuckles and gave her a reassuring smile. "I think you are related to her. In fact, I know you are."

When nerves gave way to confusion, he pulled her over toward the Ivy Arch. "Let's sit down for a minute. I've got some stuff to tell you."

It was best to just say it, simply and directly. "Since I was a kid, I have been able to see and talk to people on the other side - you know - dead people." He paused and waited for her to react before he continued.

"Get outta here, really?" When he nodded, she said, "Wow, that's totally awesome."

Relieved, he continued, "I guess I get it from my mom. She can do stuff like that, too. Anyway, I don't really tell many people, because I'm still not sure how I feel about it myself."

"Oh my god, Bill, if I could talk to spirits, I'd totally tell people, at least my friends. I'd definitely tell my close friends."

Billy just smiled; it was hard to tell people who were really into it what a burden his gifts could be. "Well, some weird shit has been happening to both me and my mom, and we found out that it has to do with you and Genevieve." Her eyes grew wide as he told her of Eva Barstow's death and all the grief and misery that followed.

"Before we left for Cleveland, I had a visit from Eva Barstow, the lady who was shot in my old house. I didn't catch the resemblance at the time because she had short hair and was wearing old fashioned clothes and a hat. When I saw Genevieve, it still took a while, because her hair is blond, and Eva's was dark like yours. Anyway, she came to me again in a dream and I kept seeing her face. I woke up and I knew she looked just like you."

"And I look just like Genevieve." Sheri mumbled, stunned by what she had been told. "My grandmother was Rose Mary Barstow. What the fuck? You have a picture of my great-great grandmother, who was murdered in your old house. What the actual fuck?"

"Yeah, this is pretty serious shit. I didn't want to tell you until I had more in the way of details, more proof that what I was telling you was true."

"I know you'd never lie to me, Bill." There was too much to process to really understand the impact of the certainty behind that statement, but she would come back to it. She would definitely come back to it. "But I can't believe that my great grandmother was murdered in North Buffalo and nobody in my family ever talked about it."

"Well, those were pretty devastating years, so it kinda makes sense that no one talked about them. Her death set off a major shitstorm, resulting in the death of her husband and youngest son, the disappearance of her younger daughter, as well as the estrangement of her two older children." He went on to tell her of the trouble Jonathan had caused by trying repeatedly to take the younger two children away from Nina. "I think Genevieve has to be a direct descendent of Amelia."

Billy pulled out his phone and showed her the family tree that Abby Stevens had sent. Sheri studied it for a long time and Billy wondered if he should tell her about his mother's connection to the Barstow family via Ciara Sloane Nolan, but decided the story of his mother's past life relations could wait until another time. Sheri touched his hand and Billy realized that he had been deep in thought and hadn't heard her speak. "I wonder if Genevieve knows any of this?"

"There's only one way to find out for sure."

"Bill, we don't even know her. She'll think we're nuts."

"Well, we have your genealogy. You can contact her and tell her you were wondering if the two of you are related in any way. Tell her that you found a story about Eva Barstow that was in the newspaper and ask her if she's ever heard that story from anyone in her family. We don't have to mention any of the psychic medium stuff if you don't want to."

Sheri agreed to call Genevieve the next day and made Billy promise to be with her when she did. "Jesus, what am I going to tell my family?"

"I don't know. Are they likely to be receptive to the entire story? If not, just tell them what you tell Genevieve."

"This is freakin' crazy."

"No doubt. I don't think you should tell your family anything until you talk to Genevieve."

"Yeah, that's a plan for sure."

They were silent for a while, and finally Billy debated whether to ask her if she was upset with him for not telling her what he knew sooner. So far, her reaction indicated that she wasn't, and he wondered if he would be poking a hornets' nest for no reason. Finally, his anxiety got the better of him. "So, you're not mad at me?"

She looked at him like he had two heads. "Why would I be mad at you?"

"I didn't feel right about telling you any of this until I had more information."

Proof. He was looking for proof to ensure that she believed him. It turned out she was revisiting her feelings sooner than expected. Sheri looked at him for longer than he was comfortable with. Finally, she said, "This may sound weird, and I hope it doesn't freak you out, but I know you'd never lie to me. You knew this was a tangled mess and you were trying to untangle it before you told me. I really appreciate that, Bill."

Relief flooded through him and he took her in his arms. At first, he just held her, enjoying the comfort of it, but neither of them was content to leave it at that. All thoughts of spirits and long-lost relatives receded as lips trailed and hands roamed. They didn't notice when the light had faded away and continued their reunion by the light of the moon that peeked through the branches of an ancient Sycamore tree. With all the present business set aside, they were just two college students who hadn't yet realized they had fallen in love.

• • •

"What do you mean you're going to Cleveland again?" Don asked his youngest son. He had come back to the shop late the next morning with a few flea market finds he was eager to start repairing when he heard Billy asking his mother for use of the car.

Billy was frustrated at having to start the story all over again from the beginning. "Last night I told Sheri everything we know about the Barstows. She wanted to call Genevieve and tell her they are related. Anyway, Genevieve asked her grandfather, and he told her about how his grandmother was shot and killed in Buffalo. He wants to meet Sheri and tell her the rest of the story in person."

Don was beyond the point where news like this would surprise him. "So, when are you leaving?"

"I'm trying to get mom to loan me her car."

Don threw him a set of car keys. "Here. Take my truck."

"Don! Wait a minute." Maude hardly got the words out before Billy snatched the keys out of the air.

"Thanks, Dad, I really appreciate it." As he was running up the stairs to grab his wallet, he said, "I'll be home late tonight, and I'll tell you everything."

When he was out of earshot, Maude turned toward her husband clearly annoyed at his intervention.

"You're just going to let him take off for Cleveland? That's a three hour drive each way."

"Yeah, I know, but there are two of them. Maude, you have to let him do this."

Maude sat back in her chair and blew out a frustrated sigh. "I know. I guess I just wish he would have invited me along."

Don gave her a sympathetic smile. "Are you feeling left out?"

"Kinda."

"You know you wouldn't be this close to solving this thing if it weren't for Billy. You have to let him see it through now that he's invested in it."

"I know. I'm just used to being the one who figures it all out."

Don feigned offense. "With a bit of help."

"Yes, of course, with a bit of help from my wonderful husband." She sat for a moment, letting the details of the past few weeks float through her mind. "He's really extraordinary." She looked at Don with envy in her eyes. "His gifts come so much easier to him than mine do for me."

"Don't sell yourself short, Maudie. You found some new skills, too, this time around."

She smiled, remembering the thrill of being able to tune in to Billy's connection to the past. "I wonder if the strength of his energy had something to do with that."

"I don't know. Maybe it's the strength of your combined energy."

"Maybe."

"Hey, why don't we go out for an early dinner, then catch a movie and maybe a few drinks after?"

Maude looked at her husband suspiciously. "Are you trying to distract me, Don Travers?"

"Yes, I am. You'll be looking out the window all night otherwise. C'mon, let's have one of those date nights we're always planning but never actually follow through on."

She smiled, thinking about how they both had dismissed the concept of date night many years ago in favor of spontaneous moments of passion snatched in the middle of the night, or sometimes, in the middle of the day. "Okay, it's a date as long as I don't have to make any decisions about where we eat, what movie we see, or where we go after."

"Deal!"

Chapter Twenty-One

Billy and Sheri largely kept to their own thoughts on the drive to Cleveland. It was an easy silence, with the mellow rhythm of Bob Marley in the background. They'd agreed to drive straight through and ate from a cooler of snacks in the back seat, stopping only to use the restrooms.

Genevieve's grandfather was a widower who lived alone in Shaker Heights. When they pulled up to his enormous colonial on Woodland Road, Billy whistled in appreciation. "Looks like your long-lost relatives have some bucks."

Scanning the rest of the neighborhood, Sheri noted a mix of fancy foreign sports cars and heavyweight Caddy's parked in many of the driveways. "Wow, definitely upscale." Sheri began to squirm as second thoughts snuck into her mind. "Maybe I should have dressed nicer." She was dressed for summer in khaki shorts and a red tank top, with her long hair pulled back in a neat pony tail.

Billy reached for her hand and gave it a confident squeeze. "Relax, you look great. We're not here to get you written into the will."

Their timing was perfect because Genevieve pulled into the driveway right behind them. The girls each flew out of their respective cars and embraced in the middle of the driveway like the long-lost cousins they were. "Oh my god! I can't believe this," Sheri told her.

"Me, either!" Genevieve turned to Billy and gave him a quick peck on the cheek. "Thanks so much for coming here."

"It's all good," Billy said. "I'm just happy that you guys found each other. Your grandfather's a solid dude to take the time to talk to us."

"You're going to love him. C'mon, let's go in." Genevieve punched in a code by the garage doors and stepped back while the door rose. It was a double garage but housed a single navy-blue Cadillac. "Hey, Pop, we're here!" she called as they entered through a door into the back hall.

The kitchen was a mixture of traditional hardwood and ceramic with all the modern conveniences necessary for someone who liked to cook. Jack Murphy was just taking a tray of cookies out of the oven as the trio walked in. "Hi, Lamb Chop. Come and give me a kiss before you introduce me to your friends."

Genevieve happily wrapped her arms around the old man's neck and planted a kiss on his cheek. He was a fit man for his seventy years and had no trouble lifting her right off the ground. "You don't come over often enough, Lamb Chop."

"I've got the rest of the summer to spend with you. You'll be sick of me by the time I go back to school."

"Never! Now, who have you brought to see me this afternoon?

"Pop, this is my friend, well, actually, my cousin as it turns out, Sheri."

"My gosh, just look at you! The two of you could be twins."

"It's nice to meet you, Mr. Murphy." She reached out to shake the man's hand. "Thanks for agreeing to meet with us."

"Well now, Sheri, you can just call me Pop, and you are quite welcome. It's not every day a man finds his long-lost relatives." Turning to Billy he asked, "You must be the young man who figured all this out."

Billy was startled at first, thinking he was referring to the supernatural end of things, but then he realized Sheri had e-mailed Genevieve the family tree. "It was really my mom's friend who did the research."

"That may be, lad, but it took you to notice there was something special between these two girls, and I'd be rude not to thank you for your efforts."

Billy shrugged it off, his eyes traveling to the tray of chocolate chip cookies still warm on the stove.

"I baked some cookies. Young people still appreciate a nice treat now and again, don't they?' He smiled when the three of them nodded vigorously. "I used my Helen's special recipe. She knew her way around the kitchen, my Helen. I've put on a fresh pot of coffee, too. I figured you probably wouldn't want milk."

Billy was secretly disappointed as he typically enjoyed a cold glass of milk in which to dip his cookies but given that they would drive straight home after their visit, the coffee was a better choice. "That's great. Thanks, Mr. Murphy."

"Now, you call me Pop, too. Let's just get settled here on the screen porch where we can have a nice chat."

The screen porch ran the width of the house, with comfortable wicker furniture at one end and a bistro table set on the other. It looked out on to a beautiful English cottage style garden. The porch was tidy but comfortable and looked as if Jack spent a considerable part of his day there. Jack brought a tray of cookies and placed them on the coffee table, while Genevieve followed him with a carafe of coffee.

"Now, Lamb Chop tells me that you know of my grandparents' deaths in Buffalo." Billy and Sheri nodded, and he continued. "My mother was Amelia, and the story I'm about to tell you comes from her directly. She told me that she never had the courage to find her sister or brother and hoped that I might one day. To tell the truth, I was a busy man for most of my life and just when I got around to thinking about it again, Lamb Chop told me about you. So, get comfortable and I'll tell you what I know."

"I grew up outside of Cincinnati, in a small town called Portsmouth, about as close to Kentucky as you can get without being in it. Didn't move to Cleveland until after I graduated from medical school. Mama spent some time in Cleveland after her own mama died, which I gather you know. You may not know that her older brother lost his mind with grief after his daddy died, blamed his brother-in-law for all the family troubles and tried several times to get mama and her other brother to come and live with him."

"We know that Matt and Amelia ran away, and that Matt died not long after," Billy interrupted gently.

"Yes, so much tragedy. Mama had it rough for a few years until she was taken in by the Booths."

As Billy listened to Pop paint a picture of two small, scared young children climbing into a freight car in the middle of the night, he could see snatches of it in his mind.

The two of them had fallen asleep, huddled together in the corner, but the motion of the train leaving the station woke them. They stayed along the far wall of the car because Amelia was afraid to be near the door while the train was moving, although it was only open wide enough for them to have squeezed in. They watched the world go by for hours and hours. Amelia must have nodded off. When she woke, Matt had moved toward the sliding door of the car. He was standing, pushing on it with all his might to open it more. "I want a better view," he told her. She begged him to step back. "Don't worry; I'll be careful." As the words came out of his mouth, the train hit a bump in the track. The door jolted open, throwing Matthew off balance. He couldn't hang on and was thrown from the train. He died instantly.

Amelia screamed, too terrified to move, watching helplessly as the world rushed past, taking her further away from her brother.

Pop's voice broke through the vision. "Mama told me that the train went on for some number of hours before it stopped outside Cincinnati. By then she was beside herself. She had no clue where her brother was, or if he was alive, and she sure as heck didn't know where she was."

Terrified and alone, Amelia curled up into a ball and cried herself to sleep. She was pulled from fitful dreams hours later by the train's whistle, announcing its arrival, but to where, she didn't know. It was still dark, and the slow rocking of the train on the tracks lulled her back to sleep.

When she woke again, it was around dawn and the train had stopped. She looked around and wondered where Matthew was. She remembered him pushing at the door and falling off the train, but had it been real? It couldn't have been real. He must have gone off to find them some food. Tired, scared and hungry, she allowed herself to believe that he would be back any minute.

Amelia stood and stretched, yawning as she approached the open door and carefully looked out. She saw a man come out of a small wooden shack near the tracks and walk with purpose toward the car. Had he seen her? He wasn't a particularly large man, but he was sturdy, and had a kind face. Maybe he had seen Matthew? Maybe he was coming to take her to him?

"Now, Charles Booth couldn't have been more than twenty at the time, and recently married, when he saw a little girl in a blue dress peeking out of the freight car. He'd been working at the railroad unloading the cars for about a year by then. Anyway, he had to look twice to believe what he'd just seen, but there she was. He went right out to learn how she'd gotten in there before his foreman found out. The child would surely have been in trouble had the foreman discovered her and she looked scared enough as it was, so he just thought he'd take care of matters himself, seeing as how his shift was over."

"Mama knew it was very important not to tell anyone that they had run away, or that they had stowed away on the freight car in Cleveland, for if she did, they would surely be sent back. So, she just told the nice man that she was waiting for her brother, and Grand Daddy said as he would just wait with her, but that she might be more comfortable on the bench by the shack. Well, they waited and waited, but her brother never came."

"Grand Daddy took her back to his house in Portsmouth and his Ruth Anne was surprised to say the least when he showed up with a little princess in a blue dress. Gran always called her a little princess, even when she was a woman grown. It was a pretty dress and all, but it had seen better days to be sure. Well, Gran had that child in a hot bath and into clean clothes, seated at the table before a heapin' plate of scrambled eggs and biscuits drizzled with honey before she ever asked where the child was from, or how had she gotten into a freight car. Mama didn't have any answers, but that didn't seem to bother anyone."

"So, did she ever tell anyone about Matt?" Billy asked.

"Well now, the way mama told it, she just had a feeling like he was gone and not coming back. Now mind you, she was just a young thing at the time, alone and scared, and don't forget all the losses she had endured up until then. She was numb and couldn't face another one, and here these nice folks just took her in. She decided the best plan was to stay put with them, and that's just what she did."

"She just stayed with them? Didn't anyone wonder how she came to live with them?"

"Now, those were different times, Lamb Chop, hard times. It wasn't unusual for a child to be sent off to live with kin who were able to provide better for them."

"What about Matthew?" Sheri asked. "Somebody must have found him."

"You're a smart young lady, like my Lamb Chop here. He was found, and it took a while, but his kin from Cleveland eventually came to claim him. There were stories in the newspapers about two runaways and queries whether anyone had seen the boy's sister. Well, Gran did wonder and asked mama outright. By then she had been with them a few months and she was happy, felt safe with the Booths. She told Gran that she ran away from a bad situation and had no mind to go back. They talked it over, Gran and Grand Daddy, and they decided they had no mind to send her back, so she stayed with them. They never did have any other children of their own. Mama thought when she got older that was likely why they just took her in and kept her, so they could have a child to raise."

"Didn't anyone come looking for Amelia?" Sheri asked.

"Well, there may have been. Mama told me there was talk around the time the young boy was found. Often folks think that children pay no mind to grown up chatter, but mama heard the whispers. As I told you, the fact that the boy had a sister still missing was in the papers. Gran made it known around town that Amelia had run from a bad situation. She and Grand Daddy were well liked, so if any stranger had come to town looking for a small girl, I'm guessing they would not have been pointed in the direction of the Booths."

They were all silent for a few moments, processing what they had been told. Finally, Genevieve asked, "How come you never said anything about this to us before, Pop? I mean, if I hadn't been visiting you last night when Sheri called, I'd never have known any of this."

"Well, Lamb Chop, it's like I said: livin' a young life is time consuming business. I went to college, got married, then had a family to raise and support." He paused for a second to organize his thoughts before continuing on. "I'd always thought of the Booths as my own kin. When my daddy died, they took mama in again. I was off in college at the time and thought about dropping out to get a job to support mama and me. Grand Daddy wouldn't hear of it. They were good people and I didn't want to upset them by lookin' up people that they were determined to think less of, so it was easy to put out of my mind. Gran and Grand Daddy are long dead, and mama with them, so the way I see it, finding the Barstow kin now keeps everyone happy."

"Don't you think it's odd that nobody on your side of the family knows anything about this?" Genevieve asked Sheri.

"When Billy first told me, I was shocked. My great grandfather died before I was born, but Gramma Rosie never mentioned any family other than her two sisters and their children. Knowing how angry Jonathan Barstow was, maybe he just cut off all contact with the rest of his family and never mentioned them again. I wonder if he even knew what happened to little Matthew."

"I think he must have," Pops offered. "It seems reasonable that Nina would have contacted him when the little boy was found."

Billy was silent, his eyes closed in concentration. After a while he looked up. "Jonathan knew, and he blamed Nina for the younger children running away." He closed his eyes, wincing from the emotional turmoil he was feeling. "I sense so much grief and anger. He never got over the loss, all of the loss. I think he remained a very bitter man." When he realized what he'd just said, there was a moment of panic. In the throes of the discussion, it hadn't occurred to him to keep his special connection to the Barstow family to himself.

Pop looked at Billy for a moment, initially surprised at this revelation, but then a slow smile spread over his face. "You have the gift of sight, don't you, young man? Is that how all of this started on your end?"

There was no accusation in his tone, and Billy felt comfortable enough to come clean. "More or less. It turns out that your grandmother Eva has been trying to connect with me since I was a kid. My mom made some connections to the family recently, and it took us a while to piece together our separate experiences, but Sheri and Genevieve meeting at the Rock and Roll Hall of Fame was really what tied it all together." Pop didn't seem particularly surprised or impressed. He just accepted Billy's explanation. Billy wondered what life experiences had left the man so open-minded but figured now wasn't the time to ask.

"Well, isn't that something." Pop was silent for a moment, apparently taking it all in. "Makes me wonder if I should have pursued this while Mama was alive. It might have brought the family some peace."

"I don't think it's too late for that," Billy told him. "I feel a sense of relief, although I really can't say if it belongs to me or to them." At that moment he wished his mother had come with them. He was feeling so many emotions, and she could have helped him sort out which ones were his and which ones belonged to the other energies he was sensing. It was all so difficult to explain to the group of people sitting before him rather stunned at his revelation.

Pop seemed to understand. "I think we are all feeling some relief, and speaking for myself, I'll add a healthy dollop of gratitude. You have helped me fill an obligation to mama that I might not have been able to do on my own. I just know that she's with us now and that she knows her family has found each other again." He pulled a handkerchief from his pocket and wiped his misty eyes. Clearing his throat and turning to Sheri, he said, "Now I want to hear all about the family in Buffalo."

They spent another few hours visiting, exchanging histories and planning a get-together so that their families could meet. It took yet another hour once Billy and Sheri had decided they'd better hit the road to actually leave. They made promises to stay in contact, and the girls agreed to exchange stories about their parents' reactions when they told them of long-lost relatives.

Sheri was all smiles in the truck on the way home, and unlike the journey there, they had lots to discuss. "My mom is going to totally flip out when I tell her all of this."

"Yeah, mine, too. She's really into this stuff."

"Can you blame her? This woman, who turns out to be my great-great-grandmother, has been trying to get your attention since you were a kid. Somehow, she knew we would end up together, and that you would help her to reunite the family that was broken apart as a result of her death. That's freakin' amazing, Bill."

He smiled and wanted to agree. Now that she put it that way, it was pretty freakin' amazing, but he was stuck on the 'knew we would end up together' part. That required more thought, and maybe a talk with his dad, before he could put the feelings generated by that innocent comment into perspective.

"I think it's totally cool that you and your mom are so close," Sheri told him. She had continued talking and he was pretty sure she had said something before that, but he hadn't heard it.

"My mom's cool. Aren't you close with yours?"

"Yeah, but we don't do stuff like this together."

"Well, this is the first time, and it might be the last time, too. I don't know about all this stuff."

"Are you kidding me, Bill? I'd love to have your gifts. Look what you were able to do. You reunited two families who had been separated for almost a century. Think of the joy you have given to Pop, and the peace you have given to Eva. Why wouldn't you want to keep doing this kind of stuff?"

"It's hard to explain. Your family's story just sort of found us. From what my mom has told me, weird shit finds her all the time, and she always ends up chasing after it. She and my dad actually went to Ireland a few years ago just because her friend in Lily Dale had been visited by a ghost from there. She spends more time doing stuff like this than she does actually working at her job. I don't want to be like that. I don't like the idea of dropping everything just because some frustrated spirit gives me a cryptic message."

"Seriously? That sounds like a blast to me, particularly if you can find a way to get paid for it." Although his eyes were on the road, she saw them roll in response to her comment. "Really, Bill, you have an amazing gift. You shouldn't just blow it off."

"It's not that I want to completely blow it off. My mom was well into her second career, married, with two kids in high school when she realized her gifts. I'm still in college. I want time to do my own thing for a while, that's all."

"That makes sense."

That was all she said, and the conversation was over. She'd found a way to give him something to think about without nagging…well, actually, to give him something more to think about. It seemed now that that talk with his dad would have to include a few beers. That's what men did when there were serious things to discuss.

CHAPTER TWENTY-TWO

When he finally got home, Billy wasn't surprised to find his parents seated at the dining room table with a Scrabble game board spread out between them. He figured they'd wait up. He'd brought Sheri with him. She wanted to thank Maude for doing her part in unraveling the mystery of her estranged ancestors. His parents didn't seem surprised to see her, but he suspected they were just more interested in hearing the details of their afternoon in Ohio.

Sheri did most of the talking, which suited Billy just fine. "It's been an amazing day, and I really want to thank you, Mrs. Travers, for all of the work you put into reuniting my family. It still doesn't seem real. I can't wait until the morning so I can tell my parents." She turned and gave Billy such a radiant smile. "Bill told me he was actually able to see little Amelia and Matthew on the train, was able to follow her in his head as Pop told us the story. I'd have never known it by looking at him at the time. It was pretty awesome."

Maude felt her husband give her a gentle kick under the table. Sheri's eyes were full of affection as she spoke about Billy, which hadn't been lost on either of his parents. Maude knew her son well and tried to keep her questions to a minimum as he reluctantly told the story of Amelia Booth as seen through his mind's eye. "You needed that connection to her son in order for you to see her more clearly," Maude told him.

"Yeah, maybe that was it. It was like I heard what he was saying, but I saw so much more detail." Billy was seated at the table, rocking on the back two legs of his chair as he spoke, anxious to move the discussion away from his gifts. All the other lights were off except the one over the dining table, making the maple leaves of the Tiffany lamp pop as it cast a warm glow on the cherry wood beneath it. "Hey, is that a new lamp?"

Don laughed out loud. "The kid can see into the past yet doesn't remember the priceless lamp we found in the root cellar! Jeez, Bill."

"Huh?"

"Billy, you were pretty young when we found this lamp in the root cellar of our old basement," his mother told him. "So, it doesn't surprise me that you don't remember that, but I'm surprised that you don't remember back a few weeks ago when Mrs. Houston gave it back to us. It's been hanging here since then."

"Why would I? It's just a lamp."

"Just a lamp? Where have I gone wrong with you? Dude, this is a Louis Comfort Tiffany lamp."

"Sorry, dad, but I just don't get as excited about lamps as you do." He looked at Sheri and rolled his eyes.

"Look at the design details, the craftsmanship," Don insisted. "Oh, and it's worth a small fortune!"

Billy looked up at the lamp and his expression changed as his eyes fixed on a particular red stained-glass leaf that stood out to him. Without looking away, he said, "He bought it for her." When both of his parents gave him blank looks, he repeated it. "He bought it for her, Conrad. He bought the lamp as a birthday present for his wife. He brought it home the night she was shot."

Don looked skeptical. "I don't know about that; he likely made a decent living as a jeweler, but I doubt he made the kind of money that could buy one of these."

Maude laid her hand on Billy's shoulder. "What do you see, Billy?"

"I'm in a jewelry store; it's dark out. There's a man in the store; he's wearing one of those suits like you see old time gangsters wear."

Maude closed her eyes and focused. "I see him, too, that's him." Don and Sheri just watched and listened, mesmerized by the story she began to tell them.

Conrad Barstow pulled out his pocket watch. It was nearly time to close the shop. No sooner did the thought cross his mind to fetch his coat and hat than did the bell on the door signal the arrival of a last-minute customer. Conrad didn't mind. In his experience, those men who came at the last minute had invariably forgotten an important birthday or were looking to purchase a gift to get them out of trouble with their wives. For those kinds of men, money was usually no object. He placed the watch back in his pocket and looked toward the door.

Conrad hid his curiosity behind a friendly smile as an elderly couple entered the shop. Their coats were clean and in good repair, but not of quality wool. The woman rested heavily on her cane, and the man was carrying a wooden crate containing something carefully wrapped in old towels. The man looked to be struggling under the weight of it and Conrad quickly moved to relieve him of the burden. "Here, let me help you with that." The older man smiled but made his own way to the counter and gently placed the box atop it.

"How can I help you?" Conrad moved back behind the counter, allowing the woman to remove the wrapping.

"We'd like to sell this," the man announced, gently removing a stained-glass hanging lamp from the box.

It was easily recognizable as the work of the Tiffany Studios in New York, and the signature on the inside of the shade confirmed it. While jewelry was his area of expertise, he knew that Tiffany lamps had been all the rage a few decades ago. Those who could afford an electric hanging lamp in those days would not have been dressed in boiled wool coats. This couple was likely not the original owners of this lamp.

As if reading his mind, the older man said, "It's ours to sell. The master has no use for it now, said it was ours if we wanted it."

Conrad had no trouble believing him. It happened all the time among the upper crust of Buffalo. The folks living on the Parkways easily discarded their old treasures for the newest shiny thing. It wasn't unusual for the household servants to be the beneficiaries of such trinkets when they had fallen out of fashion. "It's not that, sir. It's just that I'm a jeweler. I buy and sell necklaces, rings and ear bobs, not lamps."

Their faces betrayed none of the disappointment of having transported the heavy box by street car, and then on foot all the way there for nothing or of the burden of continuing on until they found a buyer. He could recommend Mr. Elliot on Ellicott Street, who dealt in such ornaments, but he wouldn't give them a fair price, knowing the Tiffany style had fallen out of fashion. Conrad took a closer look at the lamp. It was truly beautiful. He hadn't seen a Tiffany design with such richly colored maple leaves, and it would look stunning on the landing of their staircase. Eva's birthday was coming up. He was sure she would love it and he felt he needed more of a gift than the beautiful frame he had made for her favorite family photo. The lamp was perfect.

"Perhaps I can help you after all."

"The children can't know; they'll never keep a secret." Conrad spoke out loud to himself as he drove home, considering the best hiding place for his new treasure. He thought about the attic. It was unfinished, and they didn't store anything up there. "I'll never get it up there without anyone seeing." The attic was accessible from a hatch on the second floor, but he'd have to drag a step ladder up just to reach the hatch. "The root cellar!" They'd never actually used it. Eva bought what they needed from the market on Hertel Avenue. He could just slip in through the back door and down the stairs. It would be safely tucked away before anyone even knew he had come home. "That just might work," he mumbled. Then, in a more confident voice: "Yes, the root cellar!"

The four of them just sat there staring at the lamp. Finally, Maude spoke, directing her remarks to Sheri. "The interesting thing is that a descendent of the lamp's original owner came into the shop and recognized it from old family photos. We ended up selling it back to her."

"Yeah, and not too long ago, she came back into the shop and insisted we take it," Don added.

"It's a gift from Eva Barstow," Sheri proclaimed, "for reuniting her family." She took Billy's hand and they both just stared like a couple of goofballs at each other, as if no one else was in the room.

Maude and Don exchanged a different look. Each of them knew that at some point down the road they'd be passing the lamp over to Sheri, perhaps as a wedding gift.

ACKNOWLEDGEMENTS

My profound thanks to all the people who helped in the writing of this book. They include:

Officer Chris Sterlace and Lynn Milligan of the Buffalo Police Department for taking the time to look for the original case file upon which Eva Barstow's murder was based.

Lt. Mike Kaska for providing insight into the BPD in the 1920's.

Geoff Gorsuch, docent for the Richardson Olmstead Campus, who showed me around the Buffalo State Hospital (formerly the Buffalo State Asylum for the Insane) and offered insights into the institution during the 1920's.

Corey Fabian-Barrett, Visitor Services Coordinator, Richardson Olmstead Campus, who provided access to the many resources that helped me to understand the Buffalo State Hospital.

Lt. Col. Lawrence Catalano, USMCR (ret.), for his knowledge of firearms.

John and Susan Tobin of the real Antique Lamp Company, and Matt Webb from Webb Exchange for their knowledge of Louis Comfort Tiffany Lamps.

Jacqueline Lunger for her guidance and insight into inner senses and Modern Spiritualism.

Cynthia Van Ness and everyone at the Buffalo History Museum Research Library for helping me to understand North Buffalo (New York) during the 1920's.

Jackie Kishbaugh, whose pictures of Forest Lawn Cemetery and The Buffalo Zoo provided inspiration for parts of the story and the cover of this book.

To Bob Higgins, Christine Hicks, Kay Lucas, Ruth Higgins, and Jacqueline Lunger for their comments on the manuscript.

Other books by Rosanne L. Higgins

Orphans and Inmates

In the spring of 1835, at the pier of Buffalo's Canal District, the most dangerous square mile in developing America, 17 year-old Ciara Sloane steps onto land, alone, save for her younger sisters, orphaned at sea on the voyage from Ireland. Turned away by her only family on this side of the Atlantic, Ciara is admitted to the almshouse, along with her younger sisters, as the nursemaid, charged with bringing order to the chaos that is the children's ward. With the help of the Christian Ladies Charitable Society, led by the formidable Mrs. Farrell, and the compassionate and charming Dr. Michael Nolan, Ciara is able to transform the children's ward from a place of loneliness and despair to one of optimism and hope. Orphans and Inmates is the first novel in a five book series about the Sloane sisters and their experiences at the Erie County Almshouse and the Buffalo Orphan Asylum. The story explores the largely ignored origins of the social welfare system through the experiences of those who were most profoundly affected by poverty, namely women and children. It depicts the ruthlessness, depravity, compassion and hope experienced by those forced to seek institutional relief.

A Whisper of Bones

Maude Travers gulped for air. Why had this man struck her? Why was she on this kitchen floor in this ramshackle tenement? Blinking hard she was instantly sitting back in the anthropology lab questioning her own sanity. Was that a vision? An hallucination? Could she really just have witnessed, or rather, felt the brutal beating of a woman who lived over 170 years ago, and if so, why? What was this woman trying to tell her? Compelled to understand this message, Maude juggles the running of her own business and her work in the lab. Her attempt to decipher the tale of an excavated skeleton from the former grounds of the Erie County Poorhouse consumes her. This quest is aided by the diary of the Keeper of the Buffalo Orphan Asylum, Ciara Sloane Nolan. A former poorhouse inmate herself, Ciara's duty is to defend and protect the homeless children of the city. Between the journal and the whispering of bones, the past and the present intertwine. Maude learns of widespread corruption at the almshouse, and a most horrifying secret is revealed.

The Seer and the Scholar

A chance discovery takes anthropologist-turned-novelist Maude Travers through a centuries-old missing person's investigation. Each piece of evidence triggers vivid dreams of the Sloane sisters as they help Buffalo's poorest residents during the cholera epidemic of 1849.

Maude is compelled to keep digging as she suspects that her dreams of Martha Sloane and the decisions she struggles with as the first female medical student might, in fact, be true. A trip to the Modern Spiritualist community of Lily Dale, New York, brings the realization that, once again, the dead still have much to tell. A psychic medium and the spirit of a nineteenth century school teacher enable Maude to reconcile the past with the present and to glimpse what the future might hold.

A Lifetime Again

"Past life regression isn't for everyone," Charlotte Lambert had advised. The psychic medium and friend to Maude Travers also warned, "you may not like what you find." Maude's scientific roots as a researcher did not prevent her from eventually accepting the idea that she had been a nineteenth century physician in a past life. The notion had first presented itself to her in vivid dreams and waking visions of Buffalo, New York, more than a century ago. A search of the historical records verified the existence of the physician and her work in the burgeoning city's insane asylum. What did it all mean, and more importantly, how would it help Maude to understand the threats to her current business? "You tend to be surrounded by the same cast of characters in each life," Charlotte told her. "Negative karma will follow you until you do something to break the cycle." Had an adversary from another lifetime come to even the score in this one? Would Maude be able to unravel her past life in time to secure her own future?

The Girl on the Shore

A ghostly message from 1835 and dreams of the Sloane sisters of Buffalo, New York in 1880 send modern day novelist Maude Travers across the wild Atlantic to a small island off the west coast of Ireland for answers. What do the Spiritualists of Lily Dale, New York, a child accused of witchcraft and the ancient Celtic legends of the Fairy Folk have to do with the mysteries hidden there? As Maude hones her ability to connect with the past, she sees that a chance encounter with a girlhood rival awakens long forgotten secrets. Old superstitions begin to take root and place the Sloane family in danger. How will the resolution of this latest supernatural quest impact a relationship in trouble in the present, another just beginning in the past and a third that was never meant to be?

About the Author

Rosanne Higgins was born in Enfield, Connecticut, however spent her youth in Buffalo, New York. She studied the Asylum Movement in the nineteenth century and its impact on disease specific mortality. This research focused on the Erie, Niagara, and Monroe County Poorhouses in Western New York. That research earned her a Ph.D. in Anthropology in 1998 and lead to the publication of her research. Her desire to tell another side of 'The Poorhouse Story' that would be accessible to more than just the scholarly community resulted in the *Orphans and Inmates* series, which chronicles fictional accounts of poorhouse residents based on historical data. She continues to write historical fiction based in Buffalo, New York.

http://www.rosannehiggins.com/blog.html

https://www.facebook.com/pages/Orphans-and-Inmates/516800631758088